"SURELY YOU DIDN'T SUSPECT THAT I WAS JUST PLOTTING SOME WAY TO GET MY HANDS ON YOUR NAKED BODY?"

Decker pretended surprise.

"Well—"

"You shock me, Miss Wentworth." Seeing no more need to talk, he kissed her.

"Are you going to seduce me?" Naomi asked huskily when he lifted his mouth.

"Yes."

He kissed her again. His hands moved, unbuttoning buttons, unzipping zippers.

She made a sound in her throat. The kiss went on for a while. "Was that an 'I'm ready' kiss?" she whispered.

"No, no." He sighed. "That was a 'you attract me' one."

"Oh. You attract me, too."

"Kiss me that way."

She lifted her hand to the back of his head and kissed him sweetly, touching his lips with her tongue. "How was that?"

"That was a 'do it' kiss," he told her, kissing her some more.

A Nothing Town in Texas

LASS SMALL

HarperPaperbacks
A Division of HarperCollinsPublishers

This is a work of fiction. The characters, incidents, and dialogues are products of the author's imagination and are not to be construed as real. Any resemblance to actual events or persons, living or dead, is entirely coincidental.

HarperPaperbacks *A Division of* HarperCollins*Publishers*
10 East 53rd Street, New York, N.Y. 10022

Copyright © 1991 by Lass Small

Cover illustration Diane Sivavec

First printing: April 1991

Printed in the United States of America

HarperPaperbacks and colophon are trademarks of HarperCollins*Publishers*

10 9 8 7 6 5 4 3 2 1

A Nothing Town in Texas

CHAPTER ONE

DRIVING SOUTH FROM SAN ANTONIO ON HIS way to his uncle's place, Decker Jones left the highway for a narrow feeder road. It was July, hot and dry, with the faintly alluring smell of the sea carried inland on the Gulf breeze.

Decker eased his mint-condition 1967 Mustang between the simple, starkly stripped cedar trunks that marked the entrance to his uncle's land. The third cedar trunk had been hoisted up sixteen feet and secured across the top of the two upright trunks. A metal *J* hung from the middle of the crossbar.

Those crooked, weathered posts and the worn double track that led to his uncle Frank's empire made it appear that Frank Jones was a humbly unostentatious man, but Frank Jones bore the nickname of Gimme.

Sourly, Decker narrowed his eyes as his still bruised body coped with the unkempt track. The route had been laid economically along the path of least resistance through the brush. Since Decker had to drive so slowly over the rough way, he shut off the air-conditioning and wound down his windows to allow the breeze to tease through the car.

As he drove along watching his slowed way, he had

1

the time to look around. Yonder, he saw buzzards circling. There was something dying under that lazy swirl of airborne birds. They had not yet begun their spiral of descent. Decker felt a tremor of dark fear in his stomach. He tore his stare from the patiently waiting scavengers and looked at the empty brush.

It wasn't really empty. He saw birds flit. There were trees in various stages of growth, their leaves stirring lazily in the breeze. There were proud oaks, wild pear, hackberry, and at one place was a grove of pecan trees. Mainly there were the prolific, damned-near-indestructible mesquite trees whose deep roots tapped the groundwater.

While Uncle Frank hadn't half planted any of his worn-out Cadillacs tails up in a surrealistic row, as one Texan had, there were the targets. Between the cedar trunk entrance and the house, the bullet-riddled, lacy metal had once been of different motifs, from an ordinary target to a replica of the conservationists. Uncle Frank loved targets. He'd say "It gives people something to do, to break the monotony, as they drive along the track."

Decker wondered if one of the powerful bullets was the reason for the circling buzzards. What creature lay dying out yonder, alone in the brush?

In that area of Jones land, the trees, cactus, and underbrush had been left in their natural state "For the deer," Uncle Frank said. In season, the deer were hunted by packs of people who often actually knew how to hunt. Only a couple of times had people been shot. By mistake, it had been ruled. But each accidental death had been someone controversial. And when that had happened, Frank had taken his cigar out of his mouth and mournfully told the TV camera, "He's a real loss to humanity."

Decker speculated on what Uncle Frank wanted of him, and why now?

Since his dad was an honest man, Decker wondered if he'd ever objected to his brother's way of doing things. There was no question of his dad's loyalty to Frank, it was like granite, and even though Decker's mother was scornful of her brother-in-law, the obligation of blood had been made a part of Decker's fiber.

Decker sighed. Because of family, here he was again, going down this miserable road to see his uncle, who wanted something from him.

Decker was not yet recovered from the horrendous ordeal of a failed covert operation in South America. Taken before he could help the others, he'd made a difficult escape. It had been like dragging himself from the closing jaws of a giant alligator.

The "alligator" had been a filthy adobe ruin. And Decker's escape had been made while he was only half dead from the beatings but not yet racked with infection. Once he, too, had lain under an interested circle of buzzards, wishing for a bullet . . . .

Ten days ago, his doctors had told him, "You don't realize that you're better. You're only thirty. You'll survive even this. The day will come when you'll find it easier to move. Then when you understand that you're really alive and feel confident again, the nightmares will fade. You're all right."

Easy for them to say.

"Come on down, boy," Uncle Frank had bellowed over the phone last week. "I need to see that you're okay again."

In this time of his long recovery, Decker didn't need any problems. He didn't really want to see Uncle Frank or the new bride. He didn't want to sit and drink too much and listen to Uncle Frank being so kind, when Decker knew that every Gimme Jones kindness held a self-serving fishhook.

Eventually the seemingly aimless track reached Gimme's perfectly done, two-story, white clapboard house. It was strung with screened porches around both floors, and shaded all around by big old oak and pecan trees. The house looked as if it had been there, treasured, for generations, when even the oaks had been lifted in by helicopter less than twelve years ago.

Frank had stridently wanted another Tara, but the designer had convinced Frank that "such a modest man" should have a more deceptively modest house. It was good for business. Frank could see that. Then while the designer had filled the place with subtle treasures, Frank had added a few touches of his own.

The very minute Decker pulled up, it was Uncle Frank who came out the door. Like the simple, welcoming host he contrived to be, his arms were as wide as his smile as he hollered, "You got here! You're here! God love you, you're finally here!" And he pulled a flinching Decker from his car and hugged him hard.

When Decker gasped with the pain, Frank released him gingerly so that he could look at his nephew. "You okay, boy?"

"Fine." He stretched his mouth into a smile as the angry muscles and nerves settled slowly.

"God Almighty, boy, you don't know what it means to me to see you again." He cleared his throat as he released Decker but kept one hand clamped on Decker's arm. Then Frank removed a full-size bandanna handkerchief from his back pocket to wipe his eyes and blow his nose.

Decker hardened his heart.

There was no one who could match his uncle Gimme. He made it seem as if he had been concerned about Decker. By then, Decker had been out of the hospital for a couple of weeks, and this was the first Frank had contacted him. This was exactly what Decker had expected. The old fraud did this same act every single damned time he saw Decker. This was how it always began.

Decker looked critically at his uncle with hostile eyes. Decker had to admit that Frank looked great. The old man must use preservatives. He appeared to be no older than forty, and he had to be over fifty. How did he do it? Good genes. He was about thirty well-carried pounds overweight and not quite as tall as Decker; but he stood straight, his hair was thick and dark, and his face was nicely weathered. It was as if Decker was looking at himself twenty years from now.

In censure, he told his uncle, "The buzzards are circling over to the east, in the brush. Somebody ought to go look."

"Yeah?" Gimme's eyes flared. He put two fingers to his mouth and gave a shrill blast. Waited. Then came a shout and running footsteps.

Feet always ran in response to Gimme's demands.

"Yeah, boss?" The new arrival's glance went to Decker to see if he was the threat and dismissed him.

The dismissal needled something recently dead inside Decker, and that reaction irritated him. So when his uncle Frank asked where he'd sighted the buzzards, Decker was kind. "Off to the right from the track about three miles, I would guess." He knew it, exactly.

Uncle Frank told the flunky, "Take the chopper, Bud," and they both watched as the flunky jogged off toward the back of the house.

"Come in out of the heat," Frank urged hospitably. "How's your family? God, I hate to think how long it's been since your folks were down here. How they keeping? Your momma still as pretty as ever?"

With a glance to the scar on Frank's forehead, Decker nodded and replied, "She's still a fighter."

Frank laughed heartily and slapped Decker's shoulder in a manly, sharing way and didn't see his nephew flinch. "Come in. Come inside and tell me all about that fracas you was in." As do all men who only pretend to have the common touch, Frank used poor grammar. "That was terrible. Your daddy said something about you being out of the country? That you landed in the middle of a local dispute that turned real ugly. How'd you ever get out of there alive?"

Decker's reply was short: "I don't know."

A good poker player, Frank gave Decker a shrewd look and changed the subject: "What you need is a cold beer. Lone Star or Pearl?" He opened the top of a waist-high, rectangular cooler sitting on the screened porch next to the house entrance. The cooler could hold several cases of beer and, placed as it was, it had almost caused the designer to have a fit. At least the cooler was painted white.

"How about iced tea?" Decker amended.

There was an assimilating pause before Frank pointed a finger at Decker to say, "You got it. Hey!

Chico? Iced tea." He looked back at Decker. "Mint? A little Southern Comfort?"

"Just the mint."

Frank repeated in a bellow, "And mint."

From the back of the house came a reply of affirmation.

Like he was doing a sleight-of-hand trick, Frank took a Coors from the cooler, and Decker had to smile. Frank laughed, opened the beer, and ushered his nephew into the house.

There was no air-conditioning. Frank thought it was un-Texan to need it. The cross-ventilation admitted the Gulf breezes that reached far into the land. The interior of the house was cool and pleasant. The colors were muted and pleasing to the eye. It was a marvelous house.

"Sit down. Sit down. Make yourself to home, boy. Good to have you back here in the good old U.S. of A." He lit a Cuban cigar.

Decker moved to a southeast window and sat in an easy chair, lowering himself carefully to allow his body's adjustment to the change of position. He closed his eyes for a minute during the worst of it.

Frank frowned. His plan might not work. He'd had no idea how bad the boy had been hurt in that fracas. Hell. Who else could he get? There was nobody this loyal. "What you need is a distraction," he began the sales pitch. "We need to find something for you to think about. I've got a thing or two that niggles. Let's see. What sort of puzzle would be interesting to you. Hmmm. This'll take a little thinking." He pretended to do that.

Chico brought the tea and smiled back at Decker

as he said in his lovely, liquid voice, "We are glad
you're safe."

"Thank you. Gimme is lucky to still have you."

Without actually shaking their heads in exasperation, they shared an enduring look before Chico left
the room.

Frank smoked his cigar as he thoughtfully studied
the ceiling.

Decker lay back in his chair and soaked in the peace
as he listened to the familiar bird songs of Texas.
Familiar? How was it that the songs were known to
him? When had he absorbed their sounds? He was
no bird fancier. About the only thing he'd ever done
with birds was shoot doves. Now the songs filled his
hungry cells. How good it was to be back in Texas.

"By Jingo, I got just the thing for you, Decker.
Simple. No strain. Just listening. By golly, this is just
the ticket!" He smiled, pleased that he'd made it seem
so spontaneous.

Decker sighed. Here it came already. Not bothering
to kill the fatted calf, Uncle Gimme just jumped right
in. Not his usual style at all. Whatever it was, it must
be one hell of an irritation. Decker decided he
wouldn't help. Let the old man sweat. He didn't look
over at Frank but simply lay there in the chair, completely relaxed, giving no indication of even polite
attention.

It was then that Frank's new wife walked in. She
was even younger than Decker, and she was dressed
in silk and heels. Her face was perfectly made up,
with her long, sun-streaked hair artfully casual. She
hesitated on the threshold and stared at Decker's body
all through Frank's effusive introductions.

"Don't try to get up, boy, just sit still. Elise knows

you're recovering. She don't mind at all, do you, honey."

Still looking at Decker, Elise shook her head very, very slowly.

Decker shivered. Frank had him another barracuda.

She walked slowly over to Decker as if she had an intimate itch and it needed scratching. Just like the rest of Gimme's women. They'd all appeared to be that way but with most of them, the itch had been for Frank's money. This one looked like the real thing. Decker wondered if Frank could handle it.

Elise leaned over, and Decker flicked a chiding glance at her for doing anything so obvious. By moving his mouth slightly at the last minute, he managed to evade her wet kiss. She lifted her head and looked into his eyes, very amused by him. He grinned back and said heartily, "How do you do, Aunt Ellie. You're number six? Or is it seven."

She straightened to give him a fuller view before she replied, "Fifth."

"Two didn't count," Gimme put in helpfully.

Decker shook his head at his uncle. "I don't see how you survive?"

"Coors beer." He crushed the empty can in one hand and threw it exactly into a wire basket against the wall, under a painting of water lilies by Monet.

Bud knocked on the open door to the veranda as he stood there looking at them.

"Yeah, Bud?" Uncle Frank lolled back in his chair and watched.

Bud came into the room, gave a slight smile and the barest nod to indicate his awareness of Elise, then he told his boss, "It musta been a ricochet from last night. It was a cougar. Nice skin for your wife." He smiled openly at Elise. "We took it and the teeth and claws."

The very callousness of Bud's statement made Decker aware of his own injured hide, and a chill touched inside him.

"Want it?" Frank asked his wife.

She was disgusted. "No."

Frank and Bud both laughed, sharing a male look. Bud coaxed Elise, "We'll fix it nice for you. It's a good skin. Make a nice rug by your bed."

Frank gave Bud a speculative look.

Bud asked, "Okay, Boss?"

"How about you, Decker, want the skin?"

Uncle Frank didn't just glance over at Decker, he turned his head and looked straight at him. That indicated to Decker that Uncle Frank didn't want Bud to dress the skin for Elise. So Decker said, "If Aunt Ellie doesn't want it, I reckon I would take it. Thanks."

Frank said to Bud, "Okay." The agreeing word was dismissive, and Bud left.

At dinner, Aunt Elise sat half facing Decker and her shoeless foot explored his leg. So after they left the table, Decker sought Chico. "I still have trouble sleeping in a house. Could we quietly rig up a hammock somewhere outside? No need to mention where. I'd hate for my aunt to feel I was rejecting her hospitality or critical of the accommodations."

Having served the dinner and become fully aware of Decker's problem, Chico listened courteously, but his eyes danced with hilarity. Not trusting his words, his reply was only a nod.

Decker then joined his kinfolk out on the screened veranda for a nightcap. He could feel Elise pulsating

across the width of the porch. She moved her knees
minutely and she moved her body in silken whisperings that excited Decker's attentive libido. He had long
ago found it difficult to ignore an excited libido.

"Honey," Frank said shortly. "Decker and I have
some business to discuss. Would you excuse us?"

"Only if Decker will go for a moonlight ride with
me later."

Decker gave a token rise and replied pithily, "I can't
ride anything for a while yet. Give me a rain check
for next year."

"You poor boy!" Elise was all concern. "We'd go
slow."

Decker lay back in his chair again and told her
weakly, "I can't even get up—on a horse—to ride."

In leaving the room, she had turned her body away,
but she looked back over her shoulder and reminded
him: "There's always the mounting block."

Along with an easily excited libido, Decker had that
strong sense of family, and Elise shocked him. He
didn't reply to her but said a firm, "See you at breakfast, Auntie."

Frank smiled. Decker was his man. He settled down
to convince Decker that what he needed was a distraction. "You remember that little nothing place between me and that dry creek bed over yonder, on the
county road along the eastern edge of my property?"

Decker shook his head.

"You don't remember going with me to the drugstore and buying wax juice babies to chew?"

The man was a genius. He'd never taken Decker
anywhere. When Gimme built that house, Decker had
been about seventeen or eighteen, and past the wax
juice baby stage. Again, Decker just shook his head.

"Well, you was just a tad then. But that place is an annoyance to me. The people don't do nothing. They just sit around and let the place rot. I was about to buy the dregs out, and by jingo, they've started fixing up the shacks."

"So?"

"I figure somebody told them I was interested in squaring off my boundaries, and they think they can run up the price. You know that old Conner place?" Frank ignored Decker's head shake and went right on: "It's all painted up, the porch railings are fixed, and you wouldn't know the old wreck. Now, why would anybody fix it up if it wasn't to run up the price?"

"Civic pride?"

"In Sawbuck?" Frank's voice squeaked up in astonishment.

"No civic pride?"

"A sawbuck is a ten-dollar bill, and that's all that town's worth. Nothing there to be prideful *about*."

"Then . . . what?"

Maybe Decker's ordeal had addled his wits, so Frank said it again, enunciating carefully, "To run up the price."

"Why do you want the place if it's so tacky? You sure as hell got more land than you'll ever need."

"I know I got no kids." He sighed deeply. "It's not from lack of trying. Hell, how many women can stay un-caught? I get only the sterile ones, or they trick me. I got no kids of my own, just nieces and nephews, but I want the borders of my property even. I want it all neat and orderly for you all . . . when I die."

In the covering darkness, Decker had to smile. Adding that "when I die" to the end of the sentence wasn't a bid for emotion—this time—it was really an after-thought, because Frank knew he would live forever.

And just then Decker heard the sound of hoofbeats leaving the stable yard. Elise was on her way, and he could relax for a while.

Decker wondered why his uncle really wanted little old Sawbuck, Texas? A few shacks along a county road? If he had wanted the place, why had he waited until now? It didn't make sense. "What's the real reason?"

The question did take Frank by surprise. Chewing on his cigar he inhaled a little too quickly and therefore he could cough a couple of times as he assimilated the fact that he would have to give some more information.

Decker's head turned and his brown eyes showed yellow and seemed to shine in the soft light from inside the house. Frank removed his cigar in something of a shock. This was no recovering fledgling, this was a full-fledged man. One who balanced and weighed. Hell.

"There's some woman stirring them up." Frank gestured with the hand holding the cigar. "She come to Sawbuck about five months ago, and I've had nothing but trouble, ever since. She's not from Sawbuck. I hear tell she's not even a Texan, for crying out loud. She's probably some Yankee from up around Oklahoma!"

Decker laughed, and relieved, Frank joined in.

Decker asked, "What's her name?"

"Naomi Wentworth."

"How old is she?"

"I don't know. Less than thirty. It would be a favor to me if you'd ease in over there and see what the hell's going on, and why. The time for that settlement

is long past. It was dying a natural death. There's no
cause for somebody to come in there and start it up
all over again. It was dead just six months ago. Now
this female"—he spat the word—"is changing things.
She's ruining everything. Find out why for me. Do
this. The place'll mostly be yours someday. You might
just as well start learning to protect your borders.
What do you say . . . son."

Now *that* tagalong was for effect, Decker recognized
that. He wasn't interested in his uncle's land, but he
was saddled with the family loyalty.

"You'd have to be underground . . . uh . . . under
cover. Covert. You know what that is—"

"Do I?" Decker's tone was bitter.

So engrossed in himself, Frank didn't hear Decker's
bitter tone. "This'll be easy. Just a simple check to find
out what the hell that woman's up to and who the hell
she is."

This will be easy, Frank had assured Decker. With
the words, his uncle had unknowingly insulted
Decker. Gimme hadn't meant to rub salt into his soul,
so Decker only asked, "You haven't had anyone check
her out?" There was real disbelief in the words.

"She just appeared. Nobody knows a thing about
her, yet. It's weird."

"I'll sleep on it."

"That's all I ask. I know you're tired. The drive
down here's a bear cat. Your daddy said to go easy
on you. So take your time. No rush. That little lady
isn't going nowhere, damn it. You got all the time in
the world."

Frank implied he had told Decker's dad all about
the town and its problems. Had he? Rising slowly,
Decker stood still as his body adjusted to standing. He

hadn't heard the hoofbeats return, so now was a good time to get out of the house. "I'll say good night."

"You've been through a bad time. You oughtta be more careful where you go. Everybody knows that place down there's a hellhole." Gimme looked disgusted. "But it's past. Let it lay back there. Stay here as long as you like. This here's a healing place. I'd never stand the heat if I didn't have this to come back to. Good night, nephew. Sleep well."

Decker knew positively that his uncle was a backroom man. A wheeler-dealer. His pores craved stale smoke as his body craved beer. His brain lived on controversy. He'd sell his soul to win. He could not stand to lose. The only reason Frank had this place was for appearances... on occasion. He was seldom here. Yet he'd just called it a healing place in order to lure his nephew into believing he felt his borders threatened. He was a manipulator and used anything handy to get his way.

Decker slowly climbed the stairs to his room and opened the door. There was Elise on his bed. Did Frank's manipulation include sharing his wife? Tacky. "Well, Auntie," he greeted the naked woman. "Cooler now?"

She rolled over like a lithe animal and propped herself on her elbows to look up at him. In the moonlight, her long legs and the curve of her buttocks were perfectly shadowed, and the backlighting on the white sheet outlined her hanging breasts. Grudgingly he agreed with his libido that she was really something.

"Why are you avoiding me?"

"There's a little problem called my uncle Frank."

"He needn't know."

"I would."

"A goody-goody?"

Carefully, he took his sports shirt off over his head, then he replied, "Yes."

But then he tossed the shirt onto the chair, and she saw his body. "My God, Decker, what happened to you?"

"I got away."

"Not soon enough."

"The others weren't even this lucky."

She studied him silently, then guessed, "You feel guilty."

There was more to Elise than that gorgeous, hungry body. He didn't reply but undid his trousers and took them off, too.

She saw his hunger and made a throat sound. But as she saw his legs, her indrawn breath betrayed her horror. "Come to me." Her voice trembled. "I can help you to sleep."

"That's very kind of you, Elise, but I can't touch you. You're a generous, kind woman, but your husband is my uncle. I know you understand. My thanks." He pulled on pajamas, put his feet into moccasins, looked over at the luscious woman on his bed, and nodded once. At the slatted door onto the screened porch, he paused. "How did you get back without my hearing your horse?"

"I didn't leave. I sent one of the men off to patrol."

Decker nodded a series of tiny nods and replied, "Clever."

"I'm going to get you."

"Don't even try."

She turned over onto her back and lay full-length in the moonlight, her hair a tangle around her head. But Decker went stiffly on out of the room, down the stairs, and outside to find the hammock. He climbed into it, very carefully, and lay back to look up through the moon-blackened tree leaves, to the night sky beyond.

The best distraction was to try to figure out what it was about a twelve-year-long tolerance of Sawbuck that now rankled like a festering thorn in Frank's consciousness. Why? After all these years, why now? It might distract Decker to find out. He wondered what Naomi Wentworth was like. She had to be a hard-nosed, squint-eyed, pushy woman's libber.

But with the gentle sway of the hammock, the hard-nosed, squinty-eyed, pushy woman became very like Elise, beautiful, pliant...insistent.

CHAPTER
TWO

IT TOOK A COUPLE OF DAYS FOR DECKER TO CONvince himself to go to Sawbuck, and Uncle Gimme was smart enough not to push. The first thing Decker did was drive over to investigate the collection of shacks that was called after a ten-dollar bill.

A dry creek bed curled past and crossed the road below the town that was laid between Uncle Frank's fence and a dry wash. Most of the unpainted shacks were on the fence side, but along with some of the shacks among the trees by the dry wash, there was a gleaming white and tidy house. It sat up on modest stilts, and there were steps leading up to a wide porch.

It was obviously the refurbished Conner house that stuck in Uncle Frank's craw.

At a curve on the other side of town and just off the road sat a cop's car heading outward. At each side of town were signs that read SLOW TO 30 MPH. With the cop watching, that way, the passing traffic took those signs seriously.

In between those signs, there were few people moving around. Decker found he was watching primarily for a squinty-eyed, hard-nosed woman. He didn't see a one. He didn't dare to stop because watching for the bus and the passing cars was the only entertainment the idle natives had.

It was really a nothing town. He doubted if it was worth even the ten dollars of its namesake.

Along each side of the road, there was a string of stores, mostly vacant. On the front edges of the stores, supported by wooden pillars, was a continuous corrugated metal roof, shading the cracked cement sidewalks. There were chairs along the way, and sitting on some of them were men leaning back against the buildings, with their hats pulled down over their eyes, doing nothing.

It was a sorry excuse for a town. Why would Naomi Wentworth want to save it?

That night at supper, Decker asked his uncle, "What do the people do there in Sawbuck? What's their excuse for staying?"

His uncle raised innocent eyes and replied, "Damned if I know."

"If someone wants them to stay—"

"That woman."

"If 'that woman' expects them to stay there, she must have a reason—"

His uncle interrupted, "My thoughts exactly! She's probably a drug runner."

"—it's only logical that she plans some means of support for the town. I don't see any industry or even any fields in crops. What keeps them?"

"It is a question," his uncle agreed.

Elise just rubbed her soft foot along Decker's tensed calf and said nothing.

Decker looked judgmentally at his uncle. Had Gimme lost all interest in women that he couldn't figure out what his wife was doing with his nephew

at his very own table? It didn't seem plausible that
Frank could be that dumb. How long had they been
married? A year? Two?

Frank then gave the opinion: "It's my notion that
whatever is going on over there, that woman is up to
no good."

In spite of himself, Decker was intrigued. It took a
lot of guts to go into a dead bunch of shacks and try
to revive the town. There was a filling station that was
open. A drugstore. A grocery. But all the other stores
were vacant, with dirty, blind glass enclosing the
empty rooms.

The only amazing thing about the town was there
were no broken windows. That only proved there
were no teenagers roaming restlessly around. No
kids? Without kids the town was doomed.

When Elise had left the room after supper, Decker
inquired of his uncle, "How much rent should I pay
for one of those vacant stores?"

Frank looked up, excited. "You going in?"

Decker's lips moved faintly with his uncle's dramatic
words. "I can't just park the Mustang and walk around
asking questions."

"Smart." Frank nodded as if impressed.

"Why do you make it sound as if I'm so wise? You
told me it would be covert."

"Did I say that? Sometimes I amaze myself."

"The number on the public phone is—"

"Let me get a pencil. Okay . . . right . . . I got it."

"Don't call."

"Got it."

That night Elise was in Decker's room, as she had
been each night, and again he turned her down.

"You're healing. That's not why you won't. What's wrong with me?"

"Nothing. Don't you try to fool me, Elise, you know damned good and well that you're a very desirable lady. It's just against my principles. Now you take that sassy little tush off my bed and quit tempting me. You're not doing either of us any favors. Let me be."

"Please."

"Good God," he snarled through his teeth. "Give it up!"

They stared at each other for a time before she slowly got off the bed and picked up her robe. Holding it against her chest, she did leave. But in leaving, she deliberately gave him an exquisite vanishing view of her bare backside.

He stared after her for a while, then harshly took off his clothes, almost as if he were punishing himself. In night clothes, he went out onto the upstairs porch and down the stairs again.

Decker had been at his uncle's for five days, and he could feel strength slowly returning. The doctors had said all he needed was time. Well, he sure had a precious lot of that.

It was easier to get into the hammock. Was it just because he was used to it? Or was he fractionally stronger? They had told him there was no reason he wouldn't have a full recovery. To do . . . what.

Bitterly he lay in the topless cocoon and looked up through the darkened leaves at the clear night sky. Another night. Tomorrow there would be another. Then another.

He cleared his mind and found the pushy, squinty eyed, hard-nosed women's libber sneering at him. He smiled at her and again she melted like hot wax. He was going to meet her. Soon now.

In another of her long-sleeved, high-necked, ankle-length gowns and wearing another of her wide-brimmed hats, Naomi Wentworth watched as the bus stopped in Sawbuck. That was unusual.

So, like most of Sawbuck, Naomi saw the man get off the bus. She watched him step down into the powdery dust alongside the pavement. He moved with such a strange cautiousness that he might be stiff from traveling far. He was about thirty and medium-sized, well-built, and anonymously male.

He wore a battered Stetson and scuffed boots that made the faded jeans look poor instead of posh. There were spurs on his boots. She shook her head in exasperation. Getting off a bus wearing spurs. A cowboy? Then she saw the driver open the baggage section under the bus and haul out a scruffy old saddle. There was nothing so pitiful as a horseless cowboy.

Then a carved wooden saddle rack was brought out, and after that was a suitcase and two heavy cardboard boxes. An itinerant cowboy, Naomi thought sourly. Goody. Just what Sawbuck needed. Giving up on him as another zero, she went on with her purchases at the drugstore, but now and then she found that she would glance at the new arrival.

Checking a piece of paper pulled from his shirt pocket, the stranger looked around carefully. He squinted at the buildings and then looked back at the paper. The bus pulled away with the exhaust fumes puffing a choking cloud of good-bye.

The lone figure scratched under the back of his hat

in a mime of confusion. Down the cement walk, Joe sat with several other idle men. In a soft voice he asked, "What you looking for, mister?"

"Number five?" Stretching the words out, Decker drawled them with hesitant charm.

Joe was a short, red-faced man, about fifty. The watchers looked at each other in question. Then another of the chair sitters asked, "Number five... what?"

With each move Decker made, there was the soft clink from his ring spurs that carried a twirling disk within each one. "I was told it was a store on this street. I'm going to move in there?" He stressed the questioning statement in the manner of most Texans in a do-you-agree way.

"Why... a store?" asked one of the men.

"It's cheaper than a house, and I'm not trying to impress nobody."

The group exchanged shrugs and the first replied, "There's been no numbers for as long as I can recall."

Another asked, "What's the number of the drugstore." In another Texas peculiarity, the question was presented as a statement.

There was a silence, then Joe said bravely, "I'll go look." With deliberation, he put his hands on his knees in a pointed preparation to rising but indicating he could still be stopped.

"No, no." Decker held up staying hands. "Thank you. I'll go. I need toothpaste anyway." And he walked down toward the store.

Another of the group called after Decker, "We'll keep an eye on your gear."

"I'd appreciate it." Decker looked back at the group and touched the brim of his antique Stetson.

From the shadows at the back of the drugstore, Naomi watched the newcomer. He was dark-haired with brown eyes and average in height. He could fit in just about anywhere in the world without any particular attention. She listened as he explained why he was looking for number five. Sawbuckers didn't know Naomi owned the stores, so she gave no help.

Nobody knew what the drugstore number was. Some went out and looked, but there was no evidence a number had ever graced the doorway. "It must of been painted over," Mr. Buckle said solemnly.

"More than likely." Decker nodded seriously as they both studied the bare, grey wood.

"Maybe old Bill knows." That was the offering of a bystander.

"Where would I find Mr. Bill?"

"It's Miz Billmont?" That was said in the Texas questioning that asked if one understands. "She's in the house over yonder with the crepe myrtles by the stoop."

Decker touched his hat brim and clinked over there.

Mrs. Billmont was really old. She opened her door and smiled at Decker as she said, "Come inside. Oh, my, you're much too thin, dear. You sit right down at the table and try some of my raspberry tarts."

Decker took off his hat and sat down, but Mrs. Billmont couldn't find any raspberry tarts anywhere. She did search under a stack of papers and in drawers. She puzzled over which store was number five along with searching for raspberry tarts. She couldn't solve either problem.

After a time, Decker distracted the old lady from what numbers were on the stores, and the raspberry tarts, in order to take his leave. With the distinguishing spur-sound, he returned to the group on the sidewalk.

It ended up with everyone along the street examining all the storefronts, and they found the bottom of an eight . . . or was it a six . . . maybe a zero. "Three?" "Five?"

Buzz Garcia offered, "I know of a place where they started numbering along one side of the street, and when the other side built up, they just went right on with the numbering on that side."

Decker finally had to call the county seat from the freestanding booth. Decker was warned the phone didn't always work.

As he dropped in his money, he was caught again by the question as to why this town was being reclaimed. Who would want it?

The clerk at the county seat wasn't at all thrilled to look up which store was which over in Sawbuck. "Just pick one. They're all empty. I drive through there, and there's nothing there."

"I'm paying rent."

"Why."

"I'm an honest, loyal, God-fearing man."

"Married?"

"Honey, I'm living in an empty store."

"Yeah. You got a point there."

"This is costing me." Decker remembered a little late for his audience. "Call me back."

"I've been looking for it." She'd turned snippy. "Here. It's the fifth one from the northwest corner. Wait. There's only three stores here. How could it be the fifth?" But she figured that since those were numbered one, three, and five, it was the third one.

Decker reported that information to the waiting

group lounging in the shade, and they all looked down the street to the last empty store. So did Decker. That was his new home. He felt a definite lack of enthusiasm.

"One nice thing, in the evening it's the shady side. And next winter, the sun'll shine in nice and warm."

Decker wasn't going to be anywhere near Sawbuck even a month from then.

The idle men watched Decker carry his saddle and suitcase into the store. The interior was really crummy. Being vacant so long, it was layered with dust over the dirt and debris. There was a lot of useless junk piled around. At the back of the store was an all-purpose sink that was cruddy. And under the window was a gas-burner stove. No oven. At the other end of that back, partitioned space was a closet toilet that had been badly neglected by "maintenance."

After this session, Gimme would owe his nephew Decker.

He found a very old broom, tried it, and it worked well enough. There was a battered bucket that had a bullet hole about three quarters of the way up. It would do. And there was a mop handle with a rusted wire holder for a towel. It would take a good deal of work before he'd need a mop.

As he worked, a couple of the sidewalk loungers came to stand in Decker's doorway. There had been several mild insults in Spanish to test Decker's knowledge of the language. Although he understood and spoke it perfectly, he didn't respond at all. It was a truism that if you were in a strange place, you learned many an odd and interesting thing if you concealed the fact that you understood what was being said. It had been especially true in Decker's experience.

Without asking permission, several of the men brought their chairs inside number five and sat around commenting in Spanish. Even the Anglos spoke and understood the language, but their accents and pronunciations had Texanized the sounds rather amazingly. And it became apparent there were a couple of the men who spoke no English at all.

Their Spanish-spoken observations were on Decker's possessions, his wearing spurs, his probable ability with a woman, and his status as a man. They speculated why such a one would have chosen to land in Sawbuck.

Decker thought that was a good question.

"What are you called?" John asked in English.

"Decker."

They nodded, accepting that he didn't elaborate. In turn, they called each other by first names, and Decker learned who they were.

Buzz Garcia was Decker's age. He was part Hispanic and maybe a part Indian. He was as tall as Decker, solid, with dark straight hair and snapping black eyes. Looking over the accumulation of discarded debris, Buzz offered information, "There's a dump down toward the pit. About three mile. You got a car?"

"I think I've got a pickup spotted that might work out okay."

"Yeah? What kind?"

Vehicles were a common touchstone with men. Motors and sports. Any man can talk to another on either subject or both, no matter where he finds another man. Thinking that, Decker forgot himself and took off his shirt.

The men fell silent at the sight of the abuse his body had survived. Not his face. Just his body. Obviously, he'd been brutally beaten. The silence was uneasy. Decker looked up into sober faces. Realizing what caused the silence, he explained, "I tried to help some friends who were in trouble, but there were more of them than us." All that he said was true.

"A woman." It was a statement.

"One was." That, too, was an honest reply, and he remembered Anne. Brave, independent Anne who had thought she was invincible.

"She had a husband." Another assumption.

"For a while," Decker agreed sadly.

With the sparseness of Decker's replies, the listeners' imaginations decided the circumstances, and they shrugged as they shook their heads. What man hadn't had woman trouble?

Not being able to hear the conversations in number five, others came in with their chairs. "What is being said?" one asked in Spanish.

"We speak of women," was the reply.

"I had a woman once who would screw anything in pants. She was very strange." Cortez frowned, thinking of the woman.

"If she screwed you, she was strange," Buzz teased.

But Cortez was serious. "She couldn't get enough of it."

"You should have given her my name," mourned John who had sticks for bones and no teeth at all. "Although I am called John, my name is really Juan, which in the language can be interpreted as 'one.' So I am The One."

There were hoots of hilarity, but John only waited until he could say, "Why do you think I look this way? I am really only forty, but women can't leave me alone."

That led to some really raunchy comments, and Decker had to be careful which ones were said in English so that he could laugh at the right times. Some of the ones in Spanish were exquisitely funny because the words were so beautifully crude.

Decker's observers couldn't stand to watch such an injured man work alone. Skinny John was first to help, but Buzz was next, and soon several of the men moved languidly and so unobtrusively as to seem not to work at all, but they did.

It was when they got to the place they could mop the floor that the beginnings of understanding came to Decker. There was no water. Decker turned the spigot over the raunchy sink and there wasn't even a sputter. He couldn't believe it.

John told him, "There's no water."

"No water? Don't you just call the service company to come and turn it on?"

"There is none." John put a bony hand on Decker's arm and looked up into his face very seriously. "That Jones, over on the other side of the fence, steals our water."

"How."

"The wells are dry. He digs deeper and takes the water that went under our land."

"He uses it to irrigate crops." Decker clarified it. There were many big projects of irrigation and water spraying all over the country that duplicated the drying up of these local farm wells. "When did the wells go dry?"

"It began five years ago."

"Six," said another.

"Four. Our truck farms dried up, too. We have no income now. The town can't support itself."

"Why do you stay?"

That question appeared to stymie them.

Finally John replied for them all, "We know of no other place. No other way. This is our home."

Decker countered, "Your people haven't been here forever. Once this land belonged to others, and your people came here and took it from them. Why don't you move on, again?"

"Our people had a better place to come to. We have no better place to go." Then John asked Decker, "Why are you here?"

"I thought I could live here very reasonably, while I heal and get back on my feet." It was the first time he'd used his injuries as a reason for anything. Who would ever have believed that terrible time could come in handy, as an excuse, but it was the perfect reply. He felt a great irony.

Reasonably, he commented, "You can't live here without water. What are you doing for water?"

"When our wells first began to spit sand, we complained to Jones. We were told we ought to move out because the town was dead. But he had no idea where we could go. We have our houses here and our friends. We argued with his man—"

Decker caught "his man." Naturally Gimme wouldn't be available to defend his actions. It would be "his man."

"—he would see what he could do. We got a well. It's over by his fence, and when they are spraying, it won't work. But we do have water."

"How do you get it to the houses?"

"Naomi set up a schedule, and we have new drums like are used for oil. We fill 'em with a hose."

Naomi, the squint-eyed, hard-nosed, prickly wom-

an's libber who was saving this useless town. Here she
was: here were Naomi's first footprints on the town.
"How do I get a barrel?" Decker inquired.

"You ask Naomi. There's no cleaning a used one.
She finds clean ones. She just might have one at her
place."

With the thought that he would meet her, he was
astonished that a lick of something like excitement
went down him, and he smiled to himself. That was
Elise's fault. Naomi had been magically turning into
the eager, forbidden Elise every night. It would be
interesting to see what this Naomi really looked like;
but then, disillusioned, what would he dream about?
Finding dreams and losing them had happened too
often lately. Dreams of freedom, dreams of being
pain-free, dreams of Elise. . . . His attention came back
to the present and he remembered the barrel and
Naomi. "How do I find this Naomi?"

"She saw you get off the bus, and watched us looking for the number, but then she went on into town."

She'd been there? He didn't remember anyone who
could have caught his eye. A zero. "So. I wait?"

The men exchanged glances and then they grinned.
"Since you're our first new citizen since Naomi and
her friend, we'll help you carry water. Don't make a
habit of this."

"Beer on the house."

"Where'd you find beer?" they wanted to know.

"The two boxes outside."

They were appalled. "We left them alone on the
sidewalk? The bus could have thought the boxes were
cargo and taken them away!"

There was a scramble to retrieve the boxes. Motors,
sports, women, and beer. All touchstones.

Decker asked offhandedly: "Who is Naomi's 'friend'?"

"Trisha."

Decker nodded slowly. Naomi and Trisha. Probably lesbians.

With the beer out the back door in a rinsed, battered tin tub filled with cold water, the men finished the cleaning. Decker passed the water-cooled cans around as the sweaty bunch surveyed their accomplishment. Even scrubbed, the store didn't look any better. The pristine toilet worked with a couple of buckets of water, but it would be easier to use one of the privies. The store interior was still dreary and scruffy, but it was easy, now, to see out the front window.

"You're going to need to tape up newspapers or you'll have the town women and any of the pass-through women all standing on the walk, every morning and every night, watching you."

Buzz offered, "Need a roomie?"

As much as the loiterers had helped, the day had taken its toll on Decker. He'd stocked a sparse supply of groceries and eaten alone. It was early evening when he hooked his hammock in one corner of the room, across a doorway for the breeze, and he slept like a dead man.

He wakened and lay in his semicocoon with a sense of . . . what? Not contentment. But that he was again getting control. It was a strange feeling for it had been a while since he'd felt that way.

He put a leg over the edge of the hammock to rise and stopped dead. Sitting ten feet away, inside his locked door, there stood a new metal oil drum standing upright on a metal-legged rack. Now, how in the *hell* had they gotten that inside without him hearing? He who could hear a man's silenced breath from a hundred feet away?

They were a den of thieves. That's how they supported themselves. They lounged around all day and were cat burglars at night. Naomi was their fence.

He got up, inspected the drum, and with an immediate inner stillness, he noted the fine sheen of moisture on the outside of it. They had not only put the drum there, they'd filled it? He touched the heft of it. It was full.

Decker's mind shifted. Was this a warning to him? He'd been followed? They knew who he was and whom he represented? He narrowed his eyes. The water was poisoned. He'd drink it, drop dead, and vanish. No. That would be too crude. As smart as they were, guided by that black widow spider of a Naomi Wentworth, this was just a touché. It was the touch of a sword point to let him know what they could do— if they chose.

He shivered. His nerves lost control. His blood went to his heart and brain, leaving his arms and legs cold and clammy. He shook. And with the last vestiges of reason, he gave credit for his breaking—at last— where it belonged, back in the jungles of South America.

He went out the door, under the open sky and over the fence onto his uncle's land. Even doing that was only symbolic. He was closer to "them" than to any help. They could come over that fence and . . . He looked back and saw Buzz coming over the fence! And Decker's feet became rooted in his nightmare of terror.

"Decker, don't come over the fence to piss. Use the

privy. Jones gets mean if we come over the fence. He has dogs. Come back." Buzz was by then close enough to see Decker clearly, and his voice changed. "Hey, man. You okay? Hey, now, what's the matter? Them guys after you? You got friends here. But come out of the field. Let me help you. What is it? Nightmares? Don't worry. You're okay here."

And Decker cried. His grief for his friends, the pain he'd endured, caught up with him, and after all that time, he finally cried. Out of practice, he did a lousy job of it. His body was racked with his shuddering, the sounds torn from his throat were harsh.

Buzz's voice gentled as if with a spooked horse. "Those bastards. What kind of men do they think they are to do this to another man. It's them that oughtta cry. Shame to them. Here. We have to get outta this field. The lines are wired. The dogs'll be here. Come on. I'll help. Where can I touch you'n not hurt you?"

Decker gave Buzz his hand, and Buzz led Decker's stumbling steps to the fence and got Decker through as the dogs shot into sight. As the two men stood safely on the other side of the fence, the dogs were in a frustrated frenzy of spittle-flecked barking.

That afternoon, Decker rode the bus into town and called Chico to come get him. Both men were silent as they returned to Frank Jones's deceptively modest house.

When Decker was lying back on Uncle Gimme's veranda, Chico put a cold glass of iced tea in his hand. Decker lifted the glass to salute the kind man. Decker was still a little pale, but that was covered by the flush caused by Elise's hungry eyes smoldering over him.

Decker felt beleaguered. He asked his uncle roughly, "Did you get the pickup?"

Frank replied, "They had to lift the body and put the new truck under it. This is a 'tour dah farce.' You got a real truck there."

In disparagement, Decker added to that: "—and anybody who opens the hood will see the new motor. How do I explain that? You're about as subtle as a baseball bat."

His uncle laughed. "You underestimate me. The motor looks used. Come see."

With effort, Decker stood up, and Elise leaped to help, brushing against him. Her hands were gentle and her nearness touched softly deep in him, weakening him further.

Frank said to his wife, "Thanks, honey, give us a couple of minutes. We have some business. Okay?"

She left reluctantly. With determination, Decker rose and his spurs clinked.

"Wearing spurs?" Gimme was incredulous.

"For ID."

Gimme was impressed. "When they hear spurs, they know it's you. Right?" He chuckled. Then he narrowed his eyes. "And if they *don't* hear that clink, they don't know you're walking?"

Decker only looked at his uncle.

"You're smarter than I thought."

The truck was perfect. As reliable as a new truck, it had the appearance of being on its last legs... wheels. Even those wheels looked as if they'd seen enough miles. "How'd you get this done so fast?"

"Money."

"It's exactly right," Decker said approvingly. "I think I'll leave it here another day or two. It's important that I seem indigent while I get to know the town."

"That sounds logical. What do you think of Saw-buck?"

"You're a first-class bastard."

Frank frowned just a bit trying to figure that out. "Why."

"The dogs."

"Great show, aren't they? They wouldn't hurt a flea." Frank laughed with much pleasure.

"They gave every indication of tearing us apart."

"They're trained that way. Money." Frank tilted his head in an interested way. "What were you doing in the fields?"

"I had the night terrors after I woke up this morning." The time contradiction was telling.

Frank lifted his brows as he pulled down his mouth. "That happen often?"

"First time."

Very soberly and with censure. "What caused it?"

"I've found I'm not invincible." Like Anne.

Old Gimme scowled and pushed out his bottom lip. "You're not going to let a bunch of losers rattle you, are you?"

"No, Uncle, I'm going to do them a favor and run them out of town."

"Good boy."

And Decker looked at his placidly serene relative and thought that's what the bastard would have said to a dog that had obeyed.

CHAPTER THREE

IT WAS CHICO WHO DROVE DECKER INTO SAN Antonio to the bus station, and Decker took the evening bus back to Sawbuck with a strange feeling of almost calm resignation. His muscles countered that mood by objecting about bus rides all the way to Sawbuck.

In the evening's last light, the sidewalk sitters were still there. The captive audience watched Decker's stiff descent from the bus. He moved so slowly that even the spurs sounded tired. There were noncommittal greetings, then one asked, "Job hunting?"

"Yep."

"Anything decent?"

"Nope."

"Better luck next time."

"Thanks."

Buzz's softened voice asked casually, "You okay, man?"

"Yeah. Thanks." Decker went on to his store and it wasn't long before he went to the hammock.

As he lay there, he heard laughter. Women had come along and were talking to the men. Later, behind the stores, there was the unique shuffling of feet that was a dance of another kind, then a flutter of sound; and Decker wondered if it was the irresistible skin-and-bones John. He sure as hell couldn't pay. What woman would need it so bad that she'd use John?

Into Decker's mind came the vision of the squint eyed woman's libber who had seen him get off the bus that first day with his suitcase. She hadn't been interested enough to wait and meet him. Decker considered her for a while, then wondered how she handled the men in Sawbuck. Was she the foot-shuffling woman with a man in back of his store? After all his dreams of her, it would be disillusioning to think she'd be that hard up.

Of course, he hadn't met all the men in Sawbuck. There might well be some studs who would fill her bill. He felt there was competition. So. After a week of having the hard-nosed Naomi turning into Elise every night in his dreams, he was just a tad possessive? He smiled and slowly shook his head.

Then Decker considered the strange day. It was interesting to him that after his nerves had shattered that morning, and Buzz had rescued him from the fields, Decker felt almost secure in the town. Was it a false security? He hoped to God that it was real. He could stand feeling safe for a little while.

As usual, he was cautious about allowing himself to sleep. His recovering body needed the sleep, while his mind didn't want to lose itself in the hell pit of unconsciousness. He knew of no way to live without sleeping, but he relinquished his hold on himself with great reluctance. If he could concentrate on one pleasant thought, the terrible realities stayed just beyond the edge in the darkness. Elise had helped him for this while. Wouldn't it amuse her to know that Frank's goody-goody nephew dreamed of her, lasciviously?

His conscience had altered Elise's temptation into being Naomi, an unknown. Unknown, she was not complicated with staid reactions, disagreeable rejections, or bodily flaws. In his mind, he'd made Naomi lush and ripe and very willing.

What would she really be like? Considering that, he slept.

In the morning, he began his routine. He dragged the saddle on its mount out onto the communal sidewalk. Then he fetched an old rusted chrome and torn vinyl chair to place alongside the block. He began to rub saddle soap into the parched leather, working it.

Idle men love to watch someone else work. Gradually Sawbuck's idlers carried their chairs over and sat around Decker. They made observations in Spanish about the saddle being beyond redemption of any kind, and in English they asked what kind of job Decker wanted. As a cowboy? What?

"One that pays more than I'm worth."

That brought grins. It was the dream of all people. The men then tilted back their chairs and talked about the kind of jobs they'd like. Most of the quick, bragging ones had to do with satisfying some insatiable woman.

"Which one of you randy goats was out behind my store last night, making those attention-getting noises?"

"Huh?" "What time?" "You mean somebody was . . . ?" The men sent quick searching looks at one another. And for the several who spoke no English, there were Spanish explanations.

Apparently, it hadn't been any of them. Interesting.

"Did you see anything?"

Decker shook his head. "I could tell one was a woman."

"How do you know that?"

"She was, uh, gasping."

There followed a very tense silence. Then they began to talk quickly for a time about looking for jobs, about not being trained to do anything but farm, and they mentioned the stream of commuter cars going through town, twice daily, on their way into and back from San Antonio.

"The people work there but they live outside of town. People around here can't make it truck farming now, without water, so they have to have other jobs. And with Jones, over there, pulling away all the water from the land, it makes it tough."

"What do you all do? How do you make a living?"

"We don't no more."

"I only ask to see what, maybe, I can do," Decker explained.

"I got a job two hours a day at the gas pump during the rush hours," Buzz mentioned.

"Yeah. The women like to look at his crotch." That was the hooting explanation.

When the teasing settled down, they got back to how it was with them. "Some of our women work. They go into town to jobs. They want to move there so we can get jobs, too. But work isn't that easy to find, and here, we can live on what the women make."

"Have you always been out of work?" Decker asked them.

"No," John replied for the lot. "We had the truck farms. We took our vegetables into town to the farmers' market and sold them there. It was a good life. Without the water, we can't grow enough to take into town. We grow for our own tables.

"Naomi found chickens from several places that were culling flocks. Since she came here, she's found chickens for almost all of us. We let them out into the fields, and some of them go over into Jones's fields for bugs. But they eat from the crops, too, and that makes the people over there very mad."

"What do they do?"

John shrugged. "The dogs."

"Yes." There was a silence, then Decker asked, "When do I meet Naomi?"

"She doesn't have much to do with us men. She talks to the women. I don't know where she gets her money, or if she works. She doesn't have a regular job. But she must have some income. We painted the Conner house for her, and she paid us. She and her friend stay there. That old pickup of hers is no good. It rattles and shakes but it doesn't bother her. It seems to keep going."

"But she works?"

"We don't know. She got the women doing snow-flakes with string for Christmas. Dolls made of cloth. The confetti eggs. We get nothing but scrambled eggs around here. The chickens, you remember. Well, the women poke a hole in one end of the egg and shake out the insides. Then they rinse the shell and dry it before they stuff the shells with confetti. People buy them to break them open at parties."

"Fill the egg with confetti through a little hole?"

"Yep," Joe said. "Then they put a little bit of tape over it and paint the eggs real pretty for all the holidays, Easter, the Fourth of July, Halloween, Christmas, and such."

"She wants us to paint the stores and sell the women's products here in Sawbuck."

Doubtfully, Decker looked around at the bare, thirsty boards. "Who buys the paint?"

"Not us."

Then Decker asked again, "How do I meet Naomi?"

"You'll see her soon enough," Buzz assured him. "In a town this size, you can't miss her."

But he did, at every turn.

It was around then that the dog came limping into town. He was an enormous thing. No one had seen anything like him. He had a beard, and was gangly and his grey coat was ruffled and untidy-looking. He sat down in a sloppy, unmannerly way and howled, not from his mouth or lungs, but from his guts. It was an impressive sound. Then he waited five minutes before he began to howl again.

Decker came out of his store and stood with his hands on his hips in pure disgust. Who had let his dog out? How had it tracked him down? "Wellington!"

But the dog wouldn't speak to him.

Decker went over and squatted down, but the dog turned his back.

The loungers gathered only close enough to hear Decker apologizing. Then they laughed, and the dog, Wellington, smiled garishly at them. The men then laughed until tears came.

Decker was disgusted. He ended up dragging the dog out of the sun and giving him a bowl of water.

"Is that misshapen creature yours?" John asked in awe.

"God knows how he found me."

Joe complained, "In twenty years, every damn dog in the county will look like that."

The thought was stunning.

"Why would you have a dog like that?"

"He . . . guards my back."

"What do you do that your back must be guarded?" Buzz slouched against a post and waited.

"I fight for truth and justice."

"Whose truth and whose justice?"

"As I see it."

"Ahhh," said John. And after that, everyone was thoughtful.

Decker bought rolls of butcher paper and covered his front window and the door panel.

John said, "The fly doesn't wish to be observed."

Buzz explained, "He doesn't wanna get caught."

Cortez laughed, asking, "Doing what?"

Decker shook his head. "My daddy taught me not to give it away."

They had a growing appreciation of Decker.

That night he heard cries of protest, from female voices on the street, about his covered windows, and he grinned to himself.

As a couple of days passed, Decker kept tabs on the Conner house. He couldn't be too obvious about that. In fact, being the only stranger and being watched constantly out of idle curiosity, he was very hampered. The Sawbuck boredom made Decker's every move interesting to the loungers.

Followed by Wellington, he had gone clinking over to Naomi's house and knocked, ostensibly to thank her for the oil drum, but no one came to her door. He couldn't show too much interest in her this soon and leave a note or anything. Where the hell was she?

By the fifth day Decker had his pickup. All the men looked it over with great interest and criticism. But they all agreed it had been a good buy. The body was very sad, bent and rusted, but the rest looked surprisingly good. Only Buzz was silent about it, and Decker waited for his questions, but there were none.

Decker finally indicated that he knew the cop car was a fake. The weeds had grown. There were no tracks in them. He drove over and ran his pickup close to the front of the fake car in order to make tracks, and the men watched in good humor.

With the truck as an excuse, Decker suggested to the men that they collect any junk they had, and he'd haul it away with the stuff he'd taken from his store. But after that, Decker said, "Why not take the town's junk? Might just as well. We got nothing else to do."

John protested, "I have to save my strength for the women."

The men were rudely indulgent "saving" the old man's strength. In the beginning, they were lethargic as they contacted all the people and began to pile the collected junk in back of Decker's store. The pile became awesome. How long had the stuff lain around? But it gave a purpose to the days. And Decker began to meet more of the people.

With great care, during that time, Decker had made a trapdoor in the ceiling of the toilet closet. He worked as carefully as a prisoner trying to escape. Working secretly, he cleared the debris, adding it to the pile to be taken away.

Spurless, he could then leave his locked store and go silently through the ceiling onto the roof. From there he could slip into the oak tree that sprawled over considerable space, and choose his descent. But

on the ground, Wellington found Decker and followed, as his breed had been trained to do long ago
as Irish war dogs. Decker hadn't been joking when
he said Wellington guarded his back.

Together they would slip into the woods along the
wash, and they watched. Men moved in the night.
Some Decker recognized. But some were strangers.
It wasn't long before Decker knew the Sawbuck men
were the watchers of those strangers. Who were they?
Why were they traveling at night?

And in those covert venturings, Decker had a star-
tling confrontation with a large eye. It was painted in
white and black on a slanting board, and it stared at
the intruder.

One night at dusk, the men met to talk lazily as they
spent time carelessly before giving up and going to
bed. A man came down the concrete walkway toward
the loungers. He walked hard with taps on his heels.
He wanted people to know he was coming. Decker
didn't look up. Someone whispered, "Big Dog," and
Decker knew it was Buzz who warned him.

"What's going on?" the intruder's rough voice
asked. Then, so that they would know who he was
and be warned, he lit a cigarette. The match flare was
deliberately held a minute so that his face was visible
to them all. He was a big hard man about forty, maybe
not quite that. He growled, "I see we got a new bum
in the place. Who're you?"

Nice, thought Decker. How come nobody mentioned this Big Dog before now? Damn. "Name's
Jones." Decker sat, leaning his chair back against the
wall, but he felt tiny tremors of fear begin in his healing body.

The other men were all silent, and Decker was especially conscious that none had greeted the newcomer.

"What you doing here?" questioned the Big Dog.

"Living." Decker then moved his boot enough so that a spur stirred with a muted macho sound.

"Why you here?"

How Decker then handled himself would be crucial. He sighed inwardly and asked with curiosity, "Why do you ask?"

"This is my town. Nobody comes here without I say so."

With discipline that awed him, Decker sat lax. "May I." His voice was very soft and consequently very dangerous as he deliberately put the conversation into the context of a child's game.

The air was suddenly electric. There was the strong odor of man. Decker thought how primitive they all were, and a part of him had time to be amused.

Oddly, instead of reaching out and hauling Decker off that chair, the Big Dog snarled, "I'll think about it."

Decker made no reply. But the man hesitated a betrayingly uncertain second before he left, striding on his hard heels back down the sidewalk.

When he was out of hearing, the men around Decker relaxed with tiny moves and became rather animated in a hushed way. Joe asked, "How'd you know how to handle that bastard?"

"I've run into bastards before."

Buzz cautioned, "It isn't over."

"Maybe," Decker replied.

"No wonder you was all beat up." Cortez almost giggled with nervousness.

Buzz said in some irritation, "Any man who moves so careful, as you still do, ought not to be waving a bloody bone, you, in a Big Dog's hungry face."

"Does he go by any known name?" Decker asked softly.

"Rual Simpson," John supplied.

"I see." Decker's voice was still that soft way, and the other men watched him.

"You find that interesting?" Buzz was the one who asked.

"We'll see."

That was accepted as Decker's reply. It was an odd one, and Decker knew that, but he didn't want to say anything more. Somewhere he'd heard Rual's name.

Then the men asked, "Jones? You any kin to... Frank Jones?" And the men all watched Decker.

"If he's a Jones, then we're connected." He couldn't lie. There was a long silence. Decker waited what he thought was enough time before he excused himself and walked down toward his store with the muted clink of his spurs.

During the day, the men went around collecting the scraps and digging out things discarded so long ago that they'd sunk into the ground. The men took apart three useless shells of long-ago rusted-out cars, and added them to the pile.

Having their area tidied lifted the spirits of the natives, and there were nice comments, willing help, and more contributions to the pile.

As they cleared her yard, old Mrs. Billmont offered them all raspberry tarts but, knowledgeable now, even Decker declined with thanks.

It was John who took Decker to meet Magdalena.

She was ancient, John said. "She doesn't just look old, she is. We believe she is more than one hundred years. She doesn't move much. Naomi loves her. She said the sun was too bright for Magdalena's old eyes. See the tree there? Naomi made us dig three up and plant them by Magdalena's window, but two died.

"We worked very hard, but we did get the trees transplanted. We used Naomi's truck to pull the trees into place. Naomi has the children carrying water every Saturday to see to it that this tree survives." John shrugged. "It is possible."

It was a mimosa, lacy and fragile. A good size, it was as tall as the eaves of the house, and it did give a sparse shade.

As they went to Magdalena's door, where John knocked, Decker thought it was just the kind of tree a woman would dig up and move. Not a good sturdy tree, but a mimosa.

Magdalena's granddaughter wakened the old lady and helped her to come into the main room of the shack. Old Magdalena's words were infrequent and very slow. In Spanish, she asked Decker, "You wear spurs?"

Decker replied in her language, "To remind me that I'm walking."

"Ahhh," said the old lady in the universal language of sound. Then she reverted to her own language, "You take the junk to the pit?"

"Pit?" he questioned in English. Then he, too, went back to Spanish, "No. I'll take it into town to be re-cycled. If there's any money in it, you'll get it. On my honor."

All the wrinkles moved into a fascinating smile for

the young man, and the old eyes were curious. "You have honor?"

Decker smiled back. "Much."

In Spanish John asked, "So you understand our language a little?"

"A little more than that." Decker looked at John. John would know that he never lied.

John grinned his toothless grimace. "I suspected it was so. Your eyes danced with our bad teasing that first day. You had trouble not laughing, at times."

"You were all terrible jokesters."

"Yes." There was pride in John.

And Decker laughed.

Magdalena wanted to know the jokes, and John selected some for her to hear. She laughed with a hand over her mouth, her eyes twinkling with sparkling lights.

Decker bet she'd been a handful when she was young.

With the bulk of the accumulating pile of junk, and the size of the small pickup, Decker now had the excuse to follow Naomi into town. But she didn't leave Sawbuck for several days. She did come out of the house. People commented on the fact that she was pleased that the junk was being picked up. She helped. But it was never when Decker was around.

Was she avoiding him?

And that was added to his dreams. She was smitten and knew they'd come together like a mating of the cosmos, and she was afraid of the devastation of their attraction. Right.

But it was very odd that in a town the size of Sawbuck, they didn't meet. It would seem the citizens would all stumble over one another during the course of any twenty-four hours, but it didn't work out that way. Decker hadn't met even half of the fewer than one hundred citizens of that sorry town.

There were the younger women who strolled by and smiled at him, but he was cautious of singling out one. He could be distracted. Then, too, he wouldn't be around long.

He'd met some of the women who stopped by his store to welcome him to Sawbuck, and they were pleasant; and he met some of the little kids who were big-eyed and peeking at him, but he didn't even catch a glimpse of her, of Naomi . . . that he knew.

Judiciously, he and Wellington continued to go out. Never on the same night of the week nor with a certain number of days between. It was random and careful.

The great eye had been moved. Why? Was it a signal?

And he discovered Rual was the man who met a woman behind Decker's store. Why there?

Slowly, every other day or so, he and Wellington took a load of junk into town, had it weighed and calculated what it would bring in prime scrap. He would divide out that amount to the amazed previous hoarders. Glass, paper, and aluminum did bring cash, but the rest was just accepted without payment.

The bits of cash stimulated an interest in the junk, which was searched out. It didn't cost Decker very much and it gave the men incentive. He was beginning to like them. They were easy, pleasant, undemanding companions. Not one was gung-ho. It was an easy, healing time.

As he waited to meet Naomi, and as he became acquainted and listened, Decker got his saddle back in good condition. It became supple, pliant, and smooth. Then he worked on his rope. It had been handwoven of strips of leather and it, too, had been neglected while he'd been out of the country. Now he worked it, and the men watched.

"Can you throw that thing?" Buzz asked one day.

"Yep."

"Let's see you do it."

It was a time when some of the littler kids were hanging around, listening; and the men had cleaned up the stories, knowing the big ears were paying attention.

Decker made the sliding knot and drew the rope through until the loop was a nice four feet in diameter. He stood up, and his spurs clinked as he stepped off into the dusty stretch by the side of the now-vacant road. He began to twirl the rope, allowing the sliding knot to be fed by the trailing end until the rope's circle measured about six feet.

Decker twirled it up, then stepped beneath the circle and allowed it to come down around his body. His movement, the whisper of the rope, and his answering spurs were primal and stirring. The skill was of another era. It had been a long time since Decker had used those muscles in that way; and he stopped, allowing the loop to collapse.

The men clapped and exclaimed, nice enough, and the bright-eyed kids clapped, too, but they giggled and their hands hid their laughter.

Decker was untying the knot and pulling the rope into order when Buzz said offhandedly, "You had everybody gawking at you. Nobody does a real rope anymore. Even Naomi was watching."

"Where?" Decker jerked around.

"There she goes, yonder."

"I've never thanked her for the oil drum." Decker set his Stetson on his head a little firmer than necessary, squinting at the slight figure in the long gown, hunkered down to listen to some little kid before she rose and walked toward her own house. "I ought to do that or my mother will wince at my manners."

"Wince." Cortez studied the word.

Decker explained, "She's a lady and she wouldn't ever shudder over a child of hers, but she might wince."

The men found that uncommonly funny. So they watched tolerantly as Decker set off, his spurs clinking, for his cosmic clash with a squint eyed, hard-nosed woman's libber named Naomi Wentworth.

She'd just closed her door not two minutes before. She had to be there, this time. She had no excuse not to answer his knock. Ignoring the bell, he pounded on the barrier.

She opened it almost instantly, and he stared down at her. She was short. She was pretty. Her eyes were enormous. And she was quiet. No spark at all. She was a mouse. The dress wasn't only long, it was long-sleeved and high-necked. She was a zero. She was one hell of a disappointment. He relaxed and said, "I'm Decker Jones. I live in store number five? Thank you for the oil drum for the water. I can pay for it."

She didn't smile or ask him in, as any cordial person would do to a fellow citizen. She snubbed him. She didn't even speak. She took his money, nodded, and closed the door.

All his dreams of the pliable, insistent, voracious lover evaporated. Without a vision, with no hope of one, he turned, went down the steps and back to the store, his spurs sounding melancholy to his ears.

He'd never been so disappointed in all his life. She wasn't squint eyed or hard-nosed or strident. She was really fragile and quite lovely, but she was a mouse. That was disillusioning. She hadn't said one word. He'd handed her a twenty-dollar bill, and she'd taken it.

What did an empty oil drum cost? Nowhere near twenty dollars. She was a rip-off artist. She thought him a patsy? Well, she was in for a surprise.

But that night, in his hammock, he no longer had his dream of her to soothe him into sleep. How can a beleaguered man use a mouse as a protector from the dark realities of the underside of life? And he went into the void of unconsciousness without a shield. His dreams were horrific, and he saw a mouse come between them and him. A brave mouse? But she *was* there. And he wakened to lie in the still, hot night and think about a woman who wasn't anything at all but a short mouse who could come to this nothing town and try to save it. Maybe she wasn't such a mouse, after all.

When he went into town the next day, he called a friend, Pat, at the agency and asked for a check on Naomi Wentworth.

"Give me more," was the harried request.

"That's all I have."

Pat sighed. "Oh, hell."

"Find out for me."

"How urgent is it?"

"Not first wave."

Pat was sarcastic. "Goody."

"You have no respect for a fellow man."

There was a little silence, then Pat said tersely, "Oh,

yes, Decker, you have all my respect. I should have been in that hell with you."

"No!" Decker protested in anguish. "It wouldn't have changed anything. It would have made no difference at all. Remember that."

"I feel such a hell of a guilt for not being there."

"It wasn't possible. It would still have happened if you'd been there. There was no way to help."

"But I should have known."

"With a crystal ball? Don't torture yourself. If I'd thought for one minute that you were having this problem, I wouldn't have called for this. It's a woman who's come to Sawbuck, Texas, population less than one hundred, and she's trying to revive a dead town. We don't know why."

"Nothing criminal?"

"Not that we know. There's no flash. We have a Big Dog who is Rual Simpson. I find the name familiar. Check him, too, when you get the chance. Please and thank you."

"I'm glad this isn't another horror."

"Yes." Decker's voice was pensive.

CHAPTER FOUR

ON ONE OF HIS TRIPS BACK FROM SAN ANTONIO Decker saw Naomi's pickup coming toward him. As they passed, she gave him a cool look. It acknowledged she knew whose truck it was, driving back to Sawbuck, but she didn't honk or wave. She just looked at him and went on.

Where did she go? Sometimes she wouldn't come back to Sawbuck for a couple of days. That sounded like she was living a double life. Who was in the other part?

He'd seen her friend Trisha. She walked carefully and always wore a jacket, a sleeveless one of a light cloth, but it was strange that she felt the need of a jacket in the sweltering July days. She probably had poor circulation that could be cured with a little exercise.

None of the people in security that he'd contacted had yet given him any information. It seemed to Decker that was peculiar. How could the woman be untraceable? He knew full well there was no real hurry to find out about her. In this world, there were more urgent things than some squin—She wasn't squint-eyed. Her eyes were very large and thickly lashed. She looked like a cornered mouse with no fight in her at all. No spark.

He wondered if Rual gave her a hard time. He looked like the kind of bully who would harass such a woman. Decker sighed. Naomi wasn't his problem.

He'd picked up his VCR and had spent an enjoyable time in selecting special tapes. When he got back to his papered store, he set up the VCR on an old black and white television, and he cut a round eyehole in the butcher paper. Then he went outside with some black paint and put an arrow down to the peek-hole.

It didn't take long. From inside his store he could see their shadows as the curious came to peek. Then they laughed and laughed. He had old chase scenes from early, early films. He had dramatics of women chased by gorillas or lions or lots of men. He had car chases. He had six straight hours on each tape, and he would change them at two and at eight.

John said, "We should have adult pictures after ten. Something a little spicy."

"No. I don't need anyone else shuffling back and forth behind my store in the evenings."

"We watched," Cortez protested. "They's been nobody there."

"You go to bed too early," Decker replied.

John intoned with endurance, "Get an infrared camera and take their picture. I need to know this needy woman."

"I'm not sure it's the woman who's needy," Decker lied. "I think it must be John."

John laughed until tears came.

Then one of the men, a guy named Sam, asked if Decker had bought the VCR and tapes with the money from the salvage.

The "junk" had turned into "salvage." "No. I have the books, what was paid, what I paid who. You can look anytime. Ask John."

With hostility toward Sam, John agreed, "He's an honest man. You could take lessons."

That made Sam indignant. "He comes in on a bus, John. Now he's got a truck and a VCR and tapes. Where'd he get the money?"

"I had the money and the VCR before I was hurt." That, too, was an honest reply. "I can live here lots cheaper than I could in town. You have to know that, Sam. If I lived in town, I couldn't even have the truck." He had a perfectly good Mustang, with no need for a junky-looking truck.

"What do you do with the money from the leftovers. Like them cars."

"Ask John."

"We got a town fund. The extra money goes in there. Decker gets the price for a gallon of gas each trip, and he gets his share of the general cut for the extras that we find along the road."

Before he accepted the explanation, Sam grumbled a little in order to allow his indignation time to dissipate.

Then Naomi left an envelope in Decker's door with a canceled billing for one oil drum with spigot and rack, and the change from his twenty-dollar bill. How can a man be irritated by an honest mouse? Decker was.

His store peek-hole became the town's free movie. The little kids brought along stools and scared Decker as they teetered on them, pressing on the old glass storefront, all trying to see at once. So he made the hole larger, pushed the old TV up close, and let them all watch.

Then mothers came and complained: "The kids aren't getting their chores done, Decker. You ought not have the movies on all the time."

Another groused: "They aren't getting enough exercise, they spend all their time at your TV."

So Decker cut viewing hours. Life had never been so dissatisfying or so complicated.

John observed, "It was dull around here before you came along."

Decker got huffy. "I haven't done anything."

And John laughed.

Over in the Conner house, Naomi and Trisha sat on the cool side of the front porch. From there they could look across to the road, beyond to the shanties, or over to the water-smoothed white rock of the empty wash. The friends were silent as they occasionally sipped lemonade.

Naomi gazed pensively through the stunted trees toward the rows of stores on each side of the road. "Why would he want this place to be saved? They would all be better off somewhere else. There's nothing here for them."

When Naomi said "he" Trisha understood that she spoke of Brad.

"He wanted you to have something to think about, beside your grief for him."

"He was a beautiful man. Through and through."

"Granted."

In the unanswerable questioning, Naomi asked again, "How could God have taken him? He had years of giving left."

"'Only the good die young.'" Trisha sighed deeply.

There was a pause, then Naomi looked at her friend. "Do you realize you just took a deep breath, and you didn't cough?"

"I'm free of the tobacco weed." She sighed again, this time sadly.

"Hallelujah." Naomi's tone was mild.

"I wonder if I could go back and smoke again."

"No."

Sourly, Trisha explained, "I wasn't asking permission, I was wondering if I could. I didn't quit because I wanted to. This kid roiling around inside my stomach objected to nicotine." She grimaced, moving a hand as she elaborated: "—caffeine, onions. It's going to be a very picky eater."

"He'll take after Rick."

"He?"

"Twins?"

Trisha rolled her eyes at the ceiling of the porch and accused in despair, "Naomi, you have a surprising mean streak."

"When do you intend telling Rick?"

"You've mentioned that before, Naomi, and by now you are aware of the reply." Trisha enunciated in an exaggerated manner. "Rick does not want a child."

"He still should have the chance to see the kid."

"Why." It wasn't a question, but a "so" to indicate Naomi should continue.

"One of the griefs that Brad had, as he weakened, was that he couldn't get me pregnant. He wished we'd had a baby."

"He could have married you, too. Then you wouldn't have had to buy this crummy house from his estate. His family treated you—"

"You love this house."

"Yeah. It grows on you. I've begun to like the sound of the bamboo. It's like listening to rushing water."

"I wish it was really water, rushing along in the wash. We have everything we need here to help this town, but no water. If we could dam the end of the basin, down there, we could trap the next runoff. We'd have a supply for a year. Now it rains enough to have that. We need the water."

Trisha declared, "Old man Jones is a bastard."

"Probably. If not actually, then he's grown into being one."

Trisha frowned. "I've used the word 'bastard' very carelessly all of my grown years. I suppose it would behoove me to quit bandying the word about in front of my bastard child. Did you ever actually talk to this Jones?"

"No. Only to his man. You know that."

"In the months since I got here, tulip, we haven't talked a whole lot about anything. It's only since that cowboy came into town that you've seemed to come awake. He appeal to your baser instincts? It would be understandable. He's really something. I even find my insides flutter when I catch sight of that body of his"—she paused to explain "—the insides of my body that aren't entirely squashed by this kid."

"He's a drifter. He won't stay around." Naomi commented in a polite, conversational manner. "But I never could have been able to get those men to clean up the town. He's done a good job of it."

"He can't possibly get that much for the trash. What's he doing?"

"I don't know, but if he gets those men moving, that's a miracle in itself. They've hauled all the junk out of the empty stores. Did I tell you they caught a rattler in one? Right in town! And they found a real nest of them out in the bamboo. They're having a town rattlesnake roast tomorrow. Ugh. Everybody's invited."

"How do you know that?"

"John told me," Naomi replied.

"I understand rattlesnake meat is delicious."

"It must be an acquired taste. Want to go?"

"Sure. Why not? This baby process takes a long time." She put her hands at her back and her fat tummy was obvious.

"You've been a godsend to me, Trish, you must know that."

"What are friends for?"

"You've gone above and beyond the call of duty. Have I mentioned that?"

"I've been keeping track and in the eight months since Brad left us, I think this is the second time."

Naomi gasped to protest, then she smiled at her friend. "If I've never thanked you, you know I am so indebted that I could never begin to repay you for these months you've given to me."

"I'll have my payment," Trisha said in satisfaction. "You're going to be godmother to this kid. It will be a hellion, and I'll say to it, 'Guess what, Snookums, you're going to your godmother's for the whole weekend.' And you'll get the little terror all to yourself."

"My godchild will be perfect."

Trisha retorted in a very comfortable way, "Out of me, by Rick? You josh."

"What does the kid think about rattlesnake meat? Roasted rattlesnake meat and beer."

Trisha considered that.

"No strong reaction."

"Maybe it's time we checked out this cowboy. See what he's up to."

"Being a true Texan, the kid's adventuresome and curious. We'll try it."

And Naomi laughed. For the first time in—it had to be over ten months—Trisha heard Naomi laugh, and the sound brought tears to Trisha's eyes and a throat that didn't work for a while. She looked aside to the empty wash and concealed her emotional response.

In the silence between the friends, Naomi finally said, "It's very strange. I saw him get off the bus, and I felt the darndest reaction to him."

He? Naomi hadn't mentioned Decker by name. How odd. Trisha inquired, "What sort of . . . reaction?"

"He's really quite ridiculous. Those spurs. Why would he keep wearing those spurs? The closest horse belongs to the Jones outfit. He drives that old pickup around, wearing spurs. It's silly."

"So your reaction was . . . ridicule?"

"No."

Having given Naomi plenty of time for a reply that would be better than that, Trisha nudged: "Not ridicule?"

Naomi replied slowly, "A . . . yearning. . . ."

Trisha didn't move her head, but her eyes snapped open and she looked sideways toward her friend. Naomi was gazing off across the wash in such a pensive way that Trisha gave a silent groan. Naomi would now, finally, talk about Brad.

"It's so strange to feel the wanting again. I know it's body hunger. To want to be touched. I know it's just Mother Nature and body hunger, but I saw that cowboy, his name's Decker, you know. I saw him and I felt...It was strange."

"You? Lusting? Why, Naomi Wentworth, you're human!"

"Aren't we all?"

"I never realized you were that basic. Just like the rest of us. He's a morsel, he is. He's not at all like Brad." She waited, then, holding her breath. How healed was Naomi?

"No. He isn't like Brad in any way that I can see. I looked for it. The similarity. After I reacted to him so strongly, I thought maybe...you know, that maybe there was some purpose in him being here. Decker's being here. But he isn't anything at all like Brad. Maybe it's the difference that is attractive?"

"Have you spoken to him yet?"

"No. He came here to thank me for the oil drum, and he actually paid for it! I was stunned. I opened the door, ready to be disillusioned, and there he was in full color. I was tongue-tied by my reaction to him.

"I have no desire to get involved with another man. But I do have to know why he is here. Brad may have sent for him. He could be a friend of Brad's. He seems too young and too active to be a complete dropout. He has to be here because of this town.

"Since Brad made *me* come here, maybe Decker was influenced by Brad. It would be like him to try to direct my life that way, to give me a...replacement.

It tears my heart to think of him doing that, giving
me away to another man."

Rather carefully, Trisha commented, "I think your
imagination is running away with you. If Brad wanted
you and Decker to get together, then Decker would
have been here sooner."

"He's been in a hospital."

"How do you know that?" Trisha asked.

"Buzz told Magdalena."

"Buzz is the part Indian? That panther walk, that
smoldering look? If I were a free woman, I'd take
him out into the bushes."

Naomi chided, "That's shocking talk from an ex-
pectant mother."

"My stomach is all that's involved."

"And your heart."

Trisha sighed, long-suffering as she expanded the
problem: "—my lungs and taste buds and muscles. I
wasn't made to carry this belly around, this way. It's
interfering with my way of life."

"You're a sham."

"Only in your mind," Trisha demurred. "I would
have had an abortion, but I thought I missed my
periods because I was so involved with your grief for
Brad. I—"

"My dear, dear friend—"

"Don't get soggy on me. I'm emotionally unreliable,
right now, prone to be weepy and sentimental. I think
it's God's way of making me think I am involved with
this kid."

"You're not?"

"I'm resigned."

Naomi scoffed, "Ah, Trisha, you don't give in very

well. You need to tell Rick. Haven't you seen him at all?"

"I've avoided that."

"Did you split? I don't believe I ever asked that. How selfish of me. I just accept that you will be here. Does he know where you are?"

"No."

"Why not?"

"I . . . don't want him to see me . . . like this."

"You're not allowing him to share this great event."

"Rick isn't the paternal type. He isn't the least domesticated. We suit each other the way it was between us. This kid is unexpectedly complicating my life."

"Let me adopt the baby."

Trisha waited for a long time, then in a very small voice she replied, "I'll think about it."

"If you should give up the baby, let me take it. I'd love to give it a good home. You could see the kid grow up and be a favorite relative. You have to know that. And I can take care of a child. You know that, too."

"Yes." Trisha was again silent. "I'll see." Neither spoke as they considered their own thoughts, then Trisha said softly, "Do you realize this is the first time we've ever talked about this?"

Naomi was dismayed. "I've been terribly selfish. I couldn't see beyond the pain."

"But, Naomi, now you can!"

Almost offended, Naomi looked at Trisha in indignation. Then she looked thoughtfully out over the white rock basin of the wash, and she stared at it. She and that empty basin had a great deal in common. Finally, when Trisha thought Naomi was snubbing her, Naomi looked back and asked, "Do you mean the time can come when I will have only the good memories?"

"I never thought so, before today."

"Brad said I would. He told me not to grieve. That nothing would take away our time together. He said it as if he would be capable of remembering it, too, in whatever world he went. I couldn't see how that could be." And she began to weep in a different way than ever before. It wasn't grief, it was sentiment. She smiled at Trisha and said ruefully, "More tears. I thought I'd cried them all."

"These are different."

And in some surprise, Naomi said, "Yes."

Decker had asked his uncle Frank, "Have you any use for the bamboo on the south edge of the far fields?"

"God, no. It's a bane. The fool that planted that junk died off on me, and the farm is up for grabs in litigation. That damned bamboo is taking over the place." He glared at an innocent Wellington. "That dog don't come into the house until it's had a bath."

"We're short of water over in Sawbuck."

"'We're?'" His uncle Frank narrowed his eyes.

"I'm an inhabitant."

"Now, listen here, boy, just what's that mean?"

"I know that we're short on water. You siphon it all up and leave us with sandy dust. We're not as clean as we could be."

"Leave the dog outside."

"Lend me some water, and I'll wash him. You wouldn't want Wellington left out of the conversation and feeling unaccepted, would you?"

"You're getting well."

"Yeah."

"I liked you ailing and pliant."

Decker smiled.

"You recall your obligation to me? To get rid of those people?"

"Oh, yes. Have no fears. I'm trying to convince them to leave."

Uncle Frank accused, "You've been cleaning up the place."

"If the health department comes in there and finds there's no water—and why—you could have one hell of a time of it. You'd better let me do this my way."

"I'll be interested."

"And you don't mind if we take down the bamboo?"

"Go right ahead. Why are you doing that?"

"To get rid of the snakes."

Uncle Frank grinned. "Maybe you ought to leave it alone." He laughed dirty.

So Decker was out in Frank's backyard, with Chico watching him wash Wellington, when Elise came riding in on a beautiful chestnut mare. Decker rose and smiled. "Hi, Auntie."

"Decker!" She slid off the horse and called, "Eric!"

A young man ran from the barn and grinned, blushing, as he took the reins from Elisa's gloved hand. "I'll take care of her for you."

"Thank you, Eric," she said matter-of-factly as she removed her short gloves. "Chico." She turned to the houseman. "May we have some lemonade? Would you like something in it, Decker? A little gin?"

"No thanks."

"Then just the lemonade, Chico, please." She looked at Wellington who had rolled his eyes up to

her, expecting to have to accept more praise. She
asked, "What is this?"

"He is fluent in both English and Spanish. Watch
what you say."

"This is *your* dog?"

"Wellington, make your manners to the lady."

The dog dragged himself straight, woofed once in
a low, intimate way, and held up his right paw as he
grimaced a fake smile. It worked every time. Elise
bent down, took the wet paw in her hand and smiled
back.

"He's getting a bath." Decker threw a towel to Elise.

She put her hand under the hose water and rinsed
"dog" off it before she dried it on the towel, then she
cautiously smelled the towel before she continued to
dry her hand.

"You're a snob," Decker accused his aunt.

"Particular." She stepped a little closer and asked
quietly, "Are you here for the night?"

"No."

"You're stronger." She said the word in an excessively sexual way with all sorts of insinuations.

"I can stand up and squat down without undue
difficulty." He soaped down the dog.

"And take a woman?"

"Now, Auntie, we've been through all that—"

"Not yet."

"With all the eager men hereabouts, I wouldn't
think you'd have the inclination for any more."

"You ought to be slapped for that, but Frank is
upstairs, watching us, and he'd wonder why."

"That wouldn't surprise me. Why would you try to
entice me with him watching you do it?" He gave her
a scathing glance. "That give you little jollies?"

"You're rude."

"Yes, ma'am," he replied softly. "Doesn't that put you off? Or does it intrigue you? Are you an S and M freak?"

"Why can't you be nice about this?"

"Nice?" His voice was low and censuring. "All you want from me is a little 'nice' adultery. That's *nice* to you? Cut it out, Elise. Frank loves you. Behave yourself."

"Is there a woman over in Sawbuck?"

"It's possible." He thought humorously of the mouse.

"You can't be in love with her. Not this soon. You could still make love to me. It wouldn't kill you. Tonight would be a good time."

"Give your 'good times' to your husband." He stood up and gave her a hard look. He surprised the most vulnerable expression in her eyes. She was almost pathetic. He felt he'd intruded, in seeing that, and he bent his head as he sought the hose, then he busied himself in rinsing the dog's coat.

Elise didn't leave. With his harsh response to her, he would have thought she'd storm off. Or that she would just . . . leave him there. After a long silence, he glanced up at her. She was looking off through the trees. Decker's glance quickly followed hers to see whom she was watching, but no one was there.

He frowned down at the dog's wet coat, wondering what ailed Elise. What, besides an itchy crotch.

If it was only the itch, why was she so cool toward the men on the place? She'd snubbed Bud when he'd offered her the cougar skin. And with Eric, she was aloof. No secret smiles. No indications she was tumbling in the hay with the help. Or maybe she was just a real good actress.

But if she was getting it from all those available and obviously willing males, why was she inviting him? He gave up trying to figure her out.

She was still there when Chico came out with the lemonade. "Tell me, Chico, what do people need around here?"

"Water? Money?"

"No. What tools or services? How about bamboo rakes?"

"Yes."

"Anything at all you know about, hear about?"

"I'll inquire."

"I'd appreciate it."

Before he left, Decker asked his uncle Frank if that cougar skin was ready to go home with him? And it was. It had been beautifully done. The pelt was soft and supple. He put it in his truck and looked at it on the way back to Sawbuck. Why had he wanted it? And he thought of the mouse. It would amuse him to see what a mouse did with a cougar pelt. He smiled at Wellington and commented, "You smell better."

Wellington drew in his tongue, then pulled his head back inside the truck cab, looked at his driver, and wuffed a polite response.

The next day the loungers strung lights through the trees along the wash and Decker helped. They set up sawhorses made from scraps of wood, and they took off doors from inside the empty stores to serve as tables.

Decker was surprised there were still inside doors that hadn't been taken to be used elsewhere. It said something for the residents that the doors had been left alone until then, and Decker found himself somewhat proud of the town. He was surprised basic honesty meant anything to him. He frowned, thinking about it, then gave it up with a shrug.

As the trash mesquite-wood fire was being lighted to roast the rattlesnake portions, the evening wave of commuters began to go by. Some stopped and asked, "What's going on?"

"We're having a rattlesnake and beer party for the town."

"Great!" was the response. And the initial commuters included themselves. With those cars stopped, others also stopped, some went for spouses and returned, and there was a holiday air about the whole shebang. The onslaught of commuters startled the townspeople.

The male commuters especially said, "I see you guys sitting around on the sidewalk, and I envy you."

"You do that while we envy you your jobs."

"Nobody's ever satisfied."

Another said, "You guys did a pretty good job cleaning up the place."

Others looked around critically and made suggestions for additional work. They took such a proprietary interest that their hosts were amazed.

Buzz had to go for more beer and bought a lot of hamburger meat. There wasn't enough rattlesnake meat to go around so those pieces were cut into hors d'oeuvres and sampled judiciously. While everyone had more beer, Joe and Ann made some last-minute chili. Even old Magdalena helped with the tortillas, patting the dough into rounds to be laid on the griddle before being eaten as bread.

The chili was put into a big black pot over the fire, and an enormous pot of rice was cooked to be served with the chili and tortillas.

The late commuters were drawn by the scene and more stopped. It ended up being a rather loud party. There weren't enough chairs, so they moved around and they met one another.

"You drive that yellow pickup?" one queried. "Do you know you about run me into the ditch that day?"

Someone mentioned to another, "You have a back light out. You ought to check."

"Was it you had that deer last season? What'd you do with the antlers? I'd dearly like a pair, but I just can't bring myself to shoot a Bambi."

Some helped Miz Billmont look for her raspberry tarts, and they said to the townspeople, "You guys have really cleaned up the town. It looks nice. You ought to paint the stores."

The Sawbuckers could only be astonished.

CHAPTER FIVE

DECKER NOTICED THAT AMONG THE COM-
muters there were those men whose eyes saw Naomi.
Decker found he, too, was unusually conscious of the
mouse who was in a long, soft dress. With night, she'd
left off the big hat and her hair was up on top of her
head. She looked like a woman from another time.

She was hurrying around, helping with the food.
He saw that her friend, Trisha, was very pregnant.
That eliminated any lesbian affiliation. Good.

From across the fire, he watched Naomi's first taste
of the rattlesnake meat, and while he wished he was
the man giving her the nibble, he was entranced by
the way she looked as she almost reluctantly tasted it.
Then she smiled, and a shiver went through his body
in a very erotic way. Over a mouse?

That durned Naomi pretty much ignored him,
Decker thought, and he tried to see if one of the other
men had her attention. He saw that Buzz wasn't im-
mune to her, although she treated him like a friend.
She didn't touch Buzz or give him flirting looks.

But Decker saw that the Big Dog was interested in
Naomi, that he posed and postured trying to get her
attention to him, but she ignored him altogether.

So in a flaunting of his being able to do it, Decker went over to her and said, "The rakes are selling nicely."

She looked up at him with those big eyes of hers. "We have a lot of bamboo," she mentioned rather idly. Then she got to her own pet project. "If we could get the stores painted, we might be able to use one to sell the things we make. We need to look professional. We can't in such tacky stores."

"How do we get the paint?"

He really expected her to be baffled, but she said, "I've gotten some cans of discontinued colors and some damaged cans. There is almost enough. But nothing would be the same color."

"A rainbow?" He squinted.

"I think we could make a diagram of the stores and figure out how to use the colors. Would you help?"

"I'd be honored."

She blurted, "Why do you wear the spurs?"

Again he gave the same all-purpose nothing reply, "It reminds me I'm walking."

To her mind came the cowboy-without-a-horse image. The saddest circumstance a man could endure. His circumstances touched her heart; however she only nodded, as if she understood the full extent of his plight.

He smiled at her.

After everything in sight had been eaten, and the kids were getting sleepy, someone turned on his boom box to a station that played the old songs, with a mixture of country and rock. Among the songs were ones familiar to the crowd, and a good many sang the words. There were some there who were a little drunk.

Some of the women danced alone, and Trisha was one. She shimmied and the baby slid from side to side and the women all laughed until they cried. The women were distant with Naomi. They didn't feel any relationship with her, but they included Trisha as one of them.

The boom box was set louder and with the 60's song "Joy to the World," Decker got up on one cleared table and did a stomp as he sang about Jeremiah being a bull frog. His spurs jingled and he held his Stetson on his head with both hands. He curled his body in a very masculine way as he sang the verse about loving the ladies. He turned and looked for Naomi and saw that she was watching him. The look they exchanged would have powered the light for the Statue of Liberty.

Everybody laughed, except for the Big Dog. Rual. His look was a mean, smoldering one. He watched the ladies laugh at Decker in the way a man wants a woman to laugh. He didn't like Decker.

Decker didn't mind.

The commuters found an empty coffee can and stuffed it with money. It covered the food and beer, and there was some left over.

July was easing into a blistering August. Since the rattlesnake party, the commuters had known the cop car was a fake. They'd examined it. Then seeing the flat tires in the weeds, they'd lifted the hood to see the engine was gone. They'd laughed about it.

Now, as they passed through Sawbuck, they slowed down to the required thirty miles per hour, like home folks. They tooted their horns and waved. It was very friendly, and the citizens of Sawbuck waved back, still baffled by the unexpected friendliness.

John was best at rake-making. It was something for the loungers to do. All that bamboo was free. It had never occurred to the citizens of Sawbuck to use the proliferating resource. It was a boon. And they made bamboo fencing to corral the broody hens during that season.

Each of the loungers made one rake, and they set them all on the sidewalk with a sign. They charged twice what Sears charged for their metal rakes, and they sold them. After that they took orders. Buzz, the mouse, and Decker said the town got one-twentieth for the pot. Naomi kept the pot.

With the success of the rakes, Naomi seized the opportunity and told John, "I've read that bamboo wind chimes are the most soothing sound ever invented by man. They aren't difficult to make."

She gave John photocopied pages from the library with directions on making bamboo wind chimes. He didn't read English, so he gave the pages to Decker.

Decker leaned his chair back against the pillar on the sidewalk, read the directions aloud, and translated for those who needed it. It took a while to prepare the bamboo. The cane had to soak in water for a year. In slowly, barely moving, *running* water. Who had that?

Decker said, "We'll make a trough. We can put a splice of the hose to drip through the trough. It makes the bamboo like iron. We have to cut the pieces first because, after that, it's too hard. This will be interesting."

"Then you'll be here for a year?" Buzz asked, watching Decker.

"Who knows?" But it did make him wonder. What was he doing there? He looked around the neatly mowed, raked weeds. He looked at the clean sidewalk. He looked at the men who weren't quite so dull-eyed. And he smiled and shook his head once, as if the whole situation was beyond him.

It was just after the rattlesnake roast that Decker got to follow Naomi into San Antonio. He'd been to his uncle Frank's, changed into city clothing, and "wore" his vintage Mustang. That was the only way to use such a car. One "wore" it like an old watch, or a grandfather's Christmas jacket. Decker wore the Mustang.

So he was approaching the crossroad when he saw Naomi's pickup go through the intersection toward San Antonio. He was schooled in trailing without seeming to, so he could follow her and see what sort of double life she led. Where would she go?

As they went along through the busy traffic, he was critical of her driving and only grudgingly admitted that she drove like a man. That mouse?

They took the bypass around the city, partway, then a throughway through the city, to Broadway, until they reached the near-north side of town. There Naomi ended up at one of the big houses built long ago on the hill between Fort Sam Houston and Broadway.

Decker waited as she pulled up in front of one big old house and got out of that tacky pickup, leaving it like a sore thumb along that curb. Then she walked up the sidewalk and the door was opened for her before she touched a thing. Someone had watched

for her. Was it a man? Did he drag her into the house
and kiss her soft mouth hungrily as his greedy hands
roamed over her nice body?

Decker got out of his Mustang and stomped up the
sidewalk, missing the jingling accompaniment of the
spurs. He noted the address on the house and went
one beyond. There, he rang the bell and waited. A
maid replied through the portal contrived by a slick
security. "Yes, sir?"

"This the Wentworth residence?"

"No, sir, Miss Wentworth be next door at the Crawford house."

"Oh. Sorry."

"'Sall right."

So. She had a love nest in San Antonio. Gimme had
said she wasn't even a Texan. Who was she? Discouraged, Decker went back to his car and sat there
for over an hour. Too long, really. He could be noticed. But she didn't come back out, and he didn't
want to think what might be going on in there, so he
drove away.

From his parents' home, there in San Antonio, he
called Pat at the agency and asked sourly, "Got anything on Wentworth?"

"So you found where she lives."

"Who saw that?"

"One of ours."

"Whose house is it?"

"Name's Crawford. Every second Tuesday of each
month, Wentworth gets five thousand deposited to
her account."

"Why?"

"No reason that I know. She's clean. No problems,

no strange acquaintances, except for some itinerant cowboy who goes around in boots—with spurs—and drives a sham dilapidated pickup."

"That's me."

"We know."

"Is she married?"

"No."

"Ah."

"That important?"

"I just wondered."

"You might be interested in knowing there's an operative in Sawbuck. He now knows about you. He's undercover. Don't be curious. If he needs you, help him."

"Okay." Decker knew better than to ask who it was. But he did ask, "He isn't there to nursemaid me, is he?"

"No."

"Good."

"Are you okay?"

"Yeah, Pat, and thanks for the meager information."

"You want to know her schools and scars?"

Decker's voice roughened. "Who's she been with."

"She was very involved with a rock star until last year. He died some time back. Like eight months ago."

"Who was he?"

"The Duke. Real name Bradley Conner of . . . Sawbuck."

"No kidding."

"No kidding."

"Well, do you suppose he set her up there?"

"No. She bought the house from his estate. His family has shunned her."

"Is he the five thou a month?"

"No."

"Do you know where she gets it?"

"No."

"Curious. How'd he die?"

"A rampant, uncontrollable bacteria. They couldn't do a thing. In two months, he was dead."

"I'll be damned. Was she with him?"

"The whole way."

"Damn."

"Yeah. He must have been one of the special ones. His group has dispersed. They're zonked."

"Any other little nuggets?"

"She is quite a woman. She's worth any effort. But it could take a while. She really loved Duke."

"Yeh." He used the brief version to get past that statement. "Thanks, Pat."

"Anytime."

"I've been out and about, looking around."

"We know."

"Oh? I've seen a big, single eye painted on a sandwich board and propped in a path. It's moved about."

"Yes."

"Just 'yes'? Do you know anything about Rual Simpson?"

"He's being watched."

Decker went in for his physical and was pronounced: "Fine. Still having nightmares?"

"Yeah."

"They'll go away, don't worry about them."

Ah, yes, but the doctors weren't the ones who stood on the nightmare brink of darkness and watched the unleashed fire demons writhe as they strained to get at him. The only one interested was the mouse. She stood with him and watched. And she put her cool hand on his hot, naked chest. Was it to protect him and give him strength and courage? Or was it to draw strength from him? He had none to share.

His parents took him to The Club for dinner that evening. He was restless. His mother watched him. They were used to him, and they knew not to question him. But, of course, his mother did. "They haven't set you to doing anything else, this soon, have they?"

"No."

She tightened her mouth and said in disgust, "You wouldn't say if they had, would you."

He smiled at her. "No."

His dad coaxed, "Leave him be."

"He looks a little better. What did the doctors say?"

"I'm fine."

"You wouldn't tell me if they'd said otherwise, would you."

"Of course. I tell you everything. Come dance with me."

"There must be someone your age who'll dance with you."

His dad laughed, "Doesn't that sound as if she's shy? You should have seen her in her foolish youth with all the petticoats, bobby socks, and a ponytail. She was a wild woman."

"Come on, Mother, you're dying to dance. I can tell."

"Nothing rough. I've my bridge shoes on."

"Bridge shoes? Is that Dr. Scholl's."

"No, idiot, the shoes are so beautiful and silly you

can't walk in them, so they're only good for playing bridge where, if you will recall, you sit."

"I haven't played bridge since...In a very long time."

"Shall I gather a couple of tables?"

"No, thanks. You're a damned good dancer."

"Thank you."

"Let me lead for a while."

"Decker!"

At the same time, another voice said, "Decker!" It was Mark Allen, an old friend from Decker's school days. "I have a friend who wants to meet you," Mark explained as Decker hesitated in the dancing. "Meet us over by the arch after this dance? How are you, Mrs. Jones?"

"Fine." Mrs. Jones smiled at the man who'd interrupted, then she said in a sigh to Decker, "I suppose this is all the dancing I get in the whole evening."

"I'll send some of the boys around."

"No. I was being funny."

"You really are the best mother I've ever had."

"Don't slide that one in. I taught you that."

"I was just showing you that I remember all your teachings."

She tilted her head back and surveyed his beloved face.

"I wonder if you recall the number of times I told you to be careful?"

"Every one."

"Remember."

"I shall."

Decker took his mother back to their table, went in

search of two friends, and said, "Mother needs a dance or two. How about it?"

They laughed and amiably flipped a coin to see who was first.

Then Decker went to the arch to wait for Mark.

Mark came with another man. "Decker, good to see you. This is Rick Thomas from Dallas. He's looking for a woman who may be in this area. She's a friend to Naomi Wentworth who has been seen around San Antonio and—"

"You know Naomi?"

"Not well. She's younger. You forget I have almost four years on you, and I'm several more than that older than she. But Rick is searching for Trisha Peterson. She and Naomi have been dearest friends, and Naomi could know Trisha's whereabouts. You have an uncle out southeast of town, do you know of Naomi? Her family keeps refusing Rick's calls. He's desperate to contact Trisha."

"I can't give you any information. Do you have a card? I might run into Naomi, and if I do, I'll give her your card."

Rick was a restless man. He frowned at Decker, unimpressed, and said, "If you tell Naomi all this, Trisha will vanish. I have to know where Trisha is. She disappeared about seven months ago, and I haven't seen hide nor hair of her since. I have no idea what happened. I need to see her."

It didn't take a genius to understand that Rick had no idea that Trisha was pregnant. Very. Perhaps it was Rick's child? Now what would he do if he was King Solomon? "I'll see what I can find out."

"Thanks." Unconvinced, Rick left.

Mark shook hands with Decker. "Rick's okay. He was a little long settling down, but he and Trisha are a real pair. With Rick sweating these last ... what ... seven months, he knows Trisha is the one for him. I hope she hasn't found somebody else."

"It'll be interesting."

"What are you doing in this area?"

Evasively, Decker replied, "Playing cowboy."

"You're back on the rodeo circuit?" Mark's voice showed disbelief.

"Now, you *know* I've outgrown that particular mayhem."

"Well, I had thought you would, but I find you're always a surprise. You trying to impress some susceptible woman?"

"Why would you think that?"

"I've known you awhile. There was a time when you were the talk of Texas because you'd ride anything on four legs.... The meaner, the better. You were a fool for danger."

"No longer. I'm almost passed thirty, and I find my bones don't want to do 'them' things 'no more, no more.'"

Mark laughed. "Who is she?"

"Who is whom?"

"The woman who is taming you."

"There is none." He frowned.

Mark smiled just a bit, his eyes intent. His voice lowered as he said, "When can I see her. Where are you staying?"

"I don't want you nosing into my business. Do you hear me?"

"Yes."

"I want your word."

"You have it." Mark studied Decker with a small smile. "When you trust her and want to show her off, I'm first. Granted?"

"You're probably getting ready to settle down, and you're finding romance in smoke."

Mark was amused as the two said a casual good-bye and parted.

His reaction to Mark's inquiry was how Decker found out how seriously his attention had been drawn to the mouse. He didn't stay home that night, but took leave of his parents, drove to his uncle Frank's, did a nice job of testing security there, and changed into his cowboy jeans, shirt, Stetson, boots, and spurs. He collected Wellington, who wakened slowly, then sat with his front feet braced and his eyes closed in utter exhaustion. "Did they make you go out and chase rabbits?"

As Decker knew it would, the mention of rabbits opened the dog's eyes. He had to carry the big oaf out to the pickup, and roll down Wellington's window. The dog laid his tired chin on the windowsill and didn't make one comment all the way to Sawbuck.

As usual, there were the shadows that moved just a little slower than the others, but no one accosted Decker. He wondered yet again who was moving around at that time of night, and it was a comfort to think the activity was known to the agency. Who was the agent? Why not make him known to Decker?

It was insulting that they were being that cautious. It was as if they didn't trust him. Did they think if he was taken again that this time he might not keep quiet? Would he break if the beatings were repeated? Would he?

That night he dreamed of the fiery pits, the demons were closer and he could feel their breaths. They were going to . . . brand him! He wakened violently thrashing around. He found himself in the dead silence of the store with an inquiring sound—or perhaps, a snore outside the door from Wellington. Decker wondered if he'd cried out. He wasn't sure.

Where had she been? Where had his mouse been, with her cool hand. Because he was concentrating on her during the last day, why had she retreated during the night, when he had needed her?

Decker dozed for a while, into the night, but he couldn't allow himself to go into deep sleep. He dreamed of dark woods and roused himself, to pull on trousers and moccasins, then exited through the roof into the oak and vanished into the shadows, but followed then by Wellington.

He prowled, and Wellington gave no indication of anyone else being in the woods. Decker didn't see the painted eye, and searched unsuccessfully for its haunting image before he returned to his hammock to drowse.

He wakened fuzzy and out of sorts. He didn't want to get out of the hammock. Wellington suggested Decker open the door, and Decker replied, "You're so smart, why don't you learn to turn the knob yourself?"

Damned if the dog didn't rattle the knob and mutter. The damned dog had always done that. Decker knew he was the subject of a great many of the mutterings. For Wellington, a little taste of soap now and then might be a good idea.

He wondered how dogs cursed. But he wasn't really interested and he wondered if the mouse was up and if she was dressed.

Would she be receptive to an itinerant cowboy? It might be a good test. Either she would love him for himself, or she could love him for his family's place in the strata of life. Her choice would show which she valued. A good man or a place in the world. She already had a place in the world. It was equal to or better than his. So?

Could he stand to test her? Did he care which she wanted if she would give herself in exchange? What a hell of a choice for *him* to have to make. So why would he want to test her?

But he did.

By then he was absentmindedly out of the hammock, had opened the door for Wellington, and was fixing their breakfast when Buzz came by. "You're in time for breakfast," he told his guest.

"What you got?"

"Do you mean if I can't tempt you with tasty food, you won't stay?"

"That's the size of it."

"I guess I'll have to bring out eggs, bacon, home-made bread for—"

"Yours?" Buzz was incredulous.

"No. Mother's."

"The one who winces instead of shuddering."

"Right."

"I'll give it a try." Buzz sat down at the door-table that had been one of those used for the rattlesnake picnic. "I came by last night. Your truck was here, but you weren't. You out and about?"

"Why?"

"Just wondering." But Buzz left it at that.

They didn't talk anymore. They ate in silence. Wellington returned and ate his cooled eggs.

"You know that dog's a lover?"

"There are bitches who accept him?"

"Out here in the sticks, he's unusual. They think he has class."

When the two men quit laughing, Wellington asked to go out again.

Decker asked slowly, "What's going on? Why would my being out and about cause anyone to question? Are you all running something or watching something?"

"It's no concern of yours." Buzz's black eyes were flat.

Decker watched him silently, but Buzz didn't elaborate.

In his mind Decker had to smile at himself. He was just like the commuters. This was his town, too, and its business was his.

After breakfast, he left Buzz at the drugstore, and clinked down the walk, realizing that he was going to run into Rual. The Big Dog was in a state police uniform, for crying out loud, and he looked formidable. Decker nodded once to acknowledge the man, and Rual let his own glance slide past Decker whom he ignored.

Rual was a state cop? Would *he* be the agent? Naw. No way. And if Rual called on him, he was supposed to help? Decker decided he'd have to see what the bad guys had going for them. He just might side with them over Rual. But it was possible. Decker remembered once in Italy—But that was another lifetime.

This was here and now.

He sought John. "What's going on around here, nights?"

"No trouble." John shrugged.

But like the commuters, Decker was only intrigued. Now he would prowl in the night and find out what those other men were doing out there. Drugs? Whose side? Aliens? They had to be doing something and they didn't want it monitored.

He clinked over to the mouse's house and knocked on her door. She opened it and just looked up at him. Something stirred inside him. Lust.

How could such a slender, timid woman stir him to such wanting? And he wondered if it was because she was no threat to him? How could she harm him? Anything else in the world might, but this mouse wouldn't. How could he know that? What he needed to know was who had first claim on her. Who supported her?

"I came to discuss the painting."

She looked back into the house and gestured to the walls. "One of these?"

He glanced beyond her and saw the Old West paintings that lined the walls. My God, he thought, there was a fortune in paintings on those walls. He asked, "Are they insured?"

"These are careful copies. They are loaned to museums occasionally so that students can study them. And there are tribes who study them, too, because they are authentic, and the Indians can see exactly how their ancestors dressed. If you're interested, you may look at them."

How could he say only she interested him? He'd hardly even met her. A torrid, exchanged look of mutual attraction at the rattlesnake roast didn't make any kind of a commitment.

He walked slowly along the walls, studying the pictures. The Indians were Comanche. They'd been tough to pry loose from the land. They were a proud race, and Buzz held the look of them. Decker smiled at the little kids running in the pictures, their hair flying. He saw the women, and the war-painted horses. "Who was the artist?"

"No one knows. I can see why the paintings interest you, since you are a cowboy. How did you lose your horse?"

"I sold him." That was true. He'd had to, several years before. None of the others in the family was home enough, and his parents couldn't handle extra horses. They had found a good home with a teenage girl who was in love with horses. That she did salved his conscience.

"It must have been very bad for you to have to do that. To sell him."

"Yes." He was honest.

He would never guess she was his landlord. She held that secret in some delight. She asked, "Would you like one of the pictures to hang in your store as a loaner while you're here?" Then her tongue just went right on: "Is that how you were so badly hurt? Were you pitched and trampled? John said you were very badly hurt. Buzz agreed you'd had a rough time. What happened? Was it a rodeo?" She did wish her tongue would stop. He would soon know how much he fascinated her, and he'd run before she could understand why.

He didn't know how to reply, so he shrugged and

shook his head. Since she'd offered to loan him one, he then looked at the pictures differently. She followed along, and they discussed the paintings.

She was conscious of the fact that he hadn't explained his injuries. He was probably embarrassed that he'd been unseated. If she was kind, she'd let it go, but she was so curious. How could she get him to take off his shirt so that she could be sure he was all right? How long ago had he been injured?

"This one." He chose. "Maybe that one. Between these two."

She realized he was selecting a picture. "Take them both for a while."

He was exuberant. She couldn't shut him out entirely if he borrowed two of her paintings. They were beautiful. They were probably more vivid than the originals because the modern paints were so much purer. He smiled at his mouse. "What a treat for the eyes," he said, looking at her.

She blushed faintly. "Come outside on the porch and have some lemonade, coffee, tea?"

She didn't say "—or me." He chose, "Iced tea?"

"Do you like mint?"

"Yes."

"Good. I've just made up a batch of tea steeped with mint. It'll be ready." Then she did a terrible thing, she called, "Trisha, we have company."

But the gods were on Decker's side. From the back of the house, Trisha called, "Go ahead without me."

With some cynical drollness, Naomi tempted, "It's Decker. The table stomper."

"You'll have to handle him by yourself."

Decker grinned and his mouse ignored the opening to flirt. He thought it was too bad women weren't more understanding. He would allow her to handle him, but she would probably be startled if he carried her upstairs to one of the bedrooms and made love to her. Women needed preliminaries.

But he did have the opening, and he couldn't resist: "How do you intend 'handling' me?" He gave her his very best—half-closed eyes and slightly raised brows—flirting look.

She didn't back off. She looked at the drifter. Then she said coolly, "I'm going to give you iced tea."

"With mint," he pressed.

She agreed, "With mint."

"We need to talk about how we're going to paint the stores."

"Oh," she said. "You meant... When you said 'painting,' you meant... I beg your pardon. Did you even know about the paintings?"

"You're going to renege?"

"Does a cowboy know that's a common bridge term?" She was watching him, watching to see if he would reply.

"Rodeo riders do a lot of recovering on the circuit."

"I'm disillusioned that you play bridge. I thought you'd play poker and drink... rotgut."

"I prefer my whiskey like women. Smooth."

She nodded. "There you go. Now that sounds like a cowboy." She went outside onto the porch. "You had me worried. I thought you might be here under a false pretense."

CHAPTER SIX

FOLLOWING NAOMI ONTO THE PORCH, DECKER couldn't prevent a slight flush. "You doubt me?" It was best to meet things head on. He waited until she sat in a wicker chair, then he sat on the padded glider with its back to the house so that he looked out over the bank, along the empty wash.

"You don't seem the type to be idle." Naomi had the excuse to study him. "You appear to be the type to push. Were you that badly hurt?" Her study wasn't evaluating his character, she was appreciating him as a man.

He replied with slow honesty, "I think it's called regrouping. I just need some time. I'm okay. I had to let the horse go because I wasn't able to care for him, as he needed. He has a good home. I miss him, but I'm off the circuit, now. It wouldn't have been fair to the horse to see him only now and then, and have him boarded the rest of the time. He'd be lonely."

Naomi poured his mint tea and handed it to him. She realized she knew almost all she needed to know about him. John said he had a mother who would never shudder over a child of hers, but she might "wince." That, too, had told Naomi a great deal. Not only about the mother, but about the family relationship. Added to that was the fact that Decker had mentioned the incident to a group of strange men.

She listened as he explained how it was to ride on the rodeo circuit. But he didn't tell about himself, he told about the clowns whose skill kept the pitched riders from being trampled or gored. He told about horses. He told about circuit friendship and companionship.

Decker said, "It sometimes surprises me what men will do. I was watching a *National Geographic* on ice sailboats the other night? They can go a hundred miles an hour like that! Can you imagine lying along a couple of crossed sticks that are resting on blades, with an enormous three-story sail above you, skimming over *ice* at a hundred miles an hour? Now that's foolish."

And Naomi grinned. In turn she said, "Yes. Any man who did that would also think nothing of jumping off a cliff with only a harness suspended from plastic wings, or he would ride an uncomfortably bound horse to see how many *seconds* he can stay on."

He protested, "No, no, no. Horses are different."

"In what way?"

"They're a part of it all." He opened out his arms as if that was all the explanation that would be needed.

"You're implying that the horse doesn't mind being bound in that uncomfortable way?"

"The ride's a challenge, and it beats plowing."

She laughed.

And in the back of the house, Trisha heard Naomi laugh and became teary-eyed with unaccustomed emotion.

On the porch, Decker knew he'd prolonged their first real talk enough. Tempted as he was to overstay his first visit, he finished his tea and said again, "If you'll tell me the colors of the paint, I could begin to figure out what combinations we might try. Tell me the colors and how much paint you have of each kind."

"I do have a plan. I'll get it." She rose from her chair, then paused to ask, "You aren't colorblind, are you?"

"Not that I know."

She almost grinned at him but turned away and went into the house. He listened carefully to determine where she went and heard her go to a room on the first floor, at the back of the house. He wondered where her bedroom was.

He knew such a mouse would want an aerie, a place high and safe, away from prowling cats like him. Cats. That reminded him of the cougar skin. Would he be able to coax her to strip naked and wear only the softly clicking cougar teeth in a necklace and dance for him to slow, sensuous music? And would she lie back on the cougar skin, looking up at him? His body shivered as he listened to her voice murmuring at the back of the house. How would it be to have her murmur love words in his ear?

In that back room, Trisha smiled at Naomi who was digging in her desk. "Have you learned all his secrets? Or do you need my help?"

"He's nice enough."

"I didn't know you hankered after a 'nice' man. I thought you were salivating over the thought of his body."

"Hush." Naomi frowned. "He wants to see the plans for painting the stores."

"He's volunteered to do that? Does he know who you are? Is he here for a devious reason? Why would a stranger come to this dumb, decaying town and do all this work? What's his motive? You be careful, Naomi." Trisha then shook her head and began to puff and wiggle to get free of the soft chair. "I'd better come out and chaperon."

"You don't know how," Naomi scoffed.

"Don't kid yourself. I wouldn't have turned out this way if I'd been given a little freedom. I was so dreadfully monitored that my goal was to get free and do whatever I wanted."

"Was it Rick?"

"Not at first. But he knew me then, and so he wasn't surprised by me."

"He knew you . . . when?"

"When I was trying to get away."

Naomi questioned, "And he helped you?"

"I was too young, then."

Naomi had never heard Trisha speak in just this way, so she delayed in "finding" the papers. "Who helped you?"

Trisha declared, "No one. I've done everything on my own. It's all my own fault."

"Would you do it again?"

"I suppose. I had to be free. In control."

Naomi nodded but said of herself, "I needed the discipline of supervision."

"But you still went with Brad."

"He was the only one. I thought he was a god, and he came very close. Here're the papers. I need to give them to Decker." She glanced back at Trisha as she went out the door.

Idly, Trisha said, "Yes." With Naomi's last words, Trisha understood that Naomi had delayed in finding the papers so that she could hear what Trisha needed to say. Trisha realized that she'd never before faced the fact that she was responsible for herself—and now a baby. Would she give it to Naomi? The kid would be a lot better off with Naomi.

Then Trisha wondered what on earth she was doing, sitting there, nurturing a child, waiting for its birth? How very strangely lives go along, mostly carelessly unplanned.

Trisha put her hands around her stomach as the kid wiggled and thumped. It was alive and trying. The least she could do would be to try, too.

And Trisha thought about Rick Thomas up there in Dallas. She wondered whom he was seeing. What woman was the recipient of his love? Recipient. Trisha smoothed her hands over her stomach.

It had been a long time since she'd last contacted Rick. The last time she'd phoned, she'd just said, "I'm fine. I'll be in touch." Did he ever think of her? Did he ever wonder where she might be? Why she'd vanished? He had been as involved as they'd been with Brad's illness. Rick had understood when Trisha moved in with Naomi, to be her anchor in that wash of grief when Naomi had first been told there was no hope at all for Brad.

That had been terrible. Naomi hadn't been able to quit fighting. She hadn't been able to face the fact that Brad would die. Once Trisha had been in Brad's room with Naomi, when Brad's slowed voice had told her, "Don't struggle so hard for me. Relax. Let's treasure the time we have left. My love, my dearest love."

Trisha had had to leave the room. At first she had attributed the nausea to her grief for them, but it had been this baby making itself known to her.

Through Brad's final days, Trisha had been so involved with sustaining Naomi that she hadn't really noticed the signs that she was pregnant. She remembered Rick had asked, "We've not had the time together, are you okay this month?"

He had generally asked that during business separations in their relationship. Had his concern been responsibility or fear? Trisha had never been sure. He had always asked, but at that time, with Naomi so stunned, Trisha had thought his compassion was involved, and that he had asked for her own sake, in that tumultuously emotional time, that exhaustingly hopeless time of Naomi's grief.

How could Trisha have left Naomi during the time of the funeral? Brad's family had been so cool to Naomi. Having had no idea about her at all, they had acted as if she were a groupie. When they had finally known that Brad was dying, they had hovered around him and crowded Naomi aside.

Trisha wiped tears from her cheeks as she remembered Brad's filming eyes searching, searching for Naomi's face. Finding her at last, his gaze had rested on her as his mouth had almost smiled.

What a soul-tearing time. Trisha and Rick had sat in the back of the church with Naomi and had gone with her to the gravesite. They couldn't see the grave from where they were in all the madness of the photographers and gawkers, prerequisite for such a mega star. No one had recognized Naomi in her veil, for there had been so many veiled, grieving fans.

And Rick had been there with them. He had been a rock in that time. Trisha really only remembered that now. Rick had never complained or argued or chided her neglect of him. He'd done whatever he could for her and Naomi. He'd held them both as the three had stood alone at the grave those following days.

Rick had been very, very sweet. Trisha leaked more tears, wiping them away with her fingers, sniffling because it was becoming hard to get up from the chair to find the box of tissues. She admitted it belatedly; Rick had been very sweet to them.

But when she had suspected the nausea was from being pregnant, and she'd asked Rick if he would want a child, he'd said a distracted, "No, honey, the last thing we need is a kid. We need to get away for a while. You're skin and bones."

She had said sadly, "I can't leave Naomi. You have to know that."

"It might help her to be on her own for a week. Then she could notice you're around when we come back."

"No. I can't leave her. She doesn't remember to eat or to go to bed or to get up. She's a zombie."

"So are you."

She'd burst into tears.

"See? You need to get away for a week. You're making yourself sick."

"It's just that I'm so sorry for her."

"If you get really sick, you're no help to anyone," he'd said logically.

She hadn't let him stay over and sleep with her. "Think how it would be for Naomi to hear us in here when she's all alone forever?"

He had understood, for a while, but after the second month passed, he'd begun to urge some time with her. "We don't even talk," he had argued. "All we do is hold on to this lengthening wake. Brad would have a fit if he knew how you two were acting."

Trisha had railed at him as unknowing and without the most basic feelings of compassion. But she was also cognizant of the fact that she carried his unwanted child. "What kind of father would you make?" she had accused.

"A rotten one. That's why we're careful. Now, Trish, kiss me and make me feel you notice me."

In Sawbuck, the weepy, pregnant Trisha sat and realized that Rick had been very lonely during that time of her distraction from him. Well, he was better off without her. She couldn't tie a reluctant man down with an unplanned child he'd said he did not want.

He was sweetly honorable man, and if she'd told him she was pregnant, he probably would have married her. But a forced marriage wasn't anything either of them had wanted. They had been together for the delight of each other's company and the sizzlingly feverish attraction they'd shared so hotly. Actually, neither of them would have made a good parent.

Nor would she now. Even without the distraction of Rick, she wasn't mother material. She would have to come to some decision about this kid. She needed to protect its future so that it could have a good life. She ought to be thinking about that. Soon now.

But what if Rick knew she was pregnant? How would he react? One of the great temptations was to face Rick and tell him, just to see how he would handle it. People are all so strange that no one could ever anticipate how another would behave. Trisha rubbed her watery eyes. She couldn't even understand why she acted the way she did. How on earth could she know about someone else's behavior?

Well, she could fantasize.

She would go to his apartment and use her key . . . and the lock would be changed.

She would call, and they would meet at Joe's Bar. She would be sitting at a table so that he couldn't see the . . . change in her. He would hurry over, ignoring the greetings from all their bar-hopping friends. He would stand there, looking down at her with such an anguished expression on his face, then he would grin and say, "Where you been?" She would idly move her wine glass filled with just water and say pensively, "Rick, I have something to tell you." "Me first. Remember Audrey? We were married two weeks ago. She got caught. You know how I'm a little careless now and then, but what the heck."

Trisha pried herself up off the chair with bouncing heaves and pantings, and went for a box of tissues. She looked in the mirror and was shocked. She looked terrible! All blotchy and unattractive. How could she ever face a lov—ex-lover looking like this?

Restlessly Trisha walked down the hall and peeked through the living-room window. The two were sitting at the table on the wash side of the porch. That god-awful dog was sitting before the screen door and flicked an ear back to let her know that he knew she was watching him. He threw a ghastly dog smile over his shoulder and went on looking out over the seeable territory.

A dumb dog.

But that Decker was something. Trisha tried to hear what they were saying. Naomi was talking about her dam. Good grief! With a man like Decker around, you'd think she could simper a little and flirt. But she did stare at him.

That could be effective. One could never tell with men, Trisha considered as she returned toward the back of the house and allowed the soft chair to entrap her again. Why couldn't Naomi forget the dam for a while and have a nice healing little flirtation with this itinerant cowboy. He was just going to waste as it was.

Trisha had discreetly asked around, as only a woman from the big city of Dallas could do, and none of the women in the Sawbuck area had snagged Decker as yet. Naomi ought to get a taste of him before some biddy got her claws into him. God, he was built !

That part Indian was the only other male around who could come close to Decker. Buzz was really something. From the talk among the women, he was practicing on just about any female who hesitated long enough. If Trisha approached him in her condition, he would say, "Honey, it looks to me like you done been had."

That was certainly true.

What would Rick say if she confessed her glances had been pulled over to this Buzz? Rick would grin down at her and say, "You been alone too long, sugar, come give me some."

There wasn't a jealous bone in Rick's body. Of course, she'd never tested that theory. She'd never looked at another man. She'd never been tempted, enough.

Rick had known where Trisha was at all times. No matter where they were, he would call her sometime during the day and say, "Just checking up. Thinking about me?"

And she'd laugh.

"Your laugh drives me crazy," he'd say in that low, special voice that he used just on her.

Or did he? Who was he phoning now from work in the middle of the day? Would he have the *gall* to ask another woman if she was thinking about him? All men were skunks.

Out on the porch, Decker put down his glass and said, "This is a thirsty day."

"More tea?"

"Thank you. That would be just right." He might start sloshing when he moved. "Where were you raised?"

"San Antonio."

"Go to school there?"

"Um-hum." She didn't want to become too familiar with this man. She looked over at him. "You speak well. I thought cowboys said 'Yes'um' and 'No ma'am' and 'shoot.' "

"Yes'um."

She gave him a twinkling look, but she didn't actually smile.

"It's about like pulling hen's teeth to get you to talk, ma'am."

"What do you want to talk about?"

"Why are you living in this nothing town?" He waited for her reply.

She ventured, "I like the people."

"But this isn't your home."

"In a way, it is."

So she still loved that man who grew up in this house. It was a nice enough house and a great place

for kids to grow up. But she had no business here.
"How long have you been here?"

"For some months."

"How long do you plan to stay?"

"A while."

"You ought to take up cowboying, since you now
have the replies down pat."

"I've been through a . . . tough time. This place is
healing. I need it awhile longer." She looked at him.
He'd said he needed a time to regroup, maybe he
could understand.

"Yeah. Whose house was this?"

"I bought it from the Conner estate."

"They all died out?"

"No." Her voice didn't falter. "They haven't lived
here for a long time. The house had deteriorated
considerably. The men in town fixed it up. They did
quite a good job of it. The porch especially needed
new floorboards. New railings. This is a wonderful
porch. We spend a lot of time out here."

"When's Trisha's baby due?"

"She isn't exactly sure."

"She seeing a doctor?"

"Of course," Naomi said coolly.

"When's he guess?"

She smiled a little. "Not yet."

"Who's the daddy?"

She gave him a chilling look.

"She doesn't wear any rings on her left hand, and
she didn't do that by herself, and she's just got you.
Do you need any help?"

"Thank you. Everything's under control. We'll
move into town when the time comes."

"How long's that?" He was pushing.

"Not yet." Although the reply was a repeat, her voice was gentle.

He wanted her to mention Rick. He wanted to know if there was any reason not to inform Rick. "Was the daddy informed?"

"Why do you ask?

"It's tough for a woman to cope with this problem and the man ought to know so's he can help."

"There's no problem."

"You know what you're saying?"

She looked straight at him. "What." Not a question.

"You're telling me that the daddy hasn't been told. Some man doesn't know about this kid. That's cheating."

"I do agree with you, but she won't tell him."

"Why not?" His voice was very gentle now, encouraging her to tell him the whole of it.

"It's her life."

"But it's the kid's, too, and it's part of the man's. It's a dirty thing for a woman to hide from a man that he's a daddy."

"It wasn't my decision."

She was still talking straight to him. Not yet offended or not yet shutting him out. He knew she agreed with him but was being loyal to Trisha. "If you need my help in any way, at any time, ring that old triangle there on the other end of the porch. I'll come a-running."

"Thank you."

"But in the meantime, we need to talk Trisha into telling the daddy. Do you know him?"

She became reluctant and just looked at Decker.

"You do?" His tone was chiding.

"It's her choice."

"Do you realize that women are a very peculiar race? I cannot fathom a single one of you. I think God made women so men can't possibly be bored."

And she grinned.

He looked off and sighed contentedly. He'd really talked to her, and he'd gotten some answers. He wondered if the time would ever come when he could ask her if she'd ever dreamed of fire demons?

He looked at her hands. So small. How could she fight his fears? As big as he was, he couldn't. He was dreaming of her again. Would the time come when he could tell her that? "I sleep because I hold the thought of you. And when the danger is high and I'm afraid in the nightmares, there you are, watching the approach of the danger and holding it back from me."

How could a man tell a mouse-woman she was his protector? She'd think he was a coward.

Maybe he was.

CHAPTER SEVEN

DECKER GLANCED OVER AT WELLINGTON. THE dog was sitting on the top step of Naomi's porch, viewing the area like some scruffy lord who didn't realize he wasn't top drawer.

Decker looked over Naomi's porch railing at the empty rock basin. "That would be pretty with water in it." His was an idle comment. He judged the area: "About two by three blocks."

"What?"

"The length and width of the lake it'd make." He'd finished the subject.

But he'd hit a nerve in her. "Exactly. The kids and I pile stones to fill the neck to keep the water dammed, but the men aren't interested, and we can't carry big enough rocks to do any good. When the floods come, the force of the current would just carry away those we've managed to get in there."

"Where."

She looked at him sharply. "Downstream. Come look."

"I need a little more tea."

"Tea? Oh, yes, of course."

But he saw that she was distracted. So she wanted

to dam the basin. He narrowed his eyes. Why not? But let her coax first. He could say: Come sleep with me, keep the fire demons away, and I'll plug the hole for your dam. I'll plug other holes, Naomi Wentworth, and you'll forget the Duke.

She crushed the mint and served the tea. He sipped it judiciously as she watched for his reaction. He considered being asinine and making her sweat, but he smiled and said, "Just right."

"No sugar?"

"I like the mint. It cools me." Let her figure out why he needed cooling.

They didn't talk. The breeze was from the Gulf and very pleasant. It was nice, there on the porch that was shaded by an old oak, some hackberries, and a pecan. The wicker furniture had green flowered pads, and for the first time in a long time, Decker felt his body at peace. Well, almost. His muscles were relaxed, and he could move without undue pain. He smiled.

"What's funny?"

He looked over at his mouse and replied, "I like it here."

She wasn't sure how to reply. He might move in on her porch. Any man who could live in an empty store could feel quite at home on a front porch. If he were sleeping on the glider, and she was upstairs, how could she know that he would stay on the porch? Now, Naomi, he hasn't offered. *Offered?* What did she mean by that? Now just a minute, Naomi, stop this silly thinking!

"Okay."

Naomi jumped and asked, "What?"

"I'm ready to see the place I'm going to plug."

And he smiled in a way that sent shivers right up

her back and lifted her hair and peaked her breasts.
"What—?"

"The dam."

"Oh, yes!"

What *had* she been thinking? He watched her quizz-
ically, and his smile faded a little. What had distracted
her from the dam?

She readily led him down off the porch, as Wellington accompanied them, and they went around the
house to the edge of the wash. There they took a
steep path down into the basin. It was surprisingly
deep. Filled it would be over his head. They walked
downstream, along the smooth surface, with the dog
ranging around and about.

Like scoured cement, the uneven, undulating surface of the rock had been formed by rushing water.
In flood, the torn rocks had been flung by the current
and battered and rolled on the rock bed, until there
was a large basin, but along the bank beyond her
house, the rampaging water had worn a funnel that
led to the narrowed opening. It was a natural, easy
place for a dam.

Decker didn't say anything, but stood, looking
around, considering.

She gestured. "Some big rocks here, then smaller
ones to keep the water in, and there would be enough
water for the truck farms for a year."

"You forget evaporation."

"Yes."

He admitted, "But it would help."

"Oh, yes."

Looking up along the lip of the rock, he said, "You
could block this, using a tractor." He gestured where

it could be brought up to the edge of the opening easily enough.

She echoed, "A tractor."

"I might be able to borrow one."

"Oh, Decker..." She couldn't think of how to express her gratitude without throwing herself at him. And she didn't want to be so rashly forward.

"A front scoop. Fill it, dump in the rocks, pour a little cement in, to fill the holes, and you got it." He then added thoughtfully, "We could use some advice, and we might need permission before we build the dam."

"I applied and cleared it. But..." She hesitated. "But we need to put in a gate at the bottom, or the wash will fill with silt when the creek floods."

He clarified, "A gate."

"At the bottom," she specified.

"That does complicate things."

"The materials aren't too costly. There's almost enough in the town fund for it, but the labor..." She saw her hopes fading.

He smiled inside. He'd do the damned dam, but he was going to let her sweat awhile. "Let's think about this. I'm not an engineer."

"What are you?" She blurted it.

He was slow to reply. "A horse rider?" He took a step so that his spurs stirred.

"Yes." She stiffened, then said starchily, "I really must get back."

"We haven't looked at the colors for painting the stores."

"I'll show you, but we need to have a meeting and let the people decide. The paint can be moved to the store next to yours. I believe there's enough to get started."

He warned: "We'll have to see if anyone's willing to paint."

She lost heart. "Yes." She looked down at her fingers.

He gave her no encouragement. She needed to be grateful to him. Now, why should she have to do that? Well, he just wanted her to be aware of him. A little more aware. And grateful. Before he left.

He helped her out of the wash. He went up first about halfway, then reached a hand down to her and pulled her up to him. There he steadied her needlessly, turned, and put his big hand on the small of her back to support her the rest of the way up.

Under his big hand, he could feel that she was perfectly capable of getting up the bank by herself. She was as surefooted as a goat . . . as a mouse, but he had to go back for Wellington. The damned dog sat at the bottom of the incline and woofed once, calling attention to his own need for help.

"Come on," Decker told the dog.

Wellington looked off to one side with endurance and just sat.

The mouse said, "He can make it up that slope. I did."

"I helped you," Decker unfairly reminded her.

She'd been up and down that slope how many times? But if she mentioned she hadn't needed help, he wouldn't take her hand the next time. She said, "Yes."

So Decker went back down into the wash and encouraged the dog to give it a try. Wellington wasn't interested in trying. So Decker pushed from behind in an unsuccessful attempt, then he picked up that awkward, improbable combination of unruly grey hair that covered lanky bones and carried the dog up the slope. And Decker realized he could do it!

Decker set the dog down. His legs were a little wobbly and he was breathing a bit fast, but he had carried that big lug of a dog up that sharp incline! He was healing.

It was exhilarating. He gave Naomi a rather sassy look and said, "Do you want to go back down and let me carry you up?"

She merely smiled, not knowing how to reply. She couldn't jump back down the slope or she'd look willing, as if she were asking for it. That would be shocking.

It was just as well that she didn't; he might not have made it up again, carrying even her slight weight.

On that Friday night, the Sawbuck citizens dragged chairs into one of the empty stores and had their town meeting. Most of the people were present, and they included Naomi and Trisha. It was interesting to Decker that Naomi was careful to be only a member of the gathering. She said very little. John Rodriquez chaired the meeting. He did it very well.

They discussed painting the buildings. The first snag came when most of the women balked about the stores being painted.

"What about the houses?" one woman asked.

"That will come," pronounced John. "We need to paint the stores and spruce up the town. Then we'll do the houses."

The women argued that the houses needed painting much more than the empty stores. They pushed.

Naomi suggested, "For right now, how about painting just the doors of the houses?"

Decker took that up. "Choose the color, and we'll paint each door whatever color we have that you like."

They mostly wanted red. There were a couple of blue advocates. Finally they put all the colors into a hat and they got to choose and trade. It took a lot of time. Naomi was so patient that Decker was amazed by her.

With the door colors settled, they harangued about the stores. John showed them the sketched stores and Naomi's suggested color combinations. They took a while discussing it all. The drugstore wanted blue and white. There wasn't that much white. They could have dark blue and light green.

Being a store resident, Decker—out of hand—picked the colors for "his" store. He chose dark red with a mustard trim. The store next to his would be mustard with grey and the one beyond that grey with yellow.

No one signed up to paint.

Decker told the women, "Tape the paper with your color of paint on the top of your door, and I'll paint the doors."

They smiled at him and were so pleased and sweet that Joe said, "I'll help." And he was included in the approval.

Then Buzz told one woman that he'd do her door. That made another woman indignant, so he was committed to doing two.

Decker wondered about that. Buzz was involved with the two women? How would a man handle that complication in a town the size of Sawbuck?

No one had volunteered to do any of the stores.

John was persistent, so Decker said, "I'll do my store."

The grocery store owner, Mr. Stern, said, "We'll do our store."

And Mr. Buckle stated: "We'll do the drugstore."

Pete asked, "Does the gas station come in on this prettifying?"

Naomi nodded, so John replied, "Yes."

Pete then planned aloud. "Buzz'll help me paint the station, he doesn't do nothing else around there."

"I work my tail off filling gas tanks."

"Yeah. Two hours a day."

The men all laughed closed-mouthed, blowing puffs of air through their noses.

So they fairly well settled that the painting would begin.

It was August, and the Texas days were really hot and dry. The painting day was Saturday, and Decker rolled out of his hammock with comparative ease for the fire demons had been held in abeyance the night before, and he'd slept well.

He pulled on jeans, let Wellington in, and began breakfast. The kids were already tapping on his front window, wanting the VCR turned on. Decker went barefoot and shirtless to the front door and opened it to say, "Now you *know* your mommas won't allow me to start it until you all have done your Saturday chores."

"We did 'em. We did 'em!"

"Did you make your beds?"

In chorus, "Yeeesss!"

"Did you sweep the yard?" Done with homemade, twig brooms.

"Yeeessl!"

"Did you feed the chickens?"

"Yeeesss!"

"Did you water Magdalena's tree?"

There were exclamations and giggles and the kids scattered.

Decker grinned after them and turned. And there was Naomi. She wasn't in a dress. She wore denims and a blue work shirt. She was about as big as a child. She was staring at his body. She was interested in him?

She was looking at the green and yellow residue of the bruises on his body. She was frowning and her lips were parted and one hand was up as if to touch him.

He held perfectly still, hoping that she would, longing for her touch. His body was so sensitized.

She realized she was staring and blinked, moved her head and licked her lips, embarrassed. She stumbled over her words. "You were such a help last night. If you hadn't been there, and offered to do the doors, I don't believe anything would have ever been started. You shamed them into volunteering. Without you, I think they would have let it all slide. Thank you."

"Why do you want to save this town?"

She raised her gaze to his, and deep down, he could see the residue of pain. She still loved that dead man. She looked off to the side and said, "It's a nice place. These are nice people. They've been caught in between their time and high tech. They are victims of progress."

"People can't be given crutches. Obsolescence can rarely be recycled."

She did take in his meaning, but she earnestly replied, "I believe they can. We help other countries, why not think of Sawbuck as an emerging place?"

"An interesting premise."

She echoed softly, "'Obsolescence,' 'an interesting premise.'" She looked at him in speculation.

He'd slipped there. His word choices hadn't been those of an itinerant cowboy. In other circumstances, such a slip could have killed him. Stupid. It was because he didn't think of her as the enemy and he'd allowed himself to speak to her as an equal. He would have to watch himself.

Not the enemy? They were on opposite sides in Sawbuck. She was for preserving the town, and he was for emptying it. Was he? Then why was he helping to clean it up? Well, he liked the people, and he thought they'd been screwed by his uncle Gimme. The old man ought to cough up some substantial cash to coax the people into resettling somewhere else. Gimme would never miss whatever it might cost him.

But Decker wasn't entirely honest about being there as his uncle's representative.

Well, he wasn't on Gimme's payroll. He was an independent man. He could do what he damned well pleased. But if he wasn't *really* going to try to get the people to leave Sawbuck, then he should tell his uncle. He would.

He waited to see if Naomi wanted him to help. *Wanted* him? Could she?

He was watching her as if he expected her to say something. So she said, "You'll need brushes. What size do you use?"

"Four or five-inch."

"I have them."

"You going to paint?"

"I thought I might do Magdalena's door."

"I'll do hers. Why don't you get the ladies to make some lemonade? This is going to be thirsty work."

"The doors ought not take too long." She still watched him.

"They're beginning on the grocery, the drugstore, and the filling station."

"The painting is going to make such a difference. This is exciting."

He nodded, took a brush, and picked up three cans of paint. She took one can and another brush. He went into the middle of the town and yelled, "Pink? Green? Purple?"

The little kids went scrambling to see which were the doors that would be painted those colors. He waited. They came back, dancing, laughing in delight over the activity in their town.

As he began the purple door, Decker realized he'd have to go over to his uncle's house and tell him about this renovation.

But an hour later as he finished his fifth door, someone yelled, "Hey, Decker? Telephone for you!"

He looked over his shoulder, unbelieving, and and felt anger stir in him. He'd told Gimme never to call him there. He rose with a dangerous stillness that everyone watched.

A phone call for Decker? Who? The townspeople became avidly curious. Was the call from his enemies? The ones who'd beaten him?

With the slow clink of his spurs, his brown and healing body filmed in sweat, he strode in a deliberate manner over to the pay phone. Gritting his teeth, he picked it up and said, "Yeah?"

"Just what the bloody hell're you doing?"

"I'm teaching them to be neighborly." And Decker hung up.

On his way back to Mrs. Billmont's house, people

asked, "You okay?" "You in trouble?" "Somebody after you?"

Their questions touched in Decker's heart. They were anxious for him. "Everything's fine. No problem. It's okay."

But the people were not sure. They watched as Decker finished Mrs. Billmont's door while she looked for some raspberry tarts for him. He said he wasn't hungry, thanked her anyway, and moved on to the next house.

Already the doors made a difference. It was interesting how nice just that little touch of color could be, in the greyed, weathered siding of the houses. He finished the tenth door, smiled at the thanks, and looked around. All the other doors were done or being done. There was now an excess of door painters.

Decker stretched his back, crossed to the drugstore, around it to the street side, and sat down on one of the few chairs along the walk. He put his paint cans on the sidewalk and wrapped his brush in foil. Then he leaned back.

A movement caught his eye. He turned his head and saw that Naomi was coming along the walk with two tall glasses of lemonade. He almost got up, but she motioned him to sit still. She handed him one glass and sat in the chair closest to him. They sipped in companionable silence.

A car came along. That was unusual on a Saturday. It went past, slowed, swung around, and came back to pull up alongside Decker and Naomi, and a man got out. "What's going on?" he asked them.

Decker lifted the glass and questioned, "Lemonade?"

"Yeah," he decided, pleased to be asked.

Naomi got up and went to fetch another glass. She turned back and asked Decker, "Want some more?"

"I'm fine."

She nodded and went out of sight.

The guy took Naomi's chair. "You guys painting the town?"

"Yeah." Decker wondered what else they could be doing with cans of paint and brushes.

"Just all of you all? No pros?"

"Just us."

"Need some help?"

That surprised Decker. "That would be mighty nice of you."

"I'll go change my clothes. I know a couple of others who'd feel left out if they couldn't have a hand in this."

Naomi came back, and both men got up. Decker went down the sidewalk and got another chair to drag it back. The three sat down, and the guy said, "My name's Dick. I can't tell you how many times I've wanted to sit along here." He looked around at the town, viewed from another angle.

"I'm Decker and this is Naomi."

"I saw you at the rattlesnake dinner." He nodded as he said that. "This is a neat little town," he said with a proprietary smile. "It'll look great, all cleaned up and painted. We need to dam the wash and make a fishing pond over there."

Naomi and Decker exchanged a look. "We" he had said as if he were a citizen of the town. The two witnesses to this intrusive character raised their eyebrows in disbelief.

Naomi asked Dick, "What do you know about dams?"

"Nothing. But I do know an engineer. I'll call him. He doesn't have anything to do on Saturdays. His wife took off and went back to Ohio. He's a true Texan and can't understand her leaving this paradise at all."

He then drank up the last of his lemonade and said with some satisfaction, "I'd better get going, or we'll lose the best part of the day." He stood up. "Be back before you can say 'jackrabbit.'" He grinned. "Thank you for the lemonade. Is it all right if we bring back some beer?"

"Yes," Decker supplied.

Dick laughed, strode off the sidewalk to his car, and took off.

Decker and Naomi exchanged a glance. She questioned, "A real-live volunteer?"

"Looks like it."

"I am astounded."

His tongue reminded her, "I was the first one."

She loved his need for reassurance. "I remember."

"See to it that you do."

And she smiled at him.

The day was a page from *Tom Sawyer*. Not only did Dick return with four other commuters, but they brought stepladders and straight ladders on their pickup trucks. They even brought their own paintbrushes.

Then people stopped their cars and exclaimed, "You're finally taking our advice! You're painting!" They reminded the Sawbuckers that they'd mentioned the need for paint at the rattlesnake feast and asked if there would be another dinner that evening?

Decker said, "Chili . . . again" in a discouraging way.

"Oh," they said, pleased. "We'll come back."

Decker added, "—for the painters."

Decker had thought that would stop the influx of more painters, but they just said, "We can't miss a town party, we'll go change and be back."

So Naomi organized the women to start the chili pot, and John gathered volunteers to string the lights along the wash again and set out the door-tables and chairs. Naomi and Decker shook their heads in wonder over it all.

Everything that was supposed to be painted was painted that day. They finished just before sundown, and Dick said, "If the wash was dammed, we could go swimming. Hey, Ned. How about damming the wash?"

And Naomi urged, "Come look at it."

Decker got down off his ladder and went along.

Ned walked in the patient slouch of a man who knows his worth. He did a very thorough job of his survey, getting down into the basin, treading around the perimeter, eyeing it from all angles. Naomi watched avidly, respectfully silent. Ned stated, "I know a gate I can lay hands on. We need two sewer pipes about fifteen feet long."

Decker said, "Done."

Ned smiled. "I like your attitude."

Decker smiled back, but his word had been for Naomi. Decker had been jolted to have someone else moving into the hero slot on Naomi's dam.

Dick came along and asked, "Everything solved? The diving board should be right here." He gestured. "No problem. Let's mark it." He began piling stones.

Sawbuck's two most recent citizens looked on the interlopers with some indignation, but the humor of it hit them and they laughed.

By then, the lights among the trees were on, other cars were stopping, and the gate-crashers were charged for their meals. They submitted willingly and exclaimed over the changes in Sawbuck.

One said, "You all give good parties." Then it became the possessive, "We ought to give one at least once a month."

"The place looks great!" another offered, and that was repeated.

And someone added, "It was brilliant to make everything so colorful."

Rual came, walking his Big Dog strut.

That dampened the citizens, but the others treated him as if he were normal. They greeted him and included him. He was stiff-legged and territorial. The guests didn't notice because they, too, had become territorial.

The sweaty men went to the pump and hosed off. Some of the newest nonresident citizens asked about the water system and were puzzled by the curtailing of the town's water supply. They felt it wasn't very fair. "Of course, he did give you this well."

"But the farms are lying fallow," Buzz said.

"What do you do?"

He shrugged. "Nothing."

Ned asked, "So you don't have work?"

"No."

Dick said, "The bamboo rakes are a good idea. Mine is the best I've ever had."

Someone said, "Why don't you guys start selling doughnuts and coffee in the mornings?"

Someone else objected, "I need more for breakfast than rolls or doughnuts. I need cereal, eggs, and bacon, too."

Someone else said, "Pancakes."

"No rattlesnake side dishes?"

A woman's voice sounded a heartfelt "Ugh," as she turned away. Then she called, "Hurry up and come on over so's we can eat. We're waiting for the mighty painters."

"That's us," said John.

The others laughed chafingly.

Buzz asked, "What'd you paint, John?"

And he said something salacious about paintbrush handles. When the laughter settled down a little, he asked Buzz, "Where were you all afternoon?"

"I painted two doors, if you remember, and I had two grateful women."

Laughing, smelling better, the men drifted back to the group under the lights. The boom box was blaring, the food was ready, and everyone ate and talked and laughed. And forgetting they were tired, they danced. They had a good time.

Naomi sat with Trisha, Marie, Magdalena, and Ann. With their heads together, they talked with animation, gesturing. But Naomi looked up when Decker did his raw male stomp. All the other women laughed and shrieked and clapped. Naomi's eyes narrowed, but she didn't look at anyone else, just Decker. His body moved more easily. He was almost healed.

And he only glanced at the other women, but he looked back at Naomi. He danced that pagan courting lure just for her.

CHAPTER EIGHT

THE NEXT DAY WAS SUNDAY. AFTER THE newly recruited circuit preacher had completed the church service in Sawbuck, and gone on to his next stop, there was another town meeting. This one was well attended. The men had said to each other, "What else could they find for us to do? We've cleaned the grounds and we've painted. At least they won't want us to do anything else."

It was Joe's wife Ann who was spokeswoman. She stood up quickly and was very nervous. Even before they all quieted, she began, "Joe and I . . . well, you see, we've always liked cooking. Joe was an army cook during Vietnam, and he does like cooking for a lot of people, so he knows how, you see. And some of the people last night said they'd like to get coffee and doughnuts here in the mornings. We could do that. We could do that *as a town!* We'd need people to take orders and carry the stuff to the cars and make change, and keep things clean so the roaches don't move in. What do you think?"

Buzz said, "Some of them want bacon and eggs."

"We could do that. We could use that vacant store across from the drugstore and set up the door-tables

and some of the chairs. But we can start with doughnuts and sweet rolls and coffee. Right, Joe?"

Joe blushed and nodded.

There was the ever questioning about ready money.
"What do we do about change? How much would we
need?"

This time the reply was, "We'll ask at the bank."

Decker had a hard time not volunteering to fund
it all, and he knew Naomi was in an agony of not
interfering. This planning and discussing was very
exciting to all of them, but particularly exciting to the
town. It was their first giant step in doing something
positive about their own lives.

But for Naomi, it was especially emotional. It had
been nine months since Brad had set Sawbuck's recovery as a goal for her. That's how long it takes to
make a new life, so this was very like a birth to her.
She'd agonized over that town, but she'd gotten nowhere until Decker had come and tilted the odds.

As with a child, the beginnings had begun, now
came the first steps. Would the town survive? It would
be very interesting to watch. And maybe take a little
hand in things to help. She could speak to the bank
. . . first. Brad hadn't said that she had to stay completely out of it.

At that meeting, specific people were appointed to
investigate specific things like setting up a consultation
with the Small Business Advisory Board. All across
the country, members of that group were staffed by
retired executives, and their advice was free.

There were Sawbuck volunteers to seek out sources
for paper plates and cups for the coffee and doughnuts, or to price crockery. Joe was seeing to cooking
utensils and supplies.

They discussed charges, wages, and what to do with tips.

There was a committee to clean the store in question, and Naomi volunteered to see to the permission to use the store. That was no problem, she had purchased them eight months ago.

They were all to report back within two weeks.

But. There was no reason not to begin with the coffee and doughnuts as soon as the store was cleaned.

It was a busy week. They ran out of doughnuts and even coffee each of the first two days. Decker saw Naomi only now and then and didn't really get to talk to her. He'd catch a glimpse of her through the trees, walking across the grounds. She was back in her soft dresses and big hats, and again she looked like a lady from another time, another place. One not for him.

He went to see his uncle and aunt and left Wellington outside, explaining. "He's just a little ripe, and we don't have the water to spare, over in Sawbuck."

"'We'?" Uncle Frank looked like a thundercloud.

Decker exclaimed with false amazement, "Well, I declare! I've never thought you and Dad looked too much alike, but I've seen Dad look just *exactly* the way you're looking right now!"

"That doesn't surprise me one little bitty bit," Uncle Frank growled tersely, his breath held high in his chest as if he could not breathe out.

Elise said, "We could bathe Wellington."

"I appreciate that. Could you go get started? Your husband wants to say a few fulminating words to me."

"What have you done?" Elise looked between the two men.

"Not nearly enough," Decker assured her.

Elise went to her husband and said, "There's nothing important enough for you to get so angry."

Frank gave her a disbelieving look.

"Calm down, sweetie." She leaned up to him and kissed his chin.

Decker watched that with some cynicism. He figured Elise was pandering for a larger allowance.

But he noticed that Uncle Frank made an obvious effort to calm down. And he said, "Sit, nephew."

Decker sat.

Frank observed that action and said, "You're better."

"Yes."

Then Frank fooled them both. "I'm glad."

Decker smiled at his uncle and said, "Me, too. Thanks."

"But I'm a little ticked that you seem to be settling in so good over in Sawbuck. Explain this to me."

"None of the improvements was my idea," Decker told his uncle. "I'm just trying to influence and convince. Let them struggle. They'll realize they can never make it there . . . without water."

"I feel uneasy about Sawbuck. When they start painting, it's a sign that they're willing to put their sweat into a place. That's permanence. Sweat glues a community together."

"You ought to've been in advertising."

"In my way, I am." Frank got out a cigar and made a ritual of lighting it.

"When the EPA finds you and stomps out your cigars, this will be a better land."

Frank looked appalled. "Do you know what I have to pay to get real Cuban cigars?"

"Only because we're still maintaining an embargo on that little country after almost thirty years."

"Let's get back to running the people out of Saw-buck."

"Now, *this* is a free country. I can't run those people out of there, if they don't want to go. You have to know that. There's nothing crooked that I can find. There aren't any poachers into your land because you grow crops that aren't pickable by a stray, starving people. So what's your headache?"

"I want my boundaries neat and tidy."

"In all probability, you'll have your wish. These people aren't very ambitious. They're stirring a little, right now. If they had good jobs to go to, they would. They'd move out. Why don't you see if you can find them all jobs . . . somewhere else? Relocate them. Give them an incentive to leave."

"Now you gotta know that's hogwash!"

"No. It's good business."

"What's this Naomi like?"

"A mouse."

Thoughtfully, Frank digested that description as he puffed on his cigar. Watching the smoke mount and swirl, he frowned at Decker. "Wasn't there a movie called *The Mouse That Roared*?"

"Yes. About a very poor little country that managed to make one missile so they could declare war and fire the missile at the U.S. Then they could immediately surrender to us and get on the U.S. gravy train for conquered countries like Germany and Japan."

"Is this 'mouse' trying to get to my bank roll?"

"No."

"How can you be so sure?"

"She doesn't need your money."

"She's got money?"

"Apparently."

"How?"

"I don't know."

His uncle looked astounded.

Decker added, "—yet. Your plans are probably going to work. Relax. I don't know why anyone would want to live in Sawbuck. They'll make this last effort, then they'll realize the town has nowhere to go, and they'll leave. It might take as much as five years, but you have the time."

"Do I?"

"It's what we all have. Give Sawbuck a little. Not having water is their prime problem, and you control that."

"I sure do."

Decker put his hands on the arms of his chair and said, "Well, if I can borrow some water, repayable on demand, of course, I'll wash that ripe dog of mine. God only knows what he's been in to, but he sure stinks."

"I noticed."

"Be calm. I'll see you in a week or so?"

"Good enough. And, Decker, it's good to see you moving easy."

Decker smiled cautiously. When Frank started being sentimental, he wanted something more. But his uncle didn't say anything else, so Decker said good-bye. He went through the house toward the door leading to the backyard, and greeted Chico as he went through the kitchen.

Chico said, "Good to see you can move again without thinking how it'll be, Decker."

"That says it exactly, Chico. How you been doing?"

"No problems."

"Glad to hear it."

"There is some mint tea?"

"Why, thank you kindly." As he picked up the glass, he looked out the windows above the sink. "Has she started yet?"

"That dog's in hog heaven."

Decker laughed. "Us males are slaves to our senses."

Softly Chico replied, "Hallelujah, Lord."

Decker shook his head at the cook, in laughing chiding, and went on outside.

"Well, Auntie, did I take long enough for you to finish?" He looked down at the ghastly mess of a sopping-wet Wellington. The dog was unattractive dry, but wet, he was ugly. He gave Decker his "precious" look.

Elise commented, "He likes attention."

"What male doesn't?"

"You."

"Hell, I walked right into that one. What were you doing to Frank inside, being all dear and concerned, trying for a more lavish allowance?"

"No."

"How can you justify pussyfooting around me and cuddling up to Frank, too? You have the morals of an alley cat."

She turned and looked up at Decker's face, almost speaking, then her eyes changed and she looked hungrily down his body.

Elise shocked him, and he shifted uncomfortably, the spurs murmuring.

She turned back to the dog without speaking, taking up a towel and starting to dry the dog's coat. Wellington closed his eyes to keep the pleasure from spilling out.

"Let me." Decker couldn't allow a woman to work so hard drying that monster.

She said, "It's okay. I haven't anything else to do." And Wellington growled.

"Why, Wellington!" Decker said in a very shocked and offended way.

The dog understood drama and looked chastened.

"You're ruining my dog," he scolded Elise.

"Do you want me to bathe you?" She didn't look up, she just asked it in that low voice of hers.

Decker's eyes widened on her hands moving on the dog, and he exclaimed softly, "My God, woman, do you think I'm made of steel?"

"Yes," she hissed positively.

As he and a better-smelling Wellington drove back to Sawbuck, Decker replayed that conversation. It was her manner of approach and her replies that puzzled him. She hadn't spoken seductively. She had said the words and meant them but, this time, she hadn't batted an eyelash or moved her body. It was as if she were desperate for sex.

Why had she chosen him? It didn't make any sense. Maybe she'd had all the others, and he was a challenge because he just was not susceptible? But he was susceptible. God, did he want! He gritted his teeth, curled his body, and hunched his shoulders. Only it wasn't Elise's body that he wanted, it was a mouse's.

Why couldn't Naomi talk to him the way Elise did. There would be no problem if she showed any interest. But she was always squatted down talking to little kids, or trying to get someone interested in the dam, or visiting Magdalena, or walking with a very pregnant Trisha.

Maybe Trisha's condition was a deterrent to Naomi's raging passion for his body. Yeah. Sure. She was probably stone cold. Frigid.

He looked over at Wellington who was drying his tongue out the truck window. "How do you convince them?"

The dog pulled in his dry tongue and turned his chin over his shoulder. Wellington looked at Decker sadly, then sighed with great melancholy as if there was no solution for a klutz like him. Decker felt the same way.

As the week progressed, Decker realized that he spoke to Naomi every day. He kept track. But it was never about anything important. They talked about how to get the window screens repaired, or the fact that one of the commuters was inquiring about showing sports clothing in one of the painted stores, and did the town want strangers in the stores? Or her talk was something about that damned dam.

Decker got a lead on some sewer pipe and waved down commuting Ned to inquire if that was the right kind. But the pipe was mostly paper and not fired clay. They needed the clay in this instance. So he had to look farther afield. Finally, because of timing, he had to buy the sewer pipe himself. It looked new. He took it to a friend of his uncle Frank's and said, "It has to look dug up after twenty years but no damage to it."

The friend said, "It would be interesting to know how the minds of you Joneses work. You two are peculiar."

Decker just nodded. He knew it was women who were peculiar. It was just that men who age trucks and sewer pipe could never have been in any real contact with women. Women didn't need aged trucks or—Was *Naomi's* truck aged? That would be interesting to know. She would be the kind of woman who wouldn't flash a new truck in a town like Sawbuck.

That Saturday, Decker rented two films for a town showing on his VCR with Buzz's color television. They set it up on the picnic grounds, and darned if they didn't gather passersby! The commuters felt perfectly free to stop by and participate. But they brought things. Popcorn or beer or soda pop. They even brought their own folding chairs! And they didn't notice how surprised the Sawbuckers were with the horners-in.

Then halfway through the kids' show, it began to sprinkle. They had to move everything into one of the vacant stores. That made it a real adventure and much noisier.

But then Decker noticed that Naomi was agitated, and he asked, "What's the matter?"

"What if it's a gully washer and we don't have the dam ready?"

"If it is, there'll be another along before planting time."

"It *is* planting time. This area has a two-crop year."

"Then the ground will be nice and wet, and the plants can last until the next rain."

She looked as if she was being carefully tolerant of a fool.

The late show was *Someone to Watch Over Me*. The film was well done. Loyalty and permanence were underlined. After it was over, the Sawbuckers were all a little pensive and holding hands as they wandered off. And Decker got to walk Naomi . . . and Trisha . . . home in the dark, drizzly night.

It was still just a gentle sprinkling of rain. The dry earth welcomed the rain with a taunting fragrance that the people couldn't breathe deeply enough into their bodies. And the three lifted their faces to the gift of that inadequate sprinkling of moisture.

Decker watched Naomi, trying not to stare at her opened lips as she tasted the rain and licked it from around her mouth. He considered how shocked she'd be, and how she'd shriek and how upset Trisha would be, if he dragged Naomi off and made love to her in the dampened dust.

He went up on the porch and sat down as if he intended to stay. Trisha smiled encouragingly at him and said, "Good night" and she went inside! He hadn't realized Trisha was that bright.

Naomi wandered around restlessly, but she didn't suggest that he run along. She just fluttered around like a small bird that couldn't seem to light anywhere. After a time, he rose and went to her, turned her to him and kissed her.

The earth rocked, or maybe there was a Texas earthquake? He shifted, his spurs making a sound. He held her tightly to protect her from the unsteady house. But he didn't lift his mouth. He thoroughly kissed her, and his brain turned around inside his skull. Something like that did happen.

Then he groaned and put his head alongside hers and just gloried in the fact that he was holding her. She was everything. Whoever that Crawford was who lived in that house in San Antonio, he didn't count for anything.

She said in a shaky voice, "Let me go. We must not."

"Why?"

"I'm . . . you see . . . well . . ." Her voice faltered.

She didn't push back or get angry, she just gave that little inadequate protest. He kissed her again.

And she allowed it.

He became aware that she was trembling. He lifted his mouth and asked, "Are you cold?" His voice was so gentle as he smiled down at her white, indistinct face lifted to his in the darkness. She didn't duck her head or push away, but she was shivering. "Are you all right?" he asked.

"I . . ."

Then he realized she was crying. "What's the matter, Mouse? Nothing's going to get you. I'm here. You're okay."

She nodded and gulped.

Knowing she was distressed, he told her gently, "I don't understand."

"It's difficult for me to explain."

"I've lots of time."

"I can't talk now."

"Go get a sweater."

"No. You must go."

"Kiss me good night."

"I already did."

"No, no. Those were hello kisses. Can't you tell the difference?"

"No."

What a pitiful little word. "Now *this* is a good-night kiss." And he let out all the stops. He kissed her until he *had* to either stop or not even try.

She made strange sweet little gasping sounds.

"Would you dance for me, wearing a necklace of cougar teeth?" He didn't think he should mention her being naked until another time. Start easy had always been the smart way with timid women.

"Cougar teeth? Did you go out and kill a cougar?"

She sounded indignant. She was probably an environmentalist. She had to be if she was involved with saving a town. She probably protected cougars, too. "It was hit by a stray bullet and was dying. The bullet saved it from trying to fight off the buzzards."

"Really?"

"On my honor. And the skin is especially nice."

"Oh."

"I'll let you see it and feel it when you dance in the teeth."

"You *seem* civilized."

"I am."

But even as he said that, into her mind came the replay of his stomp dancing. "Not entirely." She shook her head, but she still stayed within his arms. She ought to push a little so that he would release her. But it felt so good to be hugged again. She wondered if Brad minded. And in her head she heard him chuckle. "Decker..."

He kissed along under her ear, steam-cleaning with his breath. "Yeah, Mouse?"

"Mouse?" She was back to being a little indignant.

"Yeah. How do you see yourself?"

"I really have no affection at all for mice."

"I had a pet one once."

"Why?"

"It was cute and funny and busy. Like you."

"I'm...funny?"

"You're charming." She hadn't objected to being cute and busy, only funny. He tried for another kiss, but she pushed.

"You must go."

"I'll get all wet."

"Not any wetter than you got coming out here."

"But you were with me then, and walking in the rain is fun with someone, but by yourself, you just get soggy."

She shook her head, but he could see that she smiled. She pushed again, and he loosened his arms the tiniest little bit. She pushed a little more, and he put his hands on her hips. "Sit out here with me for a while."

"I can't. I must go in. It's late, and I'm tired."

"You could lean on me and snooze."

"No. Good night, Decker."

"Did I tell you I found the right kind of sewer pipe?"

"Yes."

"I pick it up Monday. We'll be able to begin the dam."

"Go home."

"I'm a wayfaring stranger without a home."

"You know all the words."

"Obviously not enough, and not the right ones."

"You're still here, but you must go. Please."

So he released her, sighed dejectedly, and resettled his hat on his head. "I feel like a stray dog being booted on his way."

"You're as dramatic as Wellington. Did he learn all his tricks from you?"

"Naomi Wentworth, how could you say that to me?"

"It seemed so obvious."

"You're getting sassy. I probably shouldn't have kissed you. I loved it, but it's given you a big head and you think you're in control."

"Yes."

"I thought so." He was disgusted. "It just means I'll have a hell of a time keeping your hands off me now."

"I'll behave."

"Now, why would you do a silly thing like that?"

"Trisha's a fine deterrent."

"Yeah, I suppose so. But you know I'm not going to rape you. Much as I'd like to, I will refrain."

"Good."

"You *could* have said, 'Darn.'"

"I'm not that stupid."

"That is a problem we'll have to face."

"Rape?"

"No, no, no danger of that from me, but you're not stupid. That makes courtship difficult."

"Court...ship?"

"Hadn't you recognized the signs?"

"Not really."

"I'll quit being so subtle." He reached, but she backed away. He protested, "Now, cut that out. How can I do this if you don't cooperate?"

"I need to sleep."

That paralyzed him. Did his kisses affect her so much that she would not be able to sleep—either? He opened his mouth to ask, but she backed away.

He followed, but she put one hand on his chest and said, "No."

He stood still, allowing her little hand to stop him, but he complained, "'No' is a dirty word."

She moved her hand to lay it along his cheek.

"Are you seducing me into—"

"No." She was firm.

"—building your dam?"

"No."

"If I hadn't found the sewer pipe would you have let me kiss you anyway?"

"I'd better not answer that."

He hesitated. "You liked kissing me?"

"Go home."

"For a woman, a wider range of words is just about vital."

"Scoot, amscray, vamoose, depart, leave, go home."

"How about stay, stay, stay?"

"One word."

"I'm a simple man."

She laughed, turned, went into the house, and closed the screen.

He allowed that. "Good night, Mouse."

"Good night."

"Sleep tight."

"You, too."

"I wish."

But she misunderstood that was a serious problem for him, and she laughed softly.

He turned away, his spurs clinking, and there waited Wellington. He turned back and said, "Us two strays will be moseying along."

She made no reply.

"Come on, dog."

And he left.

Naomi watched him the short distance and then lost track of him. She strained to watch him move away from her, but she didn't see him again until he crossed the road.

Trisha's voice asked from the stairs, "How was it?"

"What."

"Is he a good kisser?"

There was a long silence. Trisha thought she'd offended her friend, then she heard Naomi say softly, "Very."

Someone with a sneaky little camera had taken pictures of all the activity and painting in Sawbuck. And the *San Antonio Light* carried a splash of colored pictures about the town's fix-up. The article started out with: "Not everything is deteriorating in Texas, there's Sawbuck."

On Sunday morning, Decker got another call on the pay phone from his uncle. Roused from his hammock that early, Decker pulled on jeans and groused all the way to the phone. "Yeah?"

"Get your ass over here."

"Soon enough," replied Decker and hung up.

Since Sawbuck didn't get any papers, it took some of the commuters to leave off a copy or two, and everyone in town had to see the pictures.

Decker then knew the stickerburr that was under Uncle Frank's tail. Decker had to smile. It had been bad enough to be helping with the painting, but all this publicity would just encourage the town to do more. He looked over the copy that came into his hands.

With her head wrapped in the scarf, Naomi wasn't easily recognizable, but Trisha was. She was holding a pitcher of lemonade and looking down over her belly, laughing at a small Rodriquez holding a glass almost as big as he was.

Decker went into town and bought six copies of the paper, went back to Sawbuck and gave one copy to Magdalena who was in one picture. She put her hand to her mouth and laughed. Decker squatted down beside the aged woman, and at her pace, giving her time to comment, he translated every word to her in Spanish. The old woman listened, nodding and leaking tears as sometimes happens in times of delight and amazement.

All the pictures were group pictures of busy people. The only single subject had been Buzz and he was something to see. He was straightening up as he'd looked toward the camera in a stare that could shrivel a man or excite a woman into being rash.

Decker gave a copy to Naomi who was patently relieved she wouldn't be recognized, but Trisha frowned over her own picture. "I'm that big?"

Naomi could only look at the pictures that included Decker, beautifully male, half naked, busy, never looking up. There wasn't one that was full face. She found she wanted one that was.

Decker left a copy for Rual because he hadn't helped and therefore wasn't in any of the pictures, and it would kill him that he wasn't. While Decker was a superior man, he wasn't perfect. There was just a little pinch of tit for tat mixed in his uncommon clay.

Buzz declined a copy saying, "I'll see those pictures everywhere I go." And Decker laughed.

John, of course, had to have a copy, and Decker gave one to Joe. Then Decker went back to his store and taped that section of the last copy across the front of his big window.

Probably the most interesting example of the influx of immigrants was a kid standing on a chair, reading the print under the pictures. She was reading aloud for several grown men who were in the pictures but

could not read the English words. And, even as
Decker noted that, he knew that all through time, that
same thing had happened with the restless migrations
on this planet. It was the children in a new land who
learned the words of the new language to tell them
to the more slowly assimilated adults.

Then, Decker mused, there was Magdalena who
had always been with her own and had spent all her
long life in Texas, without ever bothering to learn the
other language.

All of life was interesting, Decker thought. And
people limit themselves if they live only on the edge
of events.

CHAPTER NINE

THERE WERE MORE THAN JUST SAWBUCKERS who saw the newspaper's spread on that nothing town in Texas. In San Antonio, Mark Allen saw it. He saw Naomi and knew her in spite of her turned-away stance. She wore denims, a work shirt, and had a bandanna over her hair, but the curve of her cheek, her chin, and that slight figure were ingrained in his mind, and he knew her. Mark saw, too, that Decker Jones was very involved in that town and recalled Decker hadn't mentioned knowing where Naomi was.

With Naomi there, the baby-bellied woman with the pitcher of lemonade was probably Rick's Trisha? Did Rick know about the belly? Mentioning that to Rick was going to be tricky. As Mark put in a call to Naomi through the operator, his stare was on the picture of Naomi, lying there before him.

Mark had first noticed her playing tennis when she was about fifteen. He'd been twenty-three. He had mentally tagged her to be reinvestigated when she was a little older. Somehow she'd slipped through his fingers, and he wasn't again aware of her until after she'd become so ensnared with Brad, The Duke, that she saw no other male in focus.

Did every man have an unobtainable woman lying locked in his memories? Someone to take out in pensive might-have-been times so that he could indulge in sweet nostalgia? For Mark it was Naomi.

The operator interrupted Mark's musings, "That number is a restricted one. Sorry." So he called his mother and got the unlisted number of Naomi's parents from the housekeeper who reminded Mark, "Her mother remarried, if you recall that. Her name is Crawford."

Mark punched out that number, expecting to get an answering machine, but he talked to Naomi's mother. He introduced himself as his daddy's son and asked permission to call Naomi. He wrote the number on a pad, very patiently replied to Mrs. Crawford's friendly questions, and finally could say good-bye, disconnect, and punch out Naomi's number. The phone rang several times. And just as he was about to give up, someone lifted the receiver and queried, "Yes?"

It was a cool voice. Distanced. He said in his office voice, "This is Mark Allen in San Antonio. May I speak with Naomi Wentworth?"

"This is she. Mark? Oh, yes! I remember you. How are you?"

"Fine. And you?" It always took a while to begin. It was a little like a Chinese tea in which certain ceremonial movements had to be made. In the U.S., certain questions and replies had to be completed. It was too abrupt to simply say, "Is that Rick Thomas's Trisha with the baby belly?" Instead he had to say, "I saw your picture in the spread on . . . Sawbuck? Now what on earth are you doing in a place called *Sawbuck*. And where in the world is such a place?"

Quietly she replied, "This was Brad's hometown."

Damn. He paused before he said, "I see." Then being an astute man, and a clever one, he commented with the right amount of respect and understanding, "And you are there to rebuild the town."

"Not exactly."

With her mind on Brad, he slipped it in, "How's Trisha getting along in a place like that?"

"Just fine."

And Mark knew what he wanted to know. But his tongue went on gently, "Is there anything I can do to help?"

"Not that I know of, right now. But thank you."

"If there should ever come a time when I can do anything at all for you, Naomi, I'm here for you."

"I know you thought highly of Brad, and I appreciate your offer. I would turn to you. Thank you, Mark."

"May I see you?"

"We're very busy right now."

"I'm curious to see Sawbuck."

She laughed softly and the sound squiggled around in him. "It's a sight," she told Mark. "Because of Brad's set of rules, I had to think of a way to get it painted without seeming to buy the paint, and I bought the most god-awful colors! A gallon at a time." She chuckled. "I figured that if we could get anything on the buildings, it would act as a base coat, and we could then paint something else over it. It's really wild."

"I have to see it."

"It's worth the trip. Thanks for calling. Do stop by if you come this way."

"I shall. Good-bye for now." He hung up thinking of her saying that the town was "worth the trip." So was she. So was Naomi Wentworth.

She should be healed by now. Brad had been such a tremendous man, such a charismatic one, how could an ordinary man follow him into a woman's affections? Mark stood up and rubbed his chest thinking that Mark Allen wasn't chopped liver.

Now how was he to go about telling Rick Thomas that his woman was pregnant? What exactly should he say? He paced a while planning the conversation. Then in a miracle for this age, he dialed and reached the fourth consecutive telephone number each on the first try.

"Yeah?"

"Hello, Rick, this is Mark Allen. How are you?"

"Okay."

"I believe I have a lead on Trisha. I was just talking to Naomi Wentworth—"

"*Where?*" Rick's voice became intense.

This wasn't going as Mark intended. "There was a spread in the paper this morning and—"

"Where *is* she?"

Mark could hear from Rick's tone that he was not going to be reasonable. Mark used his courtroom voice, as with a hostile witness. "I'll meet you at The Club here, whenever, and I'll go with you. I'd like an excuse to see Naomi again."

"Where is she?"

"Naomi?"

"Trisha!" Rick snarled.

"Rick, you ought not go busting in on her. Let me go with you. You see—"

"*Where?*"

"Will you meet me? I'll be at The Club this afternoon. I have a client who believes he has the secret to golf." Mark could hear Rick's heightened breathing. More kindly, he said, "Rick, we can meet at The Club and go from there."

"Which way?"

"Now, Rick, don't go flying off in all directions. You—"

But Rick had hung up. Mark depressed the button, and again punched in the number but the phone only rang. Mark said aloud, "Hell." He had to honor the golf game with his client, but he left a regret for the evening on an answering machine. He changed his clothes and went down to his car. He had time for the golf game since Dallas was three hundred miles north. Right after the eighteenth hole, he would hunt for Rick at the clubhouse and if Rick wasn't there, he would head for Sawbuck.

In Dallas, Rick went out and scrounged the area's newsstands until he found both San Antonio papers. He hunted the article on Sawbuck, and he saw the picture of Trisha. He'd been looking for faces and it was a couple of minutes before he saw her stomach.

Heading south, the highway patrol twice arrested Rick for speeding. The first cop was an Anglo who walked up in that carefully threatening walk that seems like a stalking. The cop scrunched down cautiously and looked at Rick. "You were speeding."

"My woman is pregnant by another man."

Although the tone was kind, the words were scolding. "That's no excuse to risk other people's lives, or your own. You were going almost ninety. You are responsible for your conduct. May I see your license, sir?" As he wrote the ticket, he said, "You are to pay this fine or file an objection before this date. Drive carefully."

The second cop was Hispanic. He, too, walked up in that same stalking way. He, too, leaned down and sniffed discreetly. And he, too, said, "You've been speeding."

Rick said again, "My woman is pregnant by another man."

But this cop said, "Owww. That's killing a man. I understand. That happened even to me. Only God saved that bastard from being killed with my bare hands. God said, 'Don't do that' and I argued with Him all one night until I passed out. Go home, get drunk—don't drive—and tomorrow your head will hurt so awful, the hurt to your heart won't count. You'll see there are other women."

But he gave Rick another ticket and the same spiel about driving responsibility and paying or filing.

Rick skipped the meeting with Mark at The Club, and he arrived in Sawbuck from Dallas before Mark drove South from San Antonio.

Rick looked around that ridiculous and gaudily colorful town, squinting his eyes, and he saw the white house discreetly tucked away in the trees by the wash. He drove his car over the bumpy ground and stopped it there.

He got out, still so angry that he didn't notice how rigid he was, and he slammed the door, rocking the car. He stalked to the porch steps and deliberately stomped on each stair and across the wooden, hollow-ringing porch.

Naomi came to the screen. "Rick! Where have you been? I'm so glad to—"

Tersely through thinned lips he asked softly, "Is Trisha here?"

Trisha's voice questioned, "Rick?"

He thought her voice sounded guilty as sin, and he clenched his teeth, and then his fists in order to control himself.

All that Trisha could think was: He'll know! Then with some astonishment she thought, I'll see how he acts when he finds out. She came closer to the screen, and Naomi stepped back away, to give Trisha room.

"Come out on the porch," Rick directed her.

Trisha wished she was in a crowded room. She'd have to go out the door belly first. She comforted the bulge with one hand and opened the door shyly.

Rick stepped back stiffly. He watched her emerge. "So it's true."

She half smiled and shrugged, "Yes."

"You bitch! Who's the father? You didn't take long to screw some other guy. You whore! You told me you were all right and you'd 'be in touch' and you were *already* 'touching' some bastard. I never thought you'd do anything like this. You shock me. I'm *ashamed* of you."

Trisha was stunned. She tried to interrupt him. She said, "But, Rick—" several times, and she said, "No!" several times. Then she started crying, which wasn't that unusual lately, but she got mad, too. How dared he? How *dared* he think that of her? And she said it, "How *dare* you!"

He snarled, "How *dared* you?" Then he stormed off the porch, got into his car, roared in a dust-spewing circle, and went off to the road and out of sight.

Trisha stood helplessly, weeping racking sobs, her hands on her head and the bulge. Miserable. Hopeless. Despairing. And *furious*!

Naomi said, "For Pete's sake!"

Trisha wailed.

Naomi exclaimed, "I can't believe him. He *never* loses his temper."

Trisha sobbed and gestured meaninglessly.

"He ought to be horsewhipped, being that rude to you."

Trisha couldn't speak around her wailing, but she nodded in agreement.

"He'll be so embarrassed when he finds out the truth. He'll come crawling—"

Trisha said a guttural "No!"

Naomi frowned at Trisha. "You wouldn't punish him for being mistaken?" Trisha was into dry heaves of temper by then, and she alarmed Naomi. "Come. Lie down. Be careful, Trisha, you could upset the baby. Be calm. I know, darling. But it's simply a mistake. And it *is* our fault. We should have told Rick long ago. I was selfish not to've been paying attention. It will be all right. Calm yourself for the baby's sake. For yours. Hush now. There. I'll get some cool cloths. You're all right. I'm here. Don't fret so, love." But Naomi was crying, too.

And that's how Mark found them. He drove up, and they were still on the front porch. He got out of his car as Naomi came to the top of the stairs, holding her hands out in a stopping gesture. Trisha was lying on the glider, and Naomi was upset. Both had been crying. He asked, "What's wrong? Is it the baby?"

"Please," Naomi protested. "We aren't prepared for company. Please come another time."

With authority, Mark told her, "Let me help."

"Oh, Mark—"

Then Decker arrived. "What the *hell* is going on here? Who was that who tore out of here? What have you done to them? Mark, I swear—"

And Naomi said, "Good grief!"

But Trisha began crying again and all three turned to comfort her, and Decker didn't even know why. He assured her, "I'll cripple him. Who was it so I don't get the wrong man?"

Naomi said, "It was Rick."

Mark asked, "What happened?"

"He thinks Trisha's baby is another man's."

"It isn't?" Mark questioned.

"It's Rick's."

Mark was untypically impatient. "And no one bothered to mention the baby to Rick?"

Trisha wailed, "He doesn't *want* a baby!"

"He said that?" Decker was irritated.

"Yes!"

But Mark pushed, "He said that just now when he was here and he knew it was his?"

"No." But Trisha was crying and didn't explain.

So Naomi said, "He misunderstood. He didn't give Trisha a chance to explain."

Decker said, "I can see his problem."

Mark agreed. "If he didn't know, it wasn't his fault he was angry."

Trisha shrieked.

"Quit upsetting her!" Naomi scolded.

"Poor Rick," Mark said. "I'll see if I can find him."

Decker was glad Mark was leaving and said, "Take his car keys away from him. He's driving like a maniac."

Mark told Naomi, "I'll be back."

He'd said it like a lover. Decker frowned in disgust. Naomi was his.

Absently, Naomi replied, "Fine."

Mark smiled as if she'd just knighted him.

Decker thought any man would know that "fine" was an automatic response of a mannered lady. Naomi hadn't meant to encourage Mark. Some men weren't very bright. Like Rick tearing out of here, and now Mark being encouraged by Naomi when he had no reason, at all, to feel that way.

Then Mark said to Decker, "Can I drop you?"

And Decker replied succinctly, "No."

Mark's eyes glittered, but he said nothing more. He left with a confident walk, as if Decker would be only a minor irritation. That was galling. With Mark gone, Decker relaxed and turned to solve the ladies' conduct.

Naomi immediately suggested, "Why don't you come back another time?"

He looked at her and over at Trisha, then back to Naomi and replied, "Because I'm staying until this is settled and everything's okay again."

Naomi looked down at her fingers and said, "That isn't possible."

There was no way that he was going to ask what, when he damned well knew she meant Brad, so he just said, "I can handle anything." Well, anything but fire demons. Other people's problems were nothing. The people just made their problems complicated. He said to Trisha, "Can I take the two of you to your room?"

Her bottom lip trembled and more tears rolled down her temples into her hair. She nodded.

If he could carry Wellington, he could handle the pregnant Trisha. He squatted and his shoulders curled as he reached over to scoop her—

Naomi interfered, "It's better if she does as much as she can. That's how she handled me when I was grieving. And that's what she's doing. She's grieving. She thinks Rick is gone forever like—"

Decker deliberately interrupted, "Rick'll be back."

Trisha gulped, "No. He'd be too embarrassed."

"He loves you," Decker said. "He won't mind finding out it's his kid. He'll be back."

"You're such an expert," Trisha scoffed.

"I'm a man."

Naomi put in, "We know."

Trisha sulked. "Men."

"Look, if you want me to carry you to bed, you have to have a better attitude toward me. You have to smile a little and say, 'Please.'"

"I'll walk."

"Now why are you punishing me by being mad at me? I'm the good guy."

Trisha managed to struggle up with the aid of Decker's strong arm. She gave him a censuring look and replied, "In whose opinion?"

"Mine! I'll have you know, Trisha Peterson, that I'm becoming more and more sympathetic with *Rick*!"

Trisha's face began to crumble, and Naomi exclaimed, "Decker!"

Decker snapped, "She's past the age of consent—"

Trisha howled.

His mouse tore her hair and snarled, "Will you behave?"

But she didn't fling out her arm and tell him to get him hence. So he backed down. "Damn it, Trish, so I've still got some rough edges!"

Trisha shook her head in despair.

Naomi chided, "You can do better than that."

"I'm sorry, Trish."

She nodded.

"—for whatever it was that Rick did that you're blaming on me."

Trisha looked disgusted and healthily indignant.

"Come on, stand up. Here, let me help. I don't suppose you want me to carry you in a fireman's grasp? Would the kid object?"

"Probably." It was the first real, unemotional, normal word out of Trisha since Rick had stormed up onto the porch and confronted her.

"I hope to God you've blown your nose. I can't stand snotty women."

Trisha gave him a patient look.

"If you walk to the door, I can get it open for you and we'll take it from there. Your head hurt?"

"Yes."

"Crying does that." He nodded with the wisdom.

"The rat."

"Now, you can't *say* that. Rick must feel awful. He loves you. He's been searching everywhere for you. He didn't know what had happened to you."

"He was searching for me?" Trisha was unbelieving. "How do you know?"

"From the way he acted. He was about out of his mind. Then he finds you in this weird place and pregnant. What was he suppose to think?"

"He had no trust in me at all."

"He thinks all men are crazy for you and he feels so insecure that he thinks he doesn't have your loyalty. How could you do that to a poor guy like Rick?"

Naomi was just amazed. Here Decker had Trisha walking into the house, arguing with her enough, getting her back in balance. How had he done that? All he'd done was accuse her of not being fair to Rick. He hadn't given Trish any sympathy—But look how he handled her, gently, kindly; listen how he talked to her, scolding, soothing. He was a wily man. A woman should be very careful around such a man.

The wily man turned his dark gaze toward the wary Naomi and said, "She ought to eat a little." Then he mentioned guilessly, "It's supper time. What have you planned?"

Naomi recognized that she could not do anything other than invite him to supper. "Won't you join us?"

"Why," he said credibly surprised, "thank you." But then he smiled at her, sharing the humor.

She shook her head at him but she had to smile back.

"What's funny," Trisha asked suspiciously.

"Decker just invited himself to supper."

Trisha sighed with the weight of wisdom lately laid on her. "Men are like that. You have to be very careful around a sneaky man or you end up like me."

Being a stickler, and male, Decker corrected, "I'd bet good money Rick isn't sneaky. That's part of his problem. He's open and above board. He's a straight shooter."

The women did try, but unfortunately their glances caught and that did it. They laughed.

Decker was baffled. They refused to explain, and Trisha worsened it by patting his cheek. He was indignant.

Emotional swings during pregnancy are not uncommon, but here was the devastatedly grieving Trisha swinging wildly in the opposite direction. Decker scolded, "Behave!"

That made Naomi aware and she settled down, saying calming things to Trisha that just increased the hilarity.

Decker sternly told Naomi, "Go get supper on the table. I'll try to calm her down . . . again." He was really irritated.

But as Naomi started for the kitchen, she interrupted her departure to go to Decker, put her arms around his middle, lay head on his chest, and hug him. He was still releasing Trisha and trying to get his arms in gear when Naomi let go of him and went on off.

"You be careful of her," Trisha warned.

"Yes'um."

"Yes . . . 'um?" Trisha raised her eyebrows questioningly.

"All us here cowboys says them kind of words, altogether."

"Good Lord."

"You in control again?" he asked.

"Thank you."

"Always glad to oblige. You straighten things out with Rick," he commanded. "You've treated him rotten."

"Now you just listen here—"

He lifted his hands, palms down. "I wasn't starting any arguments or debates, I was giving sound advice! Pay attention to me. And don't make any statement without you consult with me first. Got that?"

Trisha studied Decker for a sober minute and then asked, "What's the male counterpart to 'yes'um'?"

"It's yes, *sir*! Very good, sir."

"I hadn't known."

"Practice. It'll come in handy."

"Yes, *sir*! Very good, sir."

"Not bad, for a beginner."

*   *   *

It was after supper, and Trisha had gone up to her room. Naomi had taken their glasses of wine out onto the porch, while Decker fed Wellington a plate of scraps. The two adults sat down on the glider. After a minute, Naomi said, "You just astonish me."

"Is that good or bad?"

"It's amazing. I don't see how you managed to handle Trisha in that devastating time. It makes me . . . I wonder . . ." But her words petered out.

Very, very gently with soft words he asked, "What do you wonder?"

"If you could have helped *me* to be brave some time ago."

"Yes."

"You're that sure?" She frowned at him.

"Yes."

"How can you know?"

So he told her. "Because in these weeks, even before I met you, you helped me."

"How?" She was incredulous.

He told her about the fire demons with their whips of stinging terror. As he talked, she put her hand on his arm and with the other hand, she lifted his and brought it against her soft chest. "Oh, Decker. I know, I know."

He took her into his arms and just held her. Then he said in a gravelly voice, "you can't possibly know what I'm talking about, but you've been there with me, and you aren't afraid. You give me courage."

"Why are you afraid?"

"It's very complicated. I'll tell you sometime."

"John said someone beat you."

"Many." Decker's eyes were looking down.

"Why?"

His face grim, he said, "I was in the wrong place, but for a reason."

"Why?"

"Sometime I'll tell you, maybe. It's too...I can't now."

"You lost friends there?"

His voice slowed.

"Yes. One was a woman."

"How terrible."

"It is."

She understood his use of the present tense. She kissed him. Her lips were sweetly soft and gentle, and he knew that she meant to comfort him. He could probably have coaxed her into giving herself to him, then, but when she made love with him he wanted it to be with the passion of love, not the kindness of compassion.

Compassion wasn't permanent. He wanted Naomi with permanence. He was gentle with her. His hands sought her, and she allowed that. His mouth tasted her, and she cooperated. She stood every hair he had on end, and she thrilled him with her willingness.

It took all the discipline he'd ever honed to leave her alone, but he did do that. He wasn't entirely selfless in teasing her passion, he was calculating in doing that, and while he didn't touch her intimately, his kisses steamed.

So when Decker left, walking stiffly, Naomi was a little frustrated. Restless. How remarkable to feel that again. With this man, she'd felt sexual hunger from the first minute he'd gotten off the bus on the first day that he'd arrived in Sawbuck.

With Brad, it had been the shared humor and adventure that had lured her. Before Brad she'd lived so staidly sheltered. She'd been on the sidewalk by accident when Brad and his entourage had come crowding by as the big car had pulled up for him. She'd known instantly who he was. The Duke. He'd seen her and laughed, so amused by all the foolish flurry of pushing and of the excited people around him. He'd been that one bit of sanity in the maelstrom of idiots, and his laugh had shared the insanity of such a silly time... with her. He'd winked, still grinning, and when he'd gotten in the back seat of the limo, he'd parted the crowd with a patient gesture and looked at her again. Then he'd patted the seat next to him in invitation. With no hesitation, she'd gone with him.

And she'd stayed with him for the rest of his life.

CHAPTER TEN

THAT SAME EVENING, WHEN MARK ALLEN GOT home, there was a message on his answering machine. "This is Rick," said the tired voice. "They've impounded my car and are detaining me. Come get me out."

Detaining him . . . where?

That took a while, but Mark finally networked through and found Rick just north of San Antonio. Mark went there. The police sergeant was not at all sympathetic. "Three speeding tickets today. That's more than anyone's allowed in a lifetime. Ninety miles an hour. That's stupid."

"He's been under undue stress," Mark began.

"There's nothing that allows anybody to go ninety miles an hour on highways with decent, law-abiding citizens."

Rick snapped, "Why don't you—"

Mark's voice overrode Rick's very strongly. "He regrets it. The problem won't ever arise again because no other woman—"

"You think I'm impotent?"

"He doesn't realize he's about to become a father."

165

There was a stunned silence. Then Rick said, "What the hell—"

"You didn't give Trisha a chance. You're the father. She's due anytime."

The black sergeant said, "We're not interested in his personal problems. We just don't want him in a car for . . . until next year . . . if possible."

Rick retorted hotly, "That's unreasonable."

"So're you, buster. You're just lucky you're stone-cold sober. Crazy, but sober. Your guardian angel must be worn out, trying to keep you from killing yourself . . . and *everybody else*! You're a menace. We don't need your kind."

"He'll behave. I promise. May I post bond for him?"

"I don't know why you want to let him out on the streets. We're keeping his driver's license until he goes to traffic court."

"Fine." Mark was calm. Then in order to block any more comments from Rick, Mark said kindly to him, "Why don't you sit over there until I get this done?"

Rick went over and sat down, then he blinked a couple of times and stood up as if a pin had hit his bottom. He went back over to Mark and interrupted to ask, "Did you say that she claims the baby is mine?"

The sergeant snarled, "Go sit down!"

Mark agreed but with more tact, "I'll be with you in just a few minutes."

It took longer than that. Finally Mark took Rick back to his own place, loaned Rick some clean pajamas, made him take a long, hot shower, and "nuked" a couple of frozen dinners in the microwave.

Having eaten, they pitched the plastic plates and moved into the living room where Rick flopped down in Mark's chair. "I need to go see her."

"Tomorrow. She's probably exhausted, and she's asleep by now. See her tomorrow. It's drizzling. The roads'll be slick. I'm tired, you're tired, all God's chillun is tired. Let's get some sleep."

"If it's true—"

"It is."

"She must think I'm a rat."

"She does."

Rick rubbed his face tiredly. "I've got a hell of a headache."

"Aspirin are in the cabinet in the bathroom. Sheets are in the linen closet in the hall ... first door to the right by the bath. I'll open out this sofa for you. You need the sleep."

"I've been hunting her for seven months. Not even her family knows where she is. Her family is unusual."

Mark thought aloud: "You two were together ... how long? I don't remember meeting Trisha before today."

"You were out there?"

"Right after you left."

"Was she ... all right? I said some terrible things to her."

Mark gestured vaguely. "About what you'd expect."

"She'd take it hard."

"Yes."

"I had every reason to think—"

Mark sighed. "Did you listen to her?"

"No."

"Listening is a trait that saves time."

"Yeah."

"Especially with a woman. You have to listen to all they say because they drop hints and clues while not talking about their real problems. They'll criticize someone else when they are insecure, and they'll scoff at themselves when they need praise. They move differently when they need you to notice a new dress or a new hairstyle. You have to pay attention. They're strange creatures."

"Trisha isn't like that."

"Listen to her." Mark's tone was firm.

"I'll try."

"This has been a long day, and a stressful one—"

"I'm sorry about that—"

"Your problems are common for an attorney. The stress came from having to play eighteen holes of golf so that I wouldn't clobber my client's handicap. That takes the skill of a real pro. I'm becoming so good that I think I'll close my practice and go on the tourney circuit. Think how heady it would be to play full out, to really compete and do your best."

"Golf bores me."

"I know, you like to drive racing cars." Mark cast a droll glance at his friend.

"I'll probably hear about this day, from you, for all the rest of my life."

"From me, it'll be your driving and stupidity, and from Trisha, it'll be your simple idiocy. She'll probably worry about coping with the kind of kid you've given her."

"I didn't think she'd want a baby."

"She's very protective," Mark commented. "She had her hand on her stomach to comfort it from your rejection."

"Cut it out!" Rick demanded miserably. Then he asked, "How long were you there?"

"Long enough. I'm an observer. I know women.

Trisha not only loves you so much that you devastated her, she loves that baby."

"You're making me feel like a louse."

Mark grinned. "Good beginning. You'll think of a way to square things. By the way, don't mention to either Trish or Naomi that you've met Decker."

"Why not?"

"It could be awkward."

"Okay."

"Good night, Rick. Go to sleep. Tomorrow will have to be better."

"Yeah. Thanks for all the help. I'm much obliged."

Mark started to turn away.

"I suppose you're very tired?"

Mark hesitated. He really was, but it was obvious that Rick wasn't ready to give up the day. Mark turned back and said, "Not unreasonably."

"I'd like to talk for a few more minutes."

That meant he wouldn't quit before 2 A.M. "Well, okay. For a while. Go get the aspirin and the sheets. We'll make up your bed and you can get comfortable." He sighed with disgruntled amusement. Naomi owed him for this. But along with being an almost lifetime friend, Rick was Mark's ticket for another visit with Naomi.

Rick said, "It's a little cool in here. Can we turn the air-conditioning up a little?"

"Of course." Although he had responded promptly, Mark's temper grated. He was now in his mid-thirties and had been on his own since leaving for college at eighteen. He had his life and his air-conditioner exactly as he wanted them, and it was irritating to adjust either to another's whims. He adjusted the dial.

"I'll get the aspirin," Rick stated.

"You do that."

There must have been something in Mark's tone because Rick then asked, "This isn't a burden, having me here, is it? You didn't have other plans?"

"All taken care of. No problem. You're welcome here, old friend."

"I guess I'll bore you forever, thanking you for this day."

"Forget it." Mark was kind.

"If ever—"

"I know." Mark busily opened up the sofa, willing Rick to get the aspirin. He didn't move, so Mark looked up and nudged, "We'll need the sheets."

"Yes." Rick turned away.

Mark called after him, "Take two of the supers." The plan was to get Rick to take the aspirin, get him to lie down, then they could talk lazily, no stress, and Rick *ought* to fall asleep. Or Mark would.

Mark tried a quick numbering of the times he'd figuratively held some guy's hand because of a split with his woman. There was Red, at twelve, his first sexual experience and he'd muffed it. He'd wanted to join the priesthood—

Rick called, "There's codeine!"

"That's for my shoulder! *Don't touch it*! My doctor keeps close count."

"Okay. Okay. What's wrong with your shoulder?" Rick came back into the room with a paper cup of water in his hand.

"Three months ago as I was playing with the senior partner in my firm, I realized that if I hit the ball as I was swinging the club, it would be a hole-in-one. So I adjusted the swing at the last minute and about killed myself."

"You're a conniver." Rick said that with complacency.

"No, I adjust." He waited for Rick to nod, in order to salute all the adjusting Mark had done for him that day, but the declaration went right over Rick's head. It was going to be a long evening, Mark already knew that, and Rick would feel the need to talk about Trisha. The only defense would be to ask questions and guide the talk, so that Rick could talk without telling anything too personal.

They made up the bed, and Rick willingly crawled between the sheets while Mark brought a light blanket and flipped it over the bed. Then Mark actually got to sit in his chair. It always amazed him how just about everyone who came into his apartment, including women, made a beeline for *his* chair. The only way he could sit in it was not to have company.

Rick's knees made the blanket into a hammock and he put his arms behind his head as he said pensively, "Of all the women I've known, and a couple of years there I had more than my share, Trisha—"

"You said her parents are unusual. Why?"

"They were hippies. Commune, sandals, flowers, the whole caboodle. But after they had Trisha, they turned. They became very staid, got married, became worse than their own parents. Trisha got her genes from both of those free souls, and she kicked over the traces and went free. She was wild. I got her early. I wanted to get married almost right away, but she wasn't having any of it. I had to pretend to be more liberated than she, so that she wouldn't get bored with me. I can't believe she didn't have an abortion. But it doesn't particularly surprise me that we got pregnant. She's wild. Anytime, any—"

"How do your parents like her?"

"Well, you have to know Arlene doesn't, yet, know I know about sex." He had referred to his mother as Arlene since he first went to college and got out from under her thumb.

"But they know you know Trisha."

"Oh, yes. We share a room at their house, but Arlene must think I sleep on the floor."

Mark chuckled as he knew he should. "Does that bother Trisha?"

"Naw. She thinks they're darling."

"Do you love Trisha...enough?"

Rick turned his head and looked straight at Mark before he replied, "Yes."

"With your reaction to her being pregnant, you can see I have some question about your regard for her."

"That was all testosterones. Territorial male. I saw only that she was somewhat pregnant, and she'd been gone from me for over seven months."

"She's closer to labor than that."

Rick lifted his head in alarm. "Are you sure?"

"It's your kid. You haven't seen her in seven months. Isn't that a clue?"

Hesitantly, Rick asked, "She doesn't look that pregnant. Are you sure that's my baby?"

"Aren't you? If you can't trust her, stay away from her." He got up and got the section of the paper from his desk drawer. "Look at that picture. She's contented there in Sawbuck. Don't go barging in there and unsettling her."

Rick sat up and looked at the picture. "She doesn't look that pregnant."

"If I were in your shoes, I would wait a while before

seeing her. You aren't positive. Don't go in there and stir things up until you know."

"Now, how am I ever going to know?"

"When the baby's born." Mark stated the obvious.

"Yeah. And the family birthmark will prove it's mine."

"What family birthmark?"

"I was being cynical," Rick said. "There isn't any, but that's how it works in fiction."

"Since you don't trust her, since you think she's using another man's child to blackmail you into marriage, and since you've torn her emotions apart, I strongly advise you to leave her alone. She'll recover from you. Naomi will see to it. But for her to heal, she should be left alone—by you."

"You've really laid me out."

Then Mark realized that he felt personally involved with Naomi and Trisha. In that order.

"She isn't using the baby to blackmail me into marriage. She never mentioned marriage. She ran away."

"She said that you didn't want a child."

"No! Well, that *is* what I told her, because I thought she didn't."

"You two really communicate, don't you."

"Hell. Who can understand a woman."

"There are men who try." Mark scowled.

"I thought I did. When Brad was dying, and afterward, I was there for her so that she could help Naomi. Talk about comatose, you should have seen Naomi! She was like a zombie. Trisha would get her out of a chair and lead her to the table, sit her down and hand her the fork and lift her wrist. It was incredible." He shook his head. Then he looked pensive. "She'd be a great mother."

"You two are really out of touch. Did you ever talk about anything?"

"Everything," Rick said with satisfaction.

"Everything but the basics," Mark bore in. "What would it take for you to believe her?"

Rick replied, "She'd never lie. It isn't in her. If she told me, I'd believe her if she said that tomorrow the sun would rise in the west."

That satisfied Mark. Then he guided their talk to a particular trip they'd taken one summer when they were in law school. They'd crewed a schooner across the Atlantic and had a holiday in the south of Ireland and in Wales. It had been a special time of good fellowship, good food, pretty girls, and lighthearted fun. "Do you remember..." was the beginning, and for the next two hours, they shared that time again.

As Mark had known, the memories relaxed Rick. So it was only just after 1 A.M. that the two friends said good night and Mark went to bed. He got up later and listened, but Rick was breathing deeply in solid sleep. Mark shook his head slowly and smiled as he went back to bed. Then he, too, slept.

In Sawbuck, with the drizzle continuing into the next morning, Naomi was beside herself with anxiety over the dam. "This drizzle is warning us about the coming deluge. We've *got* to get the dam going."

Trisha replied rather drearily, "Deluge? Maybe we ought to build an Ark."

Naomi said the words expressionlessly, "Ha, ha, ha."

Trisha didn't respond. She struggled out of the chair and slowly stood up, putting her hands to her back and leaning backward, straightening.

Naomi watched her. "Are you all right?"

"I feel pregnant."

"I don't believe that's uncommon."

There was a rattling knock on the screen door and someone hollered, "Miss Peterson?"

The two women looked at each other, then Naomi said, "I'll get it." She went to the front door and to the man in a delivery uniform of coveralls and cap. She questioned, "Yes?"

"Flowers for Miss Peterson." From one side he produced into view a huge floor basket of red roses. It was stunning. "You her?"

"No. But I'll sign for them."

"I need a reply," the man said. "I have to see her."

Trisha came slowly to the door. "What is it?"

His stare dropped to her stomach. "You Miss Peterson?"

"Yes," she replied gratingly.

"Got a note for you." He held it out.

Naomi unhooked the screen and took the note, handing it to Trisha. Then she opened the door farther and said, "You may bring in the basket." She turned and asked, "Rick?"

Trisha was reading and looked up at the delivery man. "Would you like some coffee on the porch? This might take a little while."

The man instructed, "He said that you were to take your time."

Naomi asked again, "Rick?"

"Yes."

Naomi said virtuously, "You needn't read *out loud!* I'll take the coffee out to the man."

And Trisha went on reading.

As Naomi passed her, carrying the coffee cup to

the porch, she commented, "He must have written a whole book!"

But Trisha just went on reading.

Naomi came back inside, and Trisha was *still* reading. Naomi straightened things in the entrance hall, which was fairly large. Two rooms, the back hall, and the stairs led from it, but there just wasn't enough to tidy. She turned impatiently and said, "He had a lot to say."

"No."

"Then what's taking you so long?"

Trisha looked up blankly at Naomi and said, "Would you like to hear what he wrote?"

"No, no. I'm sure it must be personal."

"Yes."

"What does he say!"

Trisha looked surprised. Then she read carefully, "'I love you with all my heart. When may I see you? Rick.'"

"That's *all*? Why did it take you so long?"

"It's the first time I've seen his handwriting in over a year. He says he loves me."

"I should think he would. Are you going to see him?"

"I'll go back with the delivery man."

Naomi disagreed. "No. I don't think you should go out in this weather. He should come here."

"I'll write a note," Trisha told her friend.

"This is Monday. He can come on Wednesday for tea."

Trisha was surprised. "Not until Wednesday?"

"Let him think about it for a while."

Trisha rejected waiting two days. "He can come

tomorrow. I need to wash my hair and give myself a facial."

"Well, okay." Naomi smiled. "Tomorrow."

Trisha went into the front room and opened the desk, took out a piece of stationery and picked up a pen. She wrote: *The roses are beautiful. I haven't seen that many at one time since October 10, three years ago. Please come to tea, on Tuesday at four. Trisha Peterson.* She folded the note in half, slipped it into an envelope, and wrote *Richard Thomas* on the front of it. Then she took the note to the delivery man and needlessly explained, "Here is the note," which she handed to him with a five-dollar bill.

"Thanks, lady, but I was paid. He was anxious about you." He gave her back the five dollars.

She took one of the roses from the lavish basketful and said, "Give this to him with the note."

"Yes'um." And he smiled at her.

Trisha watched the man go down the steps and into his delivery truck. He drove away, leaving tire tracks in the drizzle-dampened dirt.

At noon that day, with the soft rain, Decker came up on the porch with Wellington. They were both muddy and tired. Naomi fluttered around like an agitated butterfly. She gave Decker a stack of towels as she turned on the hose.

"You have water?"

"We dug a deeper well. Have you eaten?"

"Not a bite in days."

She laughed as if he was clever, and inside the house, Trisha narrowed her eyes. Naomi was falling in love with an itinerant cowboy? Good grief. She was only supposed to fool *around* with him, not get serious!

Decker pulled off his boots, and Naomi held the

hose so that he could wash his hands and face, and wash his feet off before he worked on the dog. She asked, "What on earth have you been doing?"

"We got the sewer pipe and the flood gate established in the break. Then we began hauling stones. We've had to put the first ones in by hand to fit them and to protect the pipe. It's been s-s-some job."

Naomi had been clasping her hands together, and holding her face, and she finally just flung herself at Decker.

He said, "Whoa, honey, I'm too dirty. I love it, but you ought not get too close to me. Well, it's too late, go ahead and hug me. You can't get any dirtier." He kissed her. "What's all this about?"

"You started the dam!"

"Why does that surprise you? You knew I had the pipe. And Ned brought the gate over here yesterday."

"But it's been sprinkling for two days, and I was afraid it couldn't be done."

"All the men have been hauling rocks all morning. They've been working like Trojans. Really. You can give me all their hugs, and when I go back, I'll *tell* them about the hugs."

So, of course, she laughed, and hugged him again and he helped. She said, "Come inside. I have a terry robe that could almost fit you."

Just inside the door, he saw the roses and became still, standing soberly and staring at them. "Who sent you those?"

"Rick sent them to Trisha."

Decker took a breath, moved and relaxed as he said a relieved "Oh." He'd thought it had been Mark sending them to Naomi.

The robe was a one-size-fits-all and it looked skimpy

on Decker. But she almost put his clothes into the washer. He objected, saying, "The guys at the dam will feel I've not been doing my share."

They moved into the kitchen, and Trisha sat listening and watching, but she didn't offer any help. Naomi scurried around making a feast for Decker, giving him samples from her fingers. She was very animated, a little flushed, casting smiles over her shoulder, knowing that Decker was watching her.

It was Decker who said to Trisha, "So Rick sent you that enormous basket of roses. He trying to impress you?"

Naomi looked at the ceiling and said warningly, "Decker."

He was very surprised and protested, "All I did was ask her if Rick was trying to impress her. What's wrong with that?"

"Was it a town of women who beat you up?"

Decker laughed with the most bubbling humor. How long since he'd had such a laugh? Years. She was teasing him. She was threatening him with mayhem. He could hardly wait. She was pretending she was going to wrestle him down. "Don't threaten me, Naomi. You know I've been working my tail off trying to get your damned dam done, and I can barely lift a finger in my defense."

Did she sympathize? She said, "Good," and gave him a sassily quelling look. She was just asking for a man's flirting swat on her nice bottom. Why didn't Trisha go off somewhere else?

Naomi asked, "If it should really rain today, would the dam hold enough water back?"

"Not yet. That dam site doesn't look deep, but it takes one hell of a lot of different sizes and shapes of rocks, and we're having to fit them carefully so they won't leak."

"Are you using cement?"

"Where we can. We're trying to get it to stick together, but if there's a real rain, it could wash away the new unset cement filler. We'd have to take the whole thing apart, and redo it from scratch. I'm getting a lot of grief on working at it today. The men say it won't, uh, will wash...away. I told them the exercise was good for them."

"What did they say to that?"

"That ever since I came to town, they've had to move around and do dumb things."

She smiled, "I suppose they would think that."

"It's just talk. They're proud of the way the town looks now. They take all the credit. If they don't mention it to you, it's because you've been so clever and sly that they don't realize what a hell of a manipulator you are."

She laughed but she blushed with pleasure. "I've already told you that if it hadn't been for you cleaning up the grounds, we never would have managed anything. That and volunteering to paint the doors, then to do your own store. You made it appear you were reluctant. I was—"

He cautioned, "Joe and Ann are putting up the breakfast signs today and plan to begin serving the meals tomorrow. This whole shebang will be out of your control before you know it. You do understand that? When people get independent and get the bit between their teeth, you might not approve of all the things that happen after that."

"I love the painted doors."

"They were your idea."

"Yes. But they look so brave, painted. I didn't paint them. You did."

"Buzz did two of them." He meant to only say a suggestive thing that she wouldn't know about, so he was surprised when she chuckled and exchanged a look with Trisha. So she knew about Buzz having to deal with two grateful women.

"Are you ready?" she asked.

He tingled in every cell. She would want to show her gratitude? She had said it right there in front of Trisha. He replied hoarsely, "Yes."

She began serving him all the kinds of foods. She had meant was he ready to eat.

After lunch, Trisha went carefully up the stairs to her room. Decker took a bowl of water out for the vigilant Wellington, then came in and helped Naomi tidy the kitchen. He said, "I sure could use a nap."

So she carried a sheet and a throw out to the *porch* and made him a nest on the *glider*! He lay in it, disappointed not to be in her bed. But she sat nearby and watched him. Impulsively, he lifted the throw and said, "Come here."

And damned if she didn't get up off that chair and come to him, to snuggle down and lie in his arms. There, in broad daylight with the drizzling rain making them cozy and . . . hotter than demon fire.

CHAPTER ELEVEN

HOW COULD ANYTHING BE HOTTER THAN FEAR? Lust. It drove a man as equally as did fear. Did Decker only lust for Naomi? Not anymore. At first, not knowing her, he had changed her into the flamboyant temptress Elise and, concentrating on her, had kept the reaching flick of the fire demons at bay.

But now Decker looked down at the dark silken hair, a glimpse of forehead and a small nose. It was all he could see of the woman close in his arms, sharing that glider, as he felt the woman-realness of her against him and the heat in him was beyond fire.

She lifted her face, and he shivered with need as he rooted down her cheek, seeking her mouth, and kissed her. It was as he'd dreamed, lying with her, holding her against him, his muscles straining isometrically to hold her close enough and still allow her to breathe.

He moved his hands on her back feeling the beautiful curve of her spine and the womanly flare of her hips. He turned, holding her, shifting until she was on top of him, then he shifted again until he could lay her down between the glider back and his hungry body.

There she had the support of the glider back to protect her from falling off as he pressed against her, trying to control his urge to take her. As wildly, mindlessly as he wanted her, he also wanted to make love to her and he didn't want to frighten her.

She was fragile. She was only emerging from a long grieving. He shouldn't shock her.

While he sought control, one big hand held her head against his bare chest. She moved a little, and he eased his hold, thinking her neck was cramped. She moved her nose and chin over his bare, hairy chest and her hot, seeking tongue found his nipple. Then her soft mouth opened on it, her tongue teased, as her free hand moved down along his side under the robe.

Hoarsely he asked, "What're you doing to me, woman?"

Her mouth squeaked as she released the peaked nipple on his hard, flat chest and tilted her face up to his. She whispered, "I'm flirting with you."

"You're flirting with disaster," he told her in an unsteady breath. "I have no protection here for you and no resistance at all."

"A pushover?"

"I suspect so."

She laughed softly in her throat. He found just the sound of that startlingly exciting and he became aware that all of his body was involved with her. He'd always just thought of his sex as the part of him being tempted. Naomi affected even his toes! He didn't *need* any more excitements slithering in him.

He told Naomi, "You're upsetting me."

She tilted her head up and propped her chin on

his chest in order to look up at him as she questioned, "In what way?"

He quickly licked his lips and whispered huskily, "Slide your hand down to the top of my lap, and you'll find the reason."

"Really?" she whispered with a wide grin.

Then she laughed that naughty, soft laugh again, and he got goose bumps all over everything. "Try it," he urged and his voice was smoky and trembly, and his breaths were uneven.

She had only barely moved her hand when he said thickly, "Wait a minute. We're tempting fate. I don't think I can handle any more. It would be the smartest thing . . . I think you'd better just carefully get up and figure how to get out of this trap I've put you in. Try not to touch me. If you can do that, I might be able to allow you to get away. Otherwise . . ."

After a minute of silence, she probed softly, "What's the 'otherwise' part?"

"Do you have any idea what you're doing to me? Don't you *know* how you affect me? You must have noticed."

She looked up at him, her chin on his chest again, and she inquired with interest, "How?"

He growled, "You're asking for it, do you understand that?"

Sassily, she queried, "For 'it'? For what?"

He moved his body against hers. "That."

But he'd made the glider squeak and bump the house.

She frowned and said, "Shhh."

He laughed, very low in his throat and almost silently. "I'm supposed to be quiet?" He whispered the question. "Quiet, when I want to bellow like a stuck bull?"

"I thought the expression was 'squeal like a stuck pig.'" It amused Naomi to be talking about frustrated shrieks in whispers.

He was emphatic in his husky reply, "I don't feel nothing like any pig, a-tall, but I do feel similar to a very needy bull."

"Control. That's the answer."

"I've had enough of control. Either get up and try to get away, or look out."

And, again, she laughed that almost-soundless, wicked laugh.

Now, what's a man to do about a woman like that? A taunting woman. A woman who is ready to tussle? So he kissed her as he wanted, and his hands moved as they wanted. She allowed that.

How nice she wore those long, soft skirts. He brought her knee up over his hip and cleared the material away over her thigh, before he released himself. Then he slid her knee down so that he was trapped at the apex of her legs.

Decker groaned in an exhaling, ragged breath, closed his eyes, and drew in air slowly through clenched teeth. Bracing one hand against the wall over her head to control the glider, he pressed his body against her.

She squeezed her thighs around his aching need. He pushed against her hold and shuddered with his almost-instant climax, his mouth opened to try to silence his laboring breath.

Gradually he relaxed for the first time since he couldn't remember when. His muscles unknotted, after having been tensed too long, and he lay spent.

After a time, she inquired, "A good deal of rabbit blood in you?"

"That is just plain rude, to make me laugh at such a euphoric time."

"Euphoria is rather hit and miss with you."

"If you're implying I'm messy, I did give you the option of getting away."

"Ho," she scoffed.

"No option?"

"None. I was trying to become acquainted with you. You're rather 'sudden.'"

"I've never before been so tempted or so tormented."

She noted that his teasing had changed.

"For a mouse, you are spectacular as a woman."

"Because I lie with you on a squeaky glider?"

"Because you breathe."

So she took a deep breath. Waited. Then she commented, "That didn't grab you."

"Just be patient."

"And keep breathing?"

"Definitely."

They lay quietly in their snug nest on the porch, listening to the only sound in their universe, as the eaves dripped in the slow drizzle. It was such a magic time. A time of never-never. The heavy mist enclosed them in another world.

It was stolen time.

He sighed. "And now I have to gird my flaccid loins and go finish working on that dam. Satisfaction isn't as great a motivator as frustration. I want to lie here with you and caress you and feel this peace."

"Which piece?"

In mock horror he inquired, "Have I become entangled with a woman who plays with words?"

She agreed. "When nothing else is available."

He laughed, hugging her to him, thinking how precious was this mouse. "I'm too strung out to laugh. You've sapped me."

"An *s*? It's supposed to be 'zapped' with a *z*."

"You've taken all my sap."

"And you accuse me of playing with words? Why don't you nap just awhile? I'll keep marauders away."

He was especially touched by her words since in his dreams she'd been doing just that without ever knowing it. He held her close to him thinking how perfect it was to have found this woman just because his uncle Gimme had—

And for the first time, it occurred to Decker that Naomi might not like the fact that he was there, in Sawbuck, to counter her objectives with that town.

What would she think if she found out he was the nephew of their dilemma? Their enemy. He was there under false pretenses. She was an honorable woman. How would she react?

As if their thoughts ran parallel, Naomi said against his chest, "I am so glad you chose Sawbuck. When you got off that bus, I thought you were useless. I thought we'd gotten another loser. And look at all you've accomplished in just—"

It was as if an icy finger slid up his spine.

"—this short time. I've been trying my best to think of a way to counter Frank Jones. That despicable man. I'm not at all sure why God allows people like him to be in the position to control other people."

"Well—"

"Just think. Some of these people's families have lived in this place for over a hundred fifty years! Jones bought that land only about a dozen years ago and look at the empire he's built. But in doing that, he took away this town's livelihood, ruined their wells. Think of just the inconvenience that he's caused these people!"

"He did have that well by the fence—"

"The Texas Joneses ought to drum him out of the corps, make him change his name. He shames all of you. When you first came, some of the people said you could be one of his breed, but John said that you were another kind of man entirely."

"Have you ever met Frank?" But even saying it, Decker knew that meeting Old Gimme would only confirm everything she thought.

"I've tried." She sighed against his chest. "All I've ever gotten is the runaround. I even asked my daddy to see him, and he agreed, but Frank put him off. He runs with a different crowd, and Daddy said he didn't have any handle to hold on the man."

"He might not be the monster that you think. He must be well insulated from a casual approach—"

"Casual? I'd like to subpoena him and make him talk to us."

"Let me see what I can do."

"Oh, Decker, you are such a good man."

But that only dug the claws of his deceit deeper into his conscience. He didn't need anything else plaguing him. In a move of self-preservation, he tried to distance himself from this latest danger. Under the colorful throw, he eased his body away, back from her, tucked his satisfied member back where it should have been all along, and pulled her skirt down over her thighs.

As he sat up and turned away, she felt him withdrawing more than his body and was puzzled by that. It was as if she'd offended him. Or was it because he didn't want to be involved in anything that wasn't connected with himself? Did he only look like a hero to her? If he were really one, would he be jobless and drifting? Maybe he was a hollow man, and he would shatter if he was tried too far?

If Brad—But Brad was no longer there. A feeling not of grief, but of melancholy descended over Naomi, blocking out hope.

Standing, Decker pulled up his jeans and fastened them. He leaned down and gently kissed her cool lips. He looked into her distanced gaze and was puzzled. She seemed a stranger now. He told her in commitment, "I've got to see about a mouse's dam."

Then he turned away, pulled on his wet wool socks and his boots, put his wet shirt back on and his wet denim jacket. He considered her, still lying there on the glider, motionless. He winked very seriously to give her courage, then he snapped his fingers at Wellington, and they left.

The rain began. It was shocking. It simply came down from the skies as if it weren't a miracle.

Naomi went upstairs to strip off her sticky clothes and shower. As she passed Trisha's room, she looked in the opened doorway. Trisha was standing by the window with her hands on her back, staring out over the rain-veiled wash.

"Trisha? Are you all right?"

She turned slowly. "Just restless." She sighed and moved awkwardly. "I feel enormous."

Naomi frowned at her. "Does the rain depress you? Or are you dreading seeing Rick again?"

"In a way. I don't feel attractive."

"You love him very much."

"Of course!" Trisha was impatient. "Why do you think I kept this baby?"

"I thought you said you didn't realize you were pregnant."

"I had all the problems. And I bought a kit right away. With the positive result, I was so scared and so excited and unbelieving—"

"Don't forget secretive! You never said *one* word!"

"You were totally concentrated on Brad. After that, you couldn't even cope with changing out of your nightgown. How was I going to burden you with my problem?"

There was a poignant pause, then in a doomsday voice Naomi stated, "I failed you."

"Oh, Naomi, you idiot." The words were impatient and a little irritated.

"I have to shower."

"I thought you already..." Trisha turned and looked at Naomi.

But Naomi just said, "Excuse me." And left.

Trisha frowned at the empty doorway, then moved restlessly and rubbed her back as she straightened. She looked out over the rainy landscape and didn't appreciate the muted shades of rain-cleansed greenery, the grey of the wet basin, or the rich black of the dirt.

In the bath, with the shower on a gentle spray, Naomi thought of lying with Decker on the glider. She shook her head to chastise herself. What foolishness had coaxed her under that throw with such a man? Ahhh, what a man. And how would he fit into her life? Or would she adjust to his? She'd adjusted to Brad's.

Life with Brad had been one that was unreal, gaudy,
noisy, one that was ridiculously serious madness. But
Brad had been as bemused by it all as Naomi. Only
he'd laughed over it, while she had only aloofly observed the tilted make-believe.

It had been a revelation when Naomi had begun to
see under the facade of wildness, under the craziness
of Brad's people, who were grabbing tooth and nail
at the instant fame in order to relish it while it lasted.
But it had lasted.

In Brad, the group had had something unique. His
"A Man and a Woman" had been written for her, and
it was glorious.

She had laughed the first time Brad had played and
sung it to her. She'd thought his "for you alone" label
of "her" song was like that of all musicians who had
one piece that was "ours"—to each woman who came
along. What could have been more anonymous than
Brad's "A Man and a Woman"? It wasn't "Brad and
Naomi," it was "A Man and a Woman."

Brad had said, "I've written a piece for us." He'd
looked over at her with his oddly yellow-brown eyes,
and he'd asked, "Want to hear it?"

She'd smiled her amusement. "Sure."

"It's not quite ready. There are some notes not exactly right. But you'll get the idea."

She had noted that Brad even had sheets of paper
with penciled notes on the music score. While she'd
known that he had written most of the group's songs,
she had also known that she had not been his first
woman.

As Brad had directed, she'd been on the sofa. With
almost shy flair and a glance that shared his bashful
humor over himself and his conduct, he'd sat at his

piano and touched the keys. He'd played the melody, and changed a note to a flat. Then he'd played it again and looked at Naomi smugly, raising his brows.

She'd laughed. Brad was practiced, she'd thought, and she'd been amused that he would make such a pretense of "composition in progress." He'd played it through. Then he had begun again, and he'd sung the words. The song was lovely. Sensual. Intimate. A man and a woman. And Brad really had written it for her.

He hadn't agreed to make a record of it until he'd sung it in concert as a surprise for her on one of their anniversaries. The stadium had gone wild over it, and demanded it again. Then word had spread about the song, and pirated taped versions were being sold. In self-defense Brad had had to record it.

When he'd done that, he'd had only Naomi in the studio. He'd laid his voice onto the completed instrumental tape while he had watched her. He'd done it in one serious take, then he'd come to her and made love to her.

In Sawbuck, Naomi watched as it continued to rain that afternoon. The ground soaked up the moisture, absorbing the water. There weren't any puddles. But in the basin, on the rock, there were the beginnings of captured water.

Naomi noted those and longed for the basin to fill. She yearned for more rain, for the skies to open up and really give them the deluge they needed. But was the dam big enough? She told Trisha, "I think I'll just go over to the dam site and see how they're getting along. I might as well take some coffee and sandwiches."

"Want me to go with you?" Trisha asked.

"In your condition, you don't need to slip and fall in the gluey mud, nor do you need to get wet and chilled."

Trisha gave her a look. "And you want to simper and smile at Decker without my censoring stare."

"Right."

"So you admit you like the guy?"

Airily, Naomi sassed, "I like a lot of people."

"But you don't lie on the glider with them. I heard that glider smash into the house."

"What big ears you have, little mother."

"I'm practicing in case this kid's a daughter. With our genes, she'd be a holy terror and no male would be safe. I'd probably have to marry her off at age twelve."

Naomi nodded, deliberately sober. "She'd be a late bloomer?"

"Don't be long . . . going down to the dam. I'm restless."

Naomi looked at her sharply, but Trisha turned away, unaware.

So after Naomi had fixed sandwiches, and had the coffee ready, she called Pete at the service station and asked, "Is there someone around who could pick up sandwiches and coffee to take out to the dam?"

"Naw. Decker's got everybody working, hauling stones. They'll probably revolt soon, and the dam will be finished with Decker's broken body somewhere inside."

"Good grief."

Philosophically Pete pronounced, "Rain does that to people. That's why we live down here in Texas. We don't have to put up with this wet stuff that louses up everything."

"Right. Getting this food over to the dam site shouldn't take long. I don't like to leave Trisha alone. Couldn't you run it over there? It isn't far."

"I got a business."

She said the obvious. "No one comes through Sawbuck this time of day."

"In the rain, somebody could get lost and need a couple of gallons of gas."

"Oh, never mind, Pete."

Trisha watched Naomi hang up. "You can leave me alone. I'm fine. Just restless."

Torn by the strangeness of Trisha's conduct, Naomi hesitated. "How long did Jim say you had?"

"Not for a couple of weeks. I haven't begun to dilate yet."

"Well, I shouldn't be long. I'll have Pete call you in a half hour. Okay? Then if I'm not back, he can take you to the station and keep an eye on you."

Trisha enunciated the words: "That place smells of oil and gas, and my kid does not like it. There is no need."

"I know, but this rain and Rick's visit have unsettled you, and I dislike leaving you alone for even a half hour."

"I did suggest going along," Trisha pointed out.

"And I canceled your going."

"I really liked you better semicomatose."

Naomi shook her head. "I must have been a real pain."

"Yeah."

Flippantly, healing, Naomi sassed, "You could have said, 'I didn't mind.'"

But Trisha explained seriously, "I thought you might die of grief."

"I was in shock. Who would ever believe we could have lost Brad to anything so simple? Bacteria. Rampant bacteria. Invisible. And it killed that good man."

"The medical staff grieved, too," Trisha reminded her.

"Did they? I couldn't see beyond my own pain."

"You are healing. I would never have believed it. Brad was so bright to give you this problem in order to distract you."

"Yes."

"He loved you."

More softly, Naomi agreed, "Yes."

"Is there a heaven?"

"I have no idea. I believe the spirit goes on. I have felt Brad with me. That was part of the distraction. I felt as if I had to concentrate on him so that he would stay with me. I thought that if my attention was diverted even a little, I would lose him."

They were silent. Trisha didn't know how to comment on that dedication.

"But he fooled me. He found something that would eventually penetrate into my consciousness, and he would be free of me."

"No," Trisha countered. "There, you have it wrong. You would be free of grief. That was what he wanted. That you wouldn't waste your life in longing backward. That you would look ahead."

"You know, Trisha, you do astonish me. You're very wise under that disguise of carefree indifference."

"I learned it all the hard way."

"I'll be back in fifteen minutes at the very latest."

"Don't break your neck."

"Stay downstairs," Naomi commanded.

"Oh, for Pete's sake!"

Naomi laughed. "I have a new jigsaw puzzle. Did you ever believe we'd sit like two old maids and do jigsaw puzzles?"

"They are underrated."

"So are you, my love. I shall return."

"That's a catch phrase. It's been overdone."

"I know." Naomi took the thermos and the basket and went out on the porch. "Lock the door."

"Here?"

"It seemed a logical thing to say."

"Just go on. Take your time. I'm perfectly all right."

"In films, the pregnant women on wagon trains and in isolated cabins and in snowstorms always say that sort of thing."

Trisha put the back of her hand to her forehead with the fingers curled outward, and said bravely, "Take your time. The snow is only waist high. I could make it the five miles to the Olsons'."

"I've only lately begun to realize you're a hambone." Naomi frowned at her friend. "How could I not have known that in all these years? You have drama in a streak a mile wide!"

"I'll be a stage mother."

"Poor kid." She patted Trisha's round stomach.

Trisha grabbed Naomi's hand and said, "Hah! Feel? High kicks! The kid's a natural!"

In sympathy, Naomi laid her hand on her concealed godchild and told it, "I'll rescue you. Don't worry. I'll see to it your wild mother and crazy father behave and let you live your own life."

"We'll go to New York and start on the stage like Ron Howard!"

"Lie down with a cool cloth, don't chill, I'll be back in fifteen minutes."

"She'll need tap-dancing lessons right away. I wonder if Gregory Hines would be available to teach her."

"He doesn't need the money."

Trisha replied as to an imbecile, "—for the satisfaction of being involved with her career!"

"Good grief." And Naomi left.

Since Naomi's pickup would go anywhere, the truck made it to the dam site. It was a quagmire up to the rock lip. The motor labored, but the wheels did move. The trip was worth it, because the men were tired and hungry. They stood around already as wet and muddy as they could get, and they ate the sandwiches and drank the hot coffee as if it were food for gods.

Naomi thought of them as supermen, just because they were actually working on the longed-for dam.

And Decker was there. She blushed as she smiled at him. He came over to her and said, "You'll have everyone believing I've made love to you, looking so pretty and pink."

"You almost did."

"I can see right now that you're going to be a woman who wants things to go her way, all your life. Just what am I doing out here in this mud?"

"You're saving a town."

Decker chewed on his mouthful and looked at his mouse. She'd just said it in clear words. She was right. He was trying to save that damned nothing town. He looked off to the side. How had this happened? He looked back at his mouse, and he knew.

CHAPTER TWELVE

NAOMI ASKED THE MEN AROUND HER TRUCK, "How is the work going?"

"Decker is a weird man," Buzz offered. "We've been okay, sitting around this town, but since he showed up, we haven't had a minute to ourselves."

Naomi noted that even as the men all made sounds of agreement, they had looks of satisfaction. They must never have adjusted to being idle. They simply hadn't had a leader. But now they had Decker.

"How's the dam?" she couldn't help but ask.

"We're getting there," Joe said forthrightly.

That was a surprise, because Joe generally was self-effacing. After he retired from the Army, he and Ann had come to Sawbuck. It had taken a while for the people to accept the outsiders. But now Joe was one of them. Well, almost. They had been accepted better than Naomi was.

"I came to inspect the works," she informed them.

They looked at her short boots doubtfully.

"I'll carry you," Decker volunteered.

The men burst out laughing. Decker was a mud man. Naomi was fairly clean.

She said stoutly, "If you all can work in this glue, I can walk in it."

Decker picked up two sandwiches, refilled his cup, and followed Naomi as he continued to eat. The footing was a little slippery, but she did very well. He mentioned an old story about a woman who slipped in the mud and made forty-five dollars before she could regain her feet. He glanced over at her to see how she'd take the joke. She tsked as she shook her head and said he was shocking. He laughed. "I was just hoping you'd slip."

"You couldn't be interested."

"Oh, yes."

But they had reached the rock lip of the basin. The water escape run was half full of rocks and their efforts were beginning to look like a serious attempt at a dam. "Oh, Decker, all that work. And the kids and I worked so hard to get that little pile of rocks."

"They've come in mighty handy as filler. You all did a good job."

"Be sure to tell the kids that."

He nodded to show he'd heard, but he said, "You were a sweetheart to bring the food. The men needed it and a break in working. They've been just great."

She smiled and looked up at him. "I wanted to see you, and it was an excuse."

Her lack of guile, her honesty, twisted the guilt claws in his conscience, but he finished chewing and swallowed before he said in satisfaction, "I think you could dance for me in the cougar teeth and lie on the skin with me."

"I guess dam building isn't as depleting as I'd supposed."

With helpfulness, he offered, "We could test that possibility."

As he took the last bite of sandwich, she looked down his mud body and grinned. "I once saw a picture of a football player who looked very like you do now."

"And he was only playing a game. We're building your dam."

Her smile faded to a gentle ghost of one as she regarded him. "You are magnificent."

"Careful. You'll have me believing it's me you like and not just getting that dam fixed."

"Do you really think I would trade myself for a dam?"

"Not for a minute. I wanted to hear you say that." He drank the last of his coffee.

Buzz came sliding over to them. "What do you think about the dam?"

"It could make a difference," she said.

"We could stock the basin with fish," Buzz suggested. "We're all good fishermen. We could still sit, but we'd be fishing."

Decker looked at Buzz. That was the first comment that Buzz had offered positively about the dam. He'd worked hard, but silently. He hadn't seemed especially interested.

Naomi offered, "Dick said we'd swim in the basin, and fish."

Buzz replied, "Yeah. It's something to hear the commuters talking about Sawbuck like they're part of it. It surprised me."

"Us, too." Decker put a hand on Naomi's shoulder. He was staking his claim. She didn't move away.

Buzz smiled a little, watching. Then he said, "Decker's made a difference here."

Decker denied it. "No. You guys have done all the work."

Buzz ignored the disclaimer. "You triggered us."

It was an acknowledgment that Buzz needed to admit, and Decker nodded once in accepting it. "I can see how you got some of your muscle, Buzz, but I wonder how you developed the muscles you've used today."

Buzz laughed.

The other men slowly came back to the dam, cheerful, tired, willing to continue. Naomi said, "I wonder if the drugstore has any muscle liniment?"

John nodded. "If Decker sticks around Sawbuck, Buckle'll need to stock up on liniment for all us victims."

"I'll stop in there on my way home. The town will put up a plaque to you guys."

"I'll keep it shined," Buzz offered.

Naomi then asked, "What will you do next?" She indicated the dam.

Decker replied, "We're putting in sand as we go along. It's not fine sand, it's gravelly. We're digging it out of the creek bed above here."

She was a stickler. "Did you get permission?"

"It belongs to the Hernandez family. He said it was okay."

"Good." She turned back to look down at the half-done dam. Then she stared out over the basin, wondering how much water a half dam would hold? But she hated to urge the tired men to additional struggle, yet today, in this morass. She ventured timidly, "You must all be very tired."

Buzz replied, "Decker has had us working for a couple of weeks, with the trash hauling and painting, so we're getting used to being on our feet."

The other men laughed, and Buzz's words were translated for the non-English–speaking listeners.

Decker walked with Naomi back to her truck. "You could pull your truck over to the side of the track, sit in the cab, and watch us work."

"I need to get back to Trisha. She's restless today."

"When's the baby due?"

"In a couple of more weeks."

"She'd be okay, if you'd like to hang around."

"I'd better get back."

"Well, okay. But behave yourself."

She grinned saucily. "We're going to work on a jigsaw puzzle."

"I'll come over later and see how you're doing."

She blushed. "All right."

"I wish there was a movie house that I could offer in entertainment. The only thing near to that is my VCR, and we'd have to sit on the sidewalk or in a store with everyone else. How about if I bring over a smoldering love story? Could you handle that without pawing me and trying to get your wily way?"

"I have great control."

He said, "Well, damn."

"Do you realize how outrageous you are?" she asked. "You're not following the rules at all."

"I've been out of the country. Have I gone too slowly?"

She laughed and shook her head. "You're long way ahead of the progression of acquaintance."

"Good!"

"You're supposed to be shocked by your breaches and offer—"

He looked down at himself. "Breeches? I'm unzipped?"

"Decker!"

"What did you have in mind for me to . . . offer?"

"I hesitate to say. You turn things around so remarkably."

"I'd like to turn you around and get you all muddy and sticky and surprised."

"I doubt you could surprise me."

"Well, I shall surely try my damnedest."

"No, no, I didn't mean that you should—"

"I can see I've confused you. I'll try to straighten you out."

By then there were yells from the dam site to Decker to get his ass back there.

"No finesse. They're animals. Well, I hate to do this, but it must be done."

"Goo . . ."

But he'd grabbed her tightly against his muddy self and he kissed her quite thoroughly. He set her aside, swatted her bottom, distributing more mud, and said, "See you tonight. As I've mentioned before, you are to behave yourself."

She looked at the sky and said, "Awk."

And he strode off like a conquering male to build her dam.

So instead of stopping off and speaking to Mr. Buckle at the drugstore, she had to go straight home and clean up. Of course, Trisha was sitting on the porch, zipped into a snug sack against the rain chill, so Naomi couldn't even get into the house unnoticed.

"Well," said Trisha enviously, "I see you encountered friendly natives. Who all was it?"

"Decker."

"He spreads mud very liberally."

Naomi grinned as she replied, "It was worth it."

Then they both laughed.

"You took longer than fifteen minutes," Trisha chided.

"They are really working hard. They're only about half done. It would hold back some of the rain runoff, but not enough. They look like a mud race. I *was* going to stop off and ask Mr. Buckle if he had any muscle liniment, but I could hardly expose myself to observation this selectively muddy."

"It would be a scandal for the town," Trisha agreed.

"Would you like to ride over into town with me? In a minute, after I clean up?"

With some drollness, Trisha reminded Naomi, "I can watch you from here."

Naomi turned her head and looked over at the town. "Yes." She came all the way up onto the porch and kept her front to Trisha.

"I'll just go change."

"Turn around."

"Why?"

"I want to see what you're hiding in back of you."

Naomi hesitated, then she slowly turned. Sure enough, there was a man's muddy hand mark on her bottom. "Did it leave a mark?"

"He did that deliberately."

"Yes."

They exchanged a laughing glance, and shedding her muddy boots, Naomi went into the house.

She returned in a few minutes in jeans, sweater,

and clean boots. "Have you been okay?" she asked
Trisha.

"Fine. I've gone to the bathroom forty thousand
times."

"In"—Naomi consulted her watch—"forty minutes? That's taken dedication."

"That's taken a crowding kid. I've explained to it
that I don't need this getting up and down, but it's
going to be independent and a real bullheaded kid."

"Like her mother."

"Surely not. Go wash out your mouth with soap."

"Come along?"

"I'll wait here, near the bathroom."

"Is it okay if I stop off to see Magdalena? I could
give her some peppermints."

"Bring me some, will you?"

"Check."

Naomi put up her umbrella and went back to her
dirty pickup, got in, waved her hand out the back
window, and turned the truck around in a sweep to
head back across the space into town. There she
stopped at the drugstore, then ran through the rain
to see Magdalena.

As with everything in such a rain, the house was
damp. Magdalena was sitting, dozing in a chair, but
her granddaughter roused her to see Naomi. Magdalena smiled and was pleased to get the bag of peppermints. The other women of the family were
working on the eggs, stuffing the shells with orange
and black confetti for Halloween.

As they painted the eggs to look like witches and
pumpkins, they all talked about the dam. They exclaimed and laughed, shaking their heads about the
commuters thinking they belonged to Sawbuck. And

they talked about the delight that so many stopped for coffee and doughnuts in the mornings on their way to work. They talked about offering the commuters drive-up main dishes for supper. They could offer pasta, Mexican foods, or roast chickens. They could take the orders in the mornings and have them ready when the commuters returned that evening.

Ann was also interested in baking bread and rolls. They discussed all sorts of things, and Naomi tried to keep track. She rose and said her good-byes. And she saw that the rain was a little heavier.

Back at home, Trisha was napping in the snug sack, waiting for Naomi. Being sure that Trisha wasn't too hot or cool, Naomi let her sleep. The eaves of the house were wide as they should be to give shade in such a sunshine climate, so the porch was dry enough, only the air was dampened by the rain.

Naomi went inside and returned with the throw Decker had used, and she curled up on the glider to nap. When she wakened, Trisha was heaving herself up from the chair. Softly, Naomi asked, "Are you okay?"

"Pregnant."

"Well," she exclaimed mildly. "How did that happen?"

"Ha, ha, ha."

Watching Trisha go into the house, Naomi decided that if she ever had children, she would investigate the advancement of test-tube incubation.

Then Naomi realized the rain had stopped. It had *stopped*? It had! It hadn't even rained enough to have a trickle of runoff.

Disgruntled, Naomi sat on the glider and glared at the breaking clouds. Her gaze was sour as the sun

spotlighted the washed leaves floating on invisible
twigs against the rain-darkened tree trunks. Nor did
she see the grasses breathing free of the dust as they
acted as background to the refreshed August wild-
flowers. She didn't see the breathtaking beauty before
her, she saw only the empty basin of the wash.

She finally saw the men's trucks coming back into
town. Muddy and moving slowly, the men got out and
stood still as they talked; and the commuters began
their nightly stream. Some slowed and called questions, some stopped and got out. There was arm waving and loud voices.

Naomi picked up her birdwatching binoculars and
focused on the center figure. Decker. But there was
an angrily gesturing man talking at Decker. It was
Ned the engineer.

Trisha shuffled out and stood still saying, "Ouch."

Naomi leaped up from the glider, rocking it back
against the house with a bang. "What's wrong?"

Trisha straightened cautiously and smiled in wonder.

"The kid just moved off my bladder! Hey! That's
better. A better bladder."

"One of life's little pleasures?"

But Trisha was looking toward the traffic jam in
town.

"What's going on?"

"A quarrel."

"A wreck?"

"No. Just an arm-waving quarrel. Decker is in the
middle, very calm. Ned is furious. They're leaving—
they're—" Naomi got up and went to the town end
of the porch and leaned out to watch as the crowd

reappeared at the end of the string of stores. "Why, it looks as if they are . . . going to the dam?"

"Go ahead, I'm very comfortable. No problems. I can even walk easier. See?"

"I am curious."

"I know. You are curious as to why Decker is in the middle of a quarrel, and you want to be there to defend him. He doesn't need you."

"Yes. He does. He told me so."

"What a line! And you took the bait." Trisha laughed.

Naomi smiled. "It's good to hear you really laugh again."

Trisha was indignant. "Quit being dear. I was laughing *at* you!"

"I know that. I don't mind. I love you, Trisha."

Trisha covered her face with her hands and gave a shriek. "I just managed to quit crying, and you get mushy. Stop it!"

"Okay, okay! I'm leaving."

"Take notes so you don't forget anything."

"Right."

Ned was furious. They'd done the dam all wrong. "Amateurs! Clods!" They would have to take it all apart and redo it that weekend.

The tired, muddy men shifted and the white glances in their mud faces moved over and landed on Decker. Was Decker discomforted? No. He said, "It seemed logical to me."

"It would have leaked. The sand would have washed away. It would have had to be redone and all the water would have been lost."

Decker defended himself. "There are earthen dams."

"They are bigger than a fifteen-foot base."

Buzz said a calm "Decker—"

Decker replied, "My fault. I'll clear this away by the weekend, and we'll get it done right."

That was just too much nobility for the men. They said exasperated versions of "Jeeeeezzzzzsss." One patient man translated the conversations to those who needed it. Then they, too, were disgruntled and unbelieving. And they, too, said Spanish words of irritation.

Decker went down off the lip and began to remove rocks. Buzz went after him and stopped him. "Tomorrow's soon enough."

The other men had lined the edge and stood watching, then John said, "We begin tomorrow."

Decker stood on the half-done dam and looked up at his friends. Slowly, he half shook his head, to show his emotion at their support and he said, "Beer's on the house."

And the men laughed.

Probably as touched by the incident as any was Ned. He *knew* how much muscle had gone into what had been done, and it would take more to undo what was in the neck of the funnel. He said, "Here's how you do it. We have to clear the neck. Roll the stones off the *downstream* side. Understand? Be careful. Roll the top ones the farthest. You've done a good stacking job. Lay them all out downstream. This weekend we'll embed the pipes in cement. That'll hold them steady so they can't slew. Then we'll build the frame for the concrete face with the gate at the bottom. See? Then the stones and rocks will be in back of that to support the concrete. The weight of the dammed water against the dam will be strong. We want a dam that'll last."

There were nods as the man watched the area they'd use and they could "see" the finished project.

Ned said, "We'll build a walkway along the top with handrails."

They "saw" that, too, and they smiled in satisfaction.

So when a clean and crisp Decker came to Naomi's porch that night, she said, "You weren't lynched."

"I wouldn't have blamed them."

"You're a little too open-minded."

He took off his antique Stetson and laid it aside. "I wanted your dam. The way we did it seemed logical to me."

She kissed him, and he wrapped his arms around her, holding her tightly. She leaned back and with the fingers of one hand, she turned his hair into a "Brutus" hairstyle. "Your dam would have lasted long enough until we won our suit for our water rights from that man over the fence."

"You're going to sue?"

"Civil rights."

"Have you talked to a lawyer?"

"I haven't yet found one who wants to go against that monster, Frank Jones."

"I may be able to find one," he said.

"I have a couple more to ask."

"A public hearing might work."

"These people have been here a long, long time. That should count for something."

"I tried to build your dam, don't I get a kiss for that?"

"I just gave you one."

"That was a hello kiss."

"Really? I thought it was a thank-you one."

"No, no, no, no. You have no sensitivity to the sub-
tleties of kissing. I can see right now that I'm going
to have to spend a lot of time and energy explaining
this to you. It's a terrible thing that you've had no real
instruction in this particular field of endeavor. I suppose now's as good a time as any for you to get started.
Come over here."

He led her to the glider that he pulled a judicious
distance from the wall of the house. "Now, sit down,"
he instructed. "Unbutton any portions of your clothing that might restrict or inhibit me."

"Clothing?" she questioned. "My face is bare. My
lips are on it. Why is my clothing involved?"

"I have to explain that, too? Now that really exas-
perates me. Just unbutton and unzip, I'll have to explain as I go along."

"I hadn't realized kissing was so involved."

"People seldom do," he acknowledged. "But you
looked like a kisser to me, so I just jumped to the
conclusion that you could."

"I've never had any complaints."

"Well, up until now I thought you were cognizant.
The only clue I've had is that you don't know the
difference between hello and good-bye kisses, and
now this problem with hello and thank-you kisses.
Since those are so basic, I am concerned for your
safety—"

"You're going to kiss me with my clothing undone
so as not to 'inhibit' you, and you are going to show
me how that's concerned with my . . . safety?"

"Yes." He was surprised. "You could give a man a
thank-you kiss when he hadn't done one damned

thing! Or you could give him an I'm-ready kiss and all hell would break loose."

She asked, "You?"

"Right."

"I see. This is for my protection."

"What in the world did you think it was about?" He pretended impatience. "Now, surely you didn't suspect that I was just plotting some way to get my hands on your naked body?"

"Well—"

"You shock me, Miss Wentworth. For you to understand male thinking to that extent and not recognize the manner of kisses involved shows a very lopsided development." He put his hands on her breasts. "But it doesn't carry through to the physical. It's just your performance we have to work to correct."

"Then you can get your hands off my chest, since they balance."

"I was just being sure," he explained.

"I would have noticed."

"How was I to know that? You have no inkling about the variety of kisses you hand out so unwillingly."

"If I am unwill—"

But he didn't see any need to talk about that, so he kissed her. When he lifted his mouth, he asked in a husky voice, "What kind was that?"

She focused her eyes with some difficulty. "Hello?"

He took a long patient breath. "That was an I'm-ready kiss."

"To ... kiss?"

He nodded. "And to fool around."

"Haven't we skipped a whole span of kinds to already be at the I'm-ready ones?"

"Yes."

"I think we should start at the beginning, and be sure I know what I'm doing."

"No."

"Then how will I learn?"

"I'll interpret yours as we go along."

She demurred. "I believe that could be very risky."

"Probably."

"Probably? You're going to seduce me?"

"Yes."

"Ahhhh."

"I had to drive into San Antonio and get a packet of sheaths. I had to do that so we didn't shock Mr. Buckle who still has his first shipment of condoms."

"It is a small town," she mentioned.

"This collection of shacks is not really a town."

"A community?"

"Are you changing the subject?" he asked suspiciously.

"I'm trying not to panic. I'm trying to go slower."

He kissed her again. His hands moved, unbuttoning buttons, unzipping zippers. One of his hands slid into her blouse and spread out over her breast, kneading it.

She made a sound in her throat. The kiss went on for a while. When he finally lifted his head and looked down at her, she allowed her flimsy neck to lay her head on his shoulder. "Was that an I'm-ready one?"

"No, no." He sighed. "That was a you-attract-me one."

"Oh. You attract me, too."

"Kiss me that way."

She lifted her hand to the back of his head and kissed him sweetly, touching his lips with her tongue. She broke the kiss and said, "How was that?"

"That was a do-it kiss."

"No kidding! I didn't mean that. I meant only to say that I am attracted to you. Since I meant only that, how could you interpret it as a do-it one? I thought you said you could tell what I intended."

He was a little distracted because with her undone clothing, he'd found that he could move his hand down onto her stomach. He pressed and swirled his hard, work-roughened hand there under her panty band, his little finger brushing along in the coarsely silken curls. Then he moved that hand back up to her stomach, along her ribs, and back over the swell of her breast which he kneaded. He said, "Ummm."

She gasped.

So he kissed her again, and he took his hand from inside her blouse and pulled up her skirt so that he could run his rough palm up the silken inside of her sensitive thigh. She stiffened, and his mouth coaxed. His sounds murmured against her mouth and the vibrations of his sound went from his chest into hers.

His breathing had changed. His concentration on her was intense. His hands were busy on her, pleasuring himself and her. She moved without meaning to, and she responded to him. Her body changed. Her movements were to entice, she became receptive, her mouth was inviting, her hands on his back, holding him, coaxing in turn.

He barely lifted his mouth from hers. "Those are I-want kisses. What do you want?"

She hesitated, then she touched his waiting lips with the tip of her tongue.

He laid her flat, rolled on a condom, lifted her skirt out of the way, and lay back down, holding his weight on his elbows. "I'm going to give you a let-me kiss.

Now pay attention." His voice was a husky whispering. As he had just that afternoon, he managed to try to be quiet. "Are you a shouter?" he asked.

"I don't know."

He raised up a little and looked at her. "You don't know?"

"I never paid any attention."

"I'll handle it. Are you ready for the let-me kiss?"

"I think so."

"I'll give you a want-you kiss first, then the let-me one. Pay attention."

But during the want-you one, he moved so that he was pressing into her heat. She gasped, and he took that gasp sweetly. His hand moved to the side of her breast, and he pressed again.

He lifted his mouth to breathe, and she whispered, "Do the let-me one."

He curled his body, pressing hard as he kissed her passionately, then he moved gently, stealthily as she widened her knees and allowed him deeper access.

She moaned into his capturing mouth and lifted her hips to meet him, to take him entirely, and his sound was of such pleasure. Furtively they moved, almost silently, and they climaxed in ecstasy, holding rigidly still against the tide of release. Then slowly they relaxed. He lifted his sound-concealing mouth from hers, trying to silence his harsh breath through opened lips, that he buried his face in the spill of her hair by her head.

Even with Brad, making love had never been that complete. Holding her new love to her, Naomi looked off into an unseen distance and wondered if she had been incomplete to Brad?

CHAPTER THIRTEEN

DECKER AND NAOMI LAY ON THE GLIDER, LATE in that cool August night. As he'd placed her once before, she was alongside him with her back to the back of the glider and her head was on his chest. He could swing them a little, and he did, noting that the glider had been oiled and didn't squeak. That made him smile inside his head. So. She'd thought he'd be back.

They talked. Having been so intimate, it was strange that their exchange, then, was on getting acquainted. They commented on their first impressions of each other.

"I really thought you were a far-traveling 'ne'er do well,' you got off that bus so stiffly. But then I didn't know you'd been so badly hurt. Where did that happen? Were you run out of some town?"

"Honey. I still can't talk . . . not about that. Not yet. When I can, I'll tell you about it."

"Are you still in danger?"

"Not from them."

"That's an odd statement. Are you in other danger?"

"Not that I know about. Why did you ask if I'd been run out of some town?"

"You do tend to take over. Here, it was for the good, but I would wonder if you hadn't liked the way things were going somewhere else, that you might well have taken an unpopular hand in things."

"I thought you'd be a squint eyed, hard-nosed woman's libber."

She loved it. "And you were right."

"I found a soft, sweet mouse who squats down to talk to little kids who in turn think they have to squat down so they can talk to you. And it amuses you."

"Little kids are so precious. But after watching Trisha, I've decided if I ever want a baby, I'm going to investigate the nurturing facilities of test tubes for prenatal care."

"Well, that proves it's just a good thing I made a quick trip into San Antonio for preventative measures."

"It beats being splattered."

He laughed. "You make me laugh at the damnedest times. You may not be hard-nosed or squinty-eyed but you are a surprise. You don't look the humorous type."

Naturally she asked, "What type do I look?"

"A Lady Elaine who floats around in soft silks and needs rescuing. I like your long dresses and those hats. I doubt there are many women in this state who wear clothes like yours."

"I sunburn."

"You could wear a Stetson and jeans."

"I didn't want to be 'one of the boys' while I was here. I needed to be aloof. Especially being single and living with just Trisha."

"So you contrived an aloof facade."

"Yes. 'An aloof facade,'" she repeated musingly.

"But now that I'm in charge of you, you can dress just like everybody else?"

"'In charge'?"

"Uh-oh."

And she laughed.

It was their soft laughter that Trisha heard. She lay in her bed in the dark night and felt alone. She was glad Rick would come the next afternoon, and they could be together again. She had missed him terribly. He'd looked for her. He hadn't just forgotten her, he'd looked for her. Trisha held that thought and slept.

Downstairs, Wellington came up on the porch and over to the lovers on the glider. Wellington could understand romance. He could smell it. He made a sound in his throat and went back to the top of the stairs, not sitting down but standing, looking back at Decker.

Decker hugged Naomi rather absently as he said in a low breath, "Something's up." Then he lifted his arm and slid his body from under Naomi before he sat up and put his feet back into his spurred boots with the muted clinks.

Decker and Wellington exchanged a stare, then Wellington started down the stairs. Decker became alert, stood and listened. He stooped down and kissed Naomi's forehead. "Go inside and lock up. I'll be back."

"What is it?"

"I don't know, but something's going on. Get inside. Do you have a gun?"

"Yes."

"Keep it close to hand. But don't shoot me. I'll whistle twice. Be careful. It might be a while."

He did an odd thing. He removed his spurs and gave them to Naomi. Then he went off the porch without his Stetson. As she watched, he disappeared.

Naomi listened very carefully for sounds close at hand, then farther away. She thought she heard a strange under-sound. She couldn't figure it out. It wasn't constant, like a motor or a machine working. But there were sounds.

She went inside and closed the door, locking it. She went around locking windows and closing shutters. Then she went upstairs and looked out into the night. She went around to windows that faced all directions, and the sound was not from the town.

She got the gun, loaded it, checked the safety, and sat in the upper hall at the top of the stairs. She did not waken Trisha.

As Decker followed the silent dog along the wash, he realized that subconsciously he'd been hearing the sound, but Naomi had distracted him. He was losing it, losing that keen edge of awareness that is the difference between living and not.

Knowing he wasn't as sharp as he should be, he took more care, so he saw the others before they saw him. He saw John and was impressed that he could move so silently. Buzz was almost invisible. How had they learned to move so stealthily? For what purpose?

He waited to see if anyone else would come along in back of him, and Joe came. He was startlingly efficient, and Decker attributed that to Joe's army training. Was he the agent?

So. What was going on? Those three men, moving ahead of Decker, were very cautious. Therefore they didn't know what was making the sound, or who was doing it.

The three dispersed, disappearing. And Decker hunkered down to wait.

It didn't take long to understand that whatever was happening was taking place at the dam site. Stones were tumbling. Someone was tearing it down? Who?

Decker had ascertained that the three ahead of him were the investigative core. He wondered if they were armed? If Sawbuck men were backup? How were they deployed? He needed to be careful since he wasn't armed.

The three materialized and met. They appeared agitated. What was going on?

In his night forays, he'd heard them signal by putting a hand backward to their faces, inserting the index finger into the opposite cheek, closing their mouths around the finger, and stiffening the finger to "pop" it from the mouth in a soft sound. As he approached them, Decker made that sound, and he startled them into jerking around toward him.

He smiled. They looked disgusted. Wellington had to show off his own expertise and walk through the middle of them before disappearing again.

Buzz came over and spoke against Decker's ear. "How long you been trailing us?"

"Once. By accident. What's going on?"

The other two were carefully close, backing to Buzz and Decker, watching around. John asked, "What the hell are you doing out here? We thought you safe on a glider and distracted."

"Wellington." That was Decker's entire reply.

"Ahhh," Buzz said. "Your ears?"

"Yes." With that admission, he had given them his trust.

They recognized that. It was John whose voice trembled with humor. "Someone is tearing down our dam."

The four then had a very hard time controlling the sounds of their laughter.

Joe said in his pragmatic way, "We won't bother them. It's healthy work."

Decker realized Joe was being unexpectedly droll! Again the four were seized with silent laughter. Finally Decker asked, "Who are they?"

"They have a lantern. Look down the funnel along this bank and you can see that the men are of that other Jones's over the fence," John explained. "They think to thwart us."

The four shook their heads and grinned widely.

Buzz commented, "I can't wait to tell the others. We'll have a free day tomorrow with all this unexpected help tonight."

But Decker added, "Unless they dynamite."

That put another slant on the night's work.

"Anybody carrying a rifle?" Decker asked. "A handgun? Anything?"

"Knives."

Yes. Silent knives. "Watch." Decker took charge. "I'll go get my rifle from my pickup."

John laid his hand on Decker's arm and whispered, "No. No guns. We've had no shootings . . . yet."

"I need to discourage dynamite. Can you see who are there?"

"Of the Jones men—Bud, Eric, a couple of others."

"Chico?"

"Naw." There was a little silence and John asked, "How do you know about Chico?"

"Know your enemy."

"You went over there?" Buzz asked, impressed.

"Yeah."

"I never could get past the perimeter. I went clear around once. I thought I'd slip in and sit next to old Jones as he slept by that young wife of his and just whisper, 'Give 'em water.' But I never got the chance. How did you do it?"

Decker's deception was getting deeper and deeper. "I'll take you with me the next time."

Buzz showed his delight with a companionable touch to Decker's shoulder.

Moving slowly, the four split and took up sentinel points. John went up an oak, and Decker would never have believed that old man could be that agile. The other three eased into the brush along the rim and watched.

The men in the funnel were carrying the rocks downstream exactly as Ned had wanted. They were kicking the gravel away. They were doing all the work that had faced Decker in dismantling the dam. But then they smashed the gates with huge rocks, and they broke the sewer pipes with other rocks.

Apparently, that was enough for them. They stood, looked around and were satisfied. They spoke softly and they laughed. They were victors. It was very hard for the watchers not to chortle.

No one got out dynamite. Apparently they thought what they had done was sufficient. They took up the lantern and walked down the dry wash, unknowing that they were carefully followed. The invaders went out of the wash far below the dam site, where a pickup waited for them. They blew out the lantern, climbed into the truck, and quietly went away.

The four, and Wellington, scouted around for another hour or so, but they could find no other evidence of intrusion. They returned to the town, and Decker split from them to go to Naomi's.

There, he mounted the porch, not being quiet, and knocked with one knuckle as he whistled twice as he'd said he would. A big-eyed Naomi cautiously opened the door. "What happened?"

"Come out on the swing."

"Come inside." She unhooked the screen.

"I'd be delighted."

She opened the screen door, and he went inside. "No problem. In fact we have to go into the kitchen and close the door so that we don't waken Trisha when I tell you. Is the safety on that gun?"

"Yes."

"Go put it away."

She obediently went up the stairs and put the gun in its hiding place. Then she came downstairs and said, "Tell me, right this minute."

"In the kitchen, with the door closed."

"What on earth?"

"Jones's men removed the dam."

She gasped indignantly as she looked at Decker who was grinning, then she laughed. She did try to control her hilarity, but she could not and she carried him back into laughter. They put their arms around each other and gave in to their smothered laughter.

She would gasp, "Tore it down?"

And he would reply, "Completely."

That word set them off again.

Then he inquired, "What on earth will I do with my free time until the weekend?"

She said, "Let's go to bed."

"Does laughter make you hot?"

"I'm exhausted from nerves. You forget I was sitting at the top of the stairs, with a loaded gun, waiting for marauders to storm the porch. I've been stretched to the limit, and I'm exhausted."

"But we can sleep tomorrow."

"I have to get my body to bed."

"I'll help with that." He picked her up and carried her up the stairs to whisper, "Which way?"

She pointed.

He stooped so that she could turn the knob, and they went into her room. It was like entering Paradise. It was a woman's room, soft, pastel, a haven. He set her down. "May I stay?"

"I suppose you ought to, so that I can sleep instead of hearing every sound and wondering what else will happen."

"I will."

"You will . . . what?" she inquired.

"Happen to you."

"Ah-hah! And I thought you meant to stay and be watchman for us."

"That, too."

"I will bet that you plan to exact a watcher fee." She gave him a slanted look.

"Yes."

"Uhhh. You want to sleep in my bed."

"That, too."

"You're hungry and want something to eat."

"That, too."

"What else?"

226

Lass Small

"It would be better if I show you."

"Are you going to kiss me?"

"Quite possibly."

"What kind are you going to do first?"

"Guess."

She sighed elaborately. "The let-me kind."

"No. The first one will be an I'm-here one. The second will be an I'm-attracted one, the third will be the let-me one."

"I'll pay attention to the nuances."

"You might be trainable." He was ponderous. "But it could take years."

"I have some idle time, right now."

"How convenient."

He took her into his arms and kissed her deliciously. His hand quickly began unbuttoning and unzipping with familiar ease, since he'd done it once before that night.

When he lifted his mouth, she said, "That was very like the let-me kiss."

"No, no, no, no. That's like this."

She couldn't see the difference at all, so he had to do it several more times. She thought she recognized the shading as she compared it with the I'm-ready one. By then she was naked, and so was he. And they crawled into her bed. She smiled and said, "Give me an I'm-ready one."

But that time he didn't wait to find out if she understood the kiss. He just went ahead. He had her writhing before he even moved his mouth down her throat and began to explore the tastes of her. He sampled as she gasped, and he didn't stop when she groaned for him not to do that. He just went right ahead and did as he chose.

He slid an insidious, rough-skinned hand up the tenderly thrilled back of her bent leg. And he kissed along her side as that hand worked at her breast. She was shivering with sensations and taking quick breaths as her insides quivered with desire.

Then he made love to her. He didn't give her any say or even the time to do anything but try to keep up. She thought they ought to wait until she caught her breath, but he didn't wait. It was like being on a runaway bike on a dark and bumpy road and not sure of balance or destination or even if she would survive.

He pushed into her sheath and rode her frantically writhing body. He smothered her gasps and encouraged her shivers and the clutchings of her hands and thighs. And he made sounds of deep pleasure.

Her hands began to slip on his filmed body, and her fingers dug into him, trying to hold on. When she thought she would explode, he stopped dead and said, "Don't move."

She jerked her head around, wide-eyed and scared. "What's the matter?"

"Hold still."

"Why?"

"I don't want to come yet."

She relaxed slowly and said, "That's all?"

"Don't move that way."

"You scared me. I thought you heard something."

"I heard you yowling like a pleasured cat. It's just lucky for the town that I was swallowing all those sexy sounds."

"I do not yowl."

"No?" He moved a little.

She lay still.

"Cooled? Indifferent?"

"Yes."

"Good. Then I can take my time?"

She yawned and stretched under him.

"Go to sleep if you like, I'll just fool around."

"I want to be on my stomach."

"Oh. Okay." He turned them over, still coupled. "How's that?"

"I would rather be on the sheets, not your sweaty body."

He said, "Okay." Then he slid her off him, but he rolled on top of her, lifted her hips, and took her from behind. "How's that?"

"My word!"

"It isn't your word that I'm playing with."

She laughed.

By her ear, he whispered, "Yowl."

"I do not yowl."

He rose, flipped her over, spread her knees, and took her again. Then he pleasured her. They'd cooled enough with the interruption that it took a while to rebuild their need. He teased her, separating, suckling, smoothing, licking, joining and working her.

Her own body filmed and she felt every cell filled with the waves of excitements. She curled her body to meet his and she lifted her breasts to be flattened by his hairy chest rubbing against her. He put his hands under her bottom and pressed hard in a swivel, and the walls came tumbling down.

As their breaths slowed, their bodies were inert in that tumbled bed. He propped himself on his elbows and complained, "You didn't yowl."

"Mew."

He groaned with his helpless attempt at laughter. "You've done it again."

He rolled free to lie still. "What a way to die."

"Die?"

"I can't get enough of you. I figure you'll be the death of me."

"There's such a thing as moderation."

"With you, it's like being in a candy shop for the first time in all my life. I just want to lick you and smell you and stuff you."

"I'm a drug?"

"Exactly." He nodded. "I'll bet the withdrawals are hell. Are you going to stick around and be my fix?"

"I don't know."

He took her hand. "I do. I'll convince you."

"Are you running from the law?"

"No. I'm a good man."

"What are you doing in Sawbuck?"

"Getting strong again. It's a quiet place. There are no demands on me."

"Other than the dam," she mentioned.

"We'll get that done. Easier, now that the first attempt has been corrected."

"It was Jones's men?"

"Yes."

"If the dam is rebuilt," she cautioned, "they'll come with dynamite."

"No."

"How can you know that?"

"I'll give them an ultimatum."

"An offer they can't refuse?" she questioned. "Like the Mafia? You have no clout. He'll just laugh at you ... and light the fuse."

"Over my dead body."

"I don't want the dam that much."

"Oh? What do you want?" He rolled back toward her and leaned over her.

"You, alive and well."

"Oh." He sounded disappointed. "I thought you wanted to make love."

"Are you insatiable?"

"No. I just didn't want a chance to go by without a rain check."

"Go to sleep."

"In a minute." He slowly rolled up and went into the bathroom. He came back with a warm wet cloth and wiped her face and body. Then he covered her with the sheet and cotton blanket. He took the cloth back to the bath, then came and got into bed with her, taking her into his arms, and they slept.

She wakened while it was still dark and saw that he was dressing. "Where are you going?"

"I can't shock Magdalena by spending the entire night."

"Come back for breakfast?" she invited.

"Thank you, but I need to go into town."

"We've used up the supply?"

"Not likely, you voracious woman." Dressed, he came to the bed and leaned down to place his hands on either side of her head. "Good morning, love." He kissed her very sweetly. "Where are my spurs?"

"On the table by the front door."

"I need them."

"To ride ... what?"

"To remind myself I'm walking."

"I could buy you a horse."

"No, thanks. I have everything I need."

"Trisha's Rick comes this afternoon."

"I remember. Want to come with me for a ride in

the beautiful Texas countryside? That would leave them alone to sort themselves out. I know a place we could skinny-dip."

"Is that right?"

"Yes'um."

"I've never skinny-dipped out in the wide-open spaces."

"Then it's high time you did." He was sure.

"I would be delighted to accompany you."

"I would be, too," he said. "See you later, how about a picnic first? I'll pick you up about twelve? One?"

"One."

"So you plot to sleep late and rest up for me?"

"For me."

"You selfish woman."

"Yes."

He kissed her sweetly, softly, lovingly. He said, "I'd better go, right now."

"Good-bye."

"No coaxing me to stay?"

She smiled.

"That was a *coaxing* smile!"

"No, no. It's like kisses. That smile was a smug, safe smile. You have to leave. Think of how shocked Magdalena would be."

"Women rule the world."

"I don't see how you can say that when—"

"I'll see you at one."

He went silently out of that squeaky house. She heard the slightest murmur from one spur. Then a slight sound as he crossed that hollow porch, and he was gone. How did he do that?

She turned over in the warm bed and stretched luxuriously contented, and she slept.

*   *   *

"Are you going to sleep all day?"

Naomi opened her eyes squintingly. It was Trisha sitting on the bed beside her. Trisha was a sight. She had her hair in giant curlers and a mud-pack on her face. She looked really weird to a woman just waking up and unbraced. "You look different."

"I'm wearing a mud pack."

"Oh."

"I'm nervous. I almost wish Rick would wait until after the kid is here, and I'm back to normal." She looked at her fingers on top of the bulge. "But I long to see him."

"I'm glad he's coming over this afternoon," Naomi said gently.

"Me, too." Trisha's voice was tiny.

"Only now have I remembered how he was *there*, before Brad died, and in those long months afterward."

"Yes."

"He's very special."

"I know," Trisha said, watery.

"Don't start crying."

"It would absolutely ruin my mud-pack."

"You don't need one, you must know that."

"It helps me kill time, since my friend has slept all morning. When did Decker leave."

Naomi started to laugh. "You don't know what happened."

"Nothing surprises me. He stayed all night?"

"Almost, but we were on the glider, and Wellington came up on the porch and made a peculiar sound in his throat. Decker became alert and stood up and listened, while the dog waited. It was as if Decker and the dog could communicate. Then Decker said for me to lock up the house and get out my gun be—"

"What? Why didn't you waken me?"

"No need," Naomi soothed. "I was on guard."

"A loose cannon like you?"

"I am always in perfect control."

Trisha scoffed. "Like the time of the house fire at school?"

"You always bring that up."

"Chaos."

Impatiently, Naomi asked, "Do you want to hear about last night?"

"If it's pornographic, I'm in no condition—"

"Jones's men tore down the dam."

"No!" Trisha exclaimed.

"Yes."

"Those rats!"

"Well, it wasn't built right," Naomi explained. "They were going to have to tear it down anyway, and were resigned to doing it, but the Jones people destroyed it and saved Sawbuck all that work."

"Don't make me laugh, I don't even have the room to breathe."

"John, Buzz, Joe, and Decker watched in high glee."

"That is hilarious."

"The Jones men laughed when they'd finished."

"Cut it out," Trisha cautioned. "I can't laugh."

"Decker thinks they might use dynamite if they really build the dam. He says he's going to see Jones and give him an ultimatum."

"A guy named Decker Jones can hardly be connected with the Mafia."

Naomi said, "That's what I thought."

"You mean he is?"

"Not that I know, but he seems to think he can influence Frank Jones."

"Maybe they are kin."

"There are millions of Joneses who aren't any relation. There isn't any way that Decker could be related to that monster across the fence."

"Wouldn't it be interesting if he was?"

"Good gravy, Trisha. Being pregnant has addled your wits."

"Addled..." Trisha tried the word thoughtfully. "That's a good word."

"It can't be the first time that you've heard it."

CHAPTER FOURTEEN

JUST BEFORE NOON, TRISHA STOOD IN THE DOOR to the kitchen and gasped, "You're going on a... picnic? Now?"

Naomi turned from the kitchen sink and replied, "Not for another hour. Why?"

"And you expect me to sit here from one until four o'clock *all by myself*, waiting for Rick?"

"Is that a problem?"

Trisha shrieked and clutched her giant curlers.

Naomi nodded one long nod, up and down, until her chin touched her chest. To clarify the situation, Naomi said, "Decker has invited me to go skinny-dipping."

"Rub it in."

"Skinny-dipping? Haven't you ever gone, either? Want to come along?"

With great irony, Trisha snarled, "It would ruin my mud pack."

"If you don't take that off, right now, your skin is liable to come off with it."

"I've never known anyone who could give another person confidence the way you do."

Naomi put an index finger to her forehead to indicate great thought. "You're nervous."

"How miraculous that you would discern that."

Naomi continued her prediction. "You want me to stick around."

"Marvelous." Trisha clapped her hands.

"Go take off the mud pack."

"Will you be here when I get back downstairs?"

"Like a leech." Naomi grinned at her friend. "Stage fright?"

"Yes," Trisha agreed mournfully.

"I don't know why you never went on the stage. Films. Your talent is wasted on me. I'm used to you."

"I've been perfectly calm for nine months."

Naomi went to her and hugged her. "I know."

"I wasn't calling in favors. This is pure friendship. For my support through Brad's sickness and your grief, I shall exact something a great deal more important."

Naomi nodded in understanding. "You want me to deliver the kid."

"Good God, no!"

"I helped Taffy deliver her pups. Remember? You were there."

"Taffy did it all," Trisha scoffed. "All you did was sit back and exclaim and brag on her."

"Is child birthing different? Would I have to do more than brag on you?"

"Just see to it that I get into San Antonio in plenty of time."

"You're moving in with your mother next week." Naomi smiled.

"You have a nasty sense of humor."

"Since you've spent so much time in mud pack and

curlers, I don't believe you'll want to go on a picnic and skinny-dip. We'll stay here until Rick arrives, then we'll go skinny-dipping. Will Rick move in or will you go back to Dallas?"

"I'll see."

"You ought to stay here. The doctor knows all about you. It might not be smart to go off to a strange doctor and start all over."

"There's no problem. I just have to get there in plenty of time."

Naomi smiled at her friend. "Rick is welcome here."

"Thank you."

Naomi smiled wider. "You're welcome. Do you want some help getting the mud pack off?"

"If you wouldn't mind."

"I would be honored."

Trisha couldn't frown because of the mud but she said, "Stuff it."

"Are you feeling a little out of sorts?"

"I'm terrified."

Naomi exclaimed, "Of *what*, for Pete's sake. Rick? He loves you!"

"He thought I'd betrayed him."

"Now he knows better," Naomi soothed. "Everything will be fine. You'll see. Let's use the bath down here. You're going to be radiant."

"I feel like a cow." Trisha's voice trembled.

"You're exaggerating. You really don't look as if you're that close to delivery."

"The kid will probably be a ten-monther."

"There's a cheerful thought." Naomi laughed. "You two can get closer, before you're separated and someone else gets to hold the kid."

They went into the downstairs bath and proceeded

to remove the mask. "There," said Naomi. "We have gilded the lily. Do you know that's a misquote? The purpose was to explain redundancy. The original quote is 'gilding gold or painting the lily white.' Both redundant. But it was corrupted to senselessness. The corruption from misusage is like the misuse of 'excuse me' in the place of 'pardon me.'"

"Our lesson for today?" Trisha gave Naomi a droll look.

"I'm nervous, too."

Trisha frowned. "Why would you be nervous? Do you think Rick is going to do something stupid?"

"Rick? Why would I worry about you two? I think I'm in really deep with Decker, and I'm not sure I'm ready for something like that."

"You're telling me this to distract me, right?"

"Yes." Naomi was impatient. "I fall in love with men so that you have something to think about. Don't be so dense."

Trisha said slowly, "Then you really are serious about Decker? You're not just using him?"

"You know me better than that."

Taking her time, Trisha commented slowly in honest evaluation, "From what I've seen of him, he's worth the effort. I wonder why he came to Sawbuck. He's no drifter."

"He is so sweet."

"Be careful of yourself," Trisha warned. "You're very vulnerable."

"I'm strong."

"Good. I like hearing that."

"And, Trisha, so are you. This meeting with Rick will be so natural. It will be as if you had never parted. You have some explaining to do, but once that's through, everything will be all right. Just watch."

"I honestly didn't know I loved Rick this much. Without him, life wouldn't be much."

"It's going to be okay. Wait and see."

"Wait! I should have gone back with the florist's delivery man. Then this meeting would be past. I am so nervous."

"You had a good night's sleep. You're going to take a calm nap, and you'll be just fine. Look at you. You're gorgeous."

Trisha stood up and looked in the mirror. She nodded at her reflection. "I think I'll take the curlers out before he gets here."

"Oh. I'm a little disappointed."

"Be quiet."

Naomi laughed. "What would you like for lunch?" She led the way back to the kitchen. "Decker will be here soon. Share with us? I'll make deviled eggs the way you like them. It's really getting warm today. A picnic lunch on the side porch would be nice. Okay?" She turned from the refrigerator and looked at Trisha.

"I'm sorry to spoil your afternoon."

With complete candor, Naomi assured her friend, "You aren't."

"A picnic and skinny-dipping would be fun."

"I can agree. With the dam finished in the next couple of weeks, and a good gully washer, we could skinny-dip right off the side porch. Think of that! You, Rick, and the kid can come down weekends and—"

"I don't want Rick skinny-dipping with you around."

"Ahhh. Jealousy? Of a mouse?"

"What mouse?"

"That's what Decker calls me."

Trisha was astonished. "He thinks you're . . ." She really laughed. Holding the bulge and groaning, she laughed. "Wait until he knows the real you."

Sanctimoniously, Naomi said, "A little at a time."

"Does he know about Brad?"

"I've tried to mention Brad a couple of times, but Decker cut me off."

"He should know."

"Brad doesn't enter into this."

"Ahhh."

"What does that mean?"

"Just a sound," Trisha explained as she watched Naomi avidly and smiled.

Naomi exchanged a long look with Trisha, and they both smiled a different way. It was the touchstone of knowing each other so well. Whatever Naomi did, Trisha could understand.

Decker came in his truck with Wellington. He came in and greeted the two women. He stood completely still but didn't change expression for two heartbeats when Naomi said they would be picnicking on the side screened porch. "The mosquitos are getting bad after the rain," she explained.

He nodded, then, accepting her decision. But Trisha couldn't allow that. She explained, "I have stage fright. Rick is coming this afternoon, and I'm nervous about talking to him again."

"It wouldn't have happened if you'd been honest with him to begin with."

"How like a man to take up for another man," Trisha flared.

"You want me to be dishonest and side with you?" He was elaborately surprised.

"Yes."

"Oh." But he didn't say anything more.

"Well?" Trisha prodded.

"I'm trying to reword my whole argument to slant your way and it's impossible."

Trisha turned to Naomi. "He is tactless."

"I'm honest!" But the claws in his conscience dug in to deny that. He snapped his mouth closed and turned aside, his spurs stirring.

There was a little silence, and then he offered, "Magdalena has a cold."

Naomi's head came up.

"It's just the sniffles," he soothed. "I went to see her to tell her about the dam." He looked over at Trisha. "Did Naomi tell you about the Jones people tearing down the dam?"

Trisha nodded, still hostile.

"Magdalena laughed a little and then said, 'There will be trouble.'"

Naomi agreed, "Yes. The dam will bring it to a head."

"Joe has an infrared camera and took pictures of them tearing the dam apart. You did have permission to block the dam in flood?"

"Yes."

"With the pictures as proof, we may have them. We took more pictures today of the broken pipe and scattered rocks."

"We'll sue," Naomi said calmly.

They carried food out to the table on the side, screened porch.

Helping the ladies into their chairs, Decker promised, "I'll see Frank Jones and explain to him that he can't walk over Sawbuck."

"How are you going to arrange that?" Naomi inquired impatiently. "He's unavailable. I've tried."

"I'll do it." He seated himself and sipped the tea. Then he took from the plate of deviled eggs and passed it, warning, "You only get one each, I get the rest."

Naomi grinned, but Trisha became indignant. "Oh, no, you don't."

In excellent competitiveness, Decker bargained, "I'll give you two ham sandwiches for your hard-boiled eggs."

"Are you crazy? How could I eat two ham sandwiches? I want my other three halves of deviled eggs."

"You're going to be a selfish mother. You have to learn to give in to other people. I'm trying to show you how things are going to be and, as usual, you can't see what you're supposed to do. You don't consider anybody else."

Trisha said, "Hah! It's you who is the selfish one. You want all the eggs!"

"That's not true. I've allowed each of you to have one half. You can ask Naomi if she'll let you have hers."

"No." Naomi then laughed. Decker had done it again! Look at Trisha. There she was, no longer faint-hearted and fearful. She was challenged, her eyes were sparkling, and she was leaning forward ready to do battle. How did Decker know how to do that?

"If you have four halves of eggs," Decker went on to Trisha, "you'll get blotchy."

"I don't blotch with eggs." Trisha was strident.

"I noticed right away that these eggs are different,"

Decker announced. "They're local eggs, right?"

"No," Naomi contributed. "These came in shells. Local eggs come in cups. The eggs are shaken out of the shells and the shells are cleaned and filled with confetti so—"

"Oh," Decker said. "Well. You can have two halves."

"I get all four. You can bargain with Naomi. You might have some influence with her. Not me."

He said to Naomi, "You do get one."

"How generous."

"For the other three, I'll take you skinny-dipping."

"You're not supposed to say such things in front of a pregnant woman," Trisha scolded. "Prenatal influence."

"I forgot. Sorry." He said to Naomi, "We'll go s-k-i-n-n-y d-i-p-p-i-n-g."

She laughed at him. "I'll give you all four."

He looked over at Trisha, "Would *you* like—"

"No."

He glanced back at Naomi before he looked at his plate, so his comment was directed to her. "We'll have to let the kid come visit so it can experience kindness and generosity."

Indignantly Trisha accused, "And you'll get all her deviled eggs!"

"Her?" Decker raised his eyebrows.

"Yes."

He looked over at Naomi. "How did Trisha figure that out?"

"She's going to be a stage actress and Trisha is going to be a stage mother."

"Yeah." Decker didn't say another word until he'd finished eating.

The two women commented and discussed the pictures taken of the dam. They decided to take pictures of the one working well.

"It would be hard to show that the other wells weren't working," Naomi commented thoughtfully. "I'm not sure how to do that."

Finished eating, Decker advised, "A video camera. Show Magdalena turning on the sink spigot and nothing coming out and have her looking sad."

"Perfect." Trisha sounded surprised.

Naomi said, "We could go into town and get one now. Okay, Trish?"

"I'll probably be riding back to Dallas with Rick. I'd better not push it. Wouldn't later be soon enough?"

Decker agreed, "Soon enough."

"I haven't packed my things. I've sorted them. But I did get out a small bag in case we decide to go right away."

"I could send your things to you."

"Do you feel I'm leaving you in the lurch?"

Naomi laughed.

But Decker said, "You're a third wheel."

Naomi protested, "Decker!"

"I was just helping ease her conscience. She was starting a guilt jag."

Even Trisha grinned.

As they cleared the table, Naomi whispered to Decker, "Don't say anything controversial, we want Trisha drowsy for a nap."

So, sleepy-eyed, Decker sat on the porch. Yawning. Saying drowsily, "Hmmm?" when addressed. He lulled both women. They began to yawn. Then Trisha said, "I can't keep my eyes open," and she trailed off upstairs.

They heard her door close and the ceiling fan go

on with its gentle hum. Naomi looked over at Decker
. . . and he was grinning, wide awake!

"You fraud."

He nodded. "One does as one must. You *did* claim
she needed a nap."

Naomi narrowed her eyes suspiciously. "Do you
really liked deviled eggs that well?"

"Tolerably." He rubbed his mouth as his sparkling
eyes danced with laughter. "We could skinny-dip in
the shower."

"You animal."

"Yeah."

"I can barely move. You were very convincing in
your sleepiness. I need a nap."

"Could we sleep on the glider? I might be too noisy
upstairs."

"Noisy?"

"When I make love to you."

"I'm taking a nap." She lifted her chin.

"That's just your brain. 'I don't need no conversation.' I just want to play with the rest of you."

He slid her the most salaciously wicked grin she'd
ever seen. She mentioned thoughtfully, "There's a
couch in the morning room at the back of the house."

"Let's give it a try."

Backless, a little wider than a sofa, it was a plush
Victorian resting couch. It rounded over at the top
like a curling wave. Decker surveyed it with a smile.
"My grandmother had one of these." He went over
and sat on it. "My God, it has the original stuffing.
It's like lying on a cloud." He stood up and gestured.
"Come here, woman, you're about to make all my
adolescent dreams come true."

She stood inert as he removed all of her clothing,

chiding her, saying, "You need to dress more simply. A sack shift, no underwear. Leave your hair down."

"I feel like an object."

"Yeah. The object of my desire."

"A warm body."

"Right."

"Any body would do."

He undid her bra but he turned her around and looked at her face. Then he tilted her chin so that he could see into her eyes. "I thought you wanted me the way I crave you." He was dead serious.

She understood him. "I want you"—she measured a hair's breadth between thumb and forefinger—"that much."

"Oh. Well. I guess I need to work on your attitude. Do you need a coaxing I'm-attracted kiss?"

"Not especially."

"Stone dead cold. My, that does present a problem." He paced over to the window while he unbuttoned and removed his shirt. Then he sat down and took off his boots, spurs and all. He shook his head and said "Hmmm" a couple of times as if he had considered and discarded solutions to her. He was out of his jeans and had skimmed off his underwear when he got back to her.

He bent her over one arm and kissed her in sipping kisses, then he wammied her with a you're-driving-me-crazy kiss. It steamed up the humid room, spiraled around inside her skin, circling her bones and disrupting her nervous system entirely.

When she was half fainting, and their breathing was erratic, he gasped, "That caught your attention, yet?"

She nodded wobblily.

"Then we move on."

He gave her the whole span of progressively alluring kisses, naming them along the way in breathless growls. But his hands were hot, his mouth scalding, and no man should *ever* have been allowed to learn to kiss that way, and move that way, and touch like that. It was scandalous.

And she purred.

He carried her over to that sinfully soft and seductive couch and laid her on it as he said, "Okay, you can go to sleep now."

But then he lay with her, and he used her body deliciously. He ventured and investigated and touched and licked and suckled and petted and squeezed and smoothed and kneaded and felt where all he chose. He used his furnace body and his scalding tongue and lips, his hot palms and his long inquisitive fingers. He kissed and nuzzled as he explored. He fitted them together in such astonishing ways that she murmured and exclaimed and reached and turned and helped.

The humid day and their exertions filmed their bodies, making them hotly slick and slippery as they entwined, and they were ready and needy. Their ache built to incredible desire and their minds were swooning with passion before he finally allowed their frantic, tumultuous, shuddering, thrilling release.

And they lay like broken, discarded dolls, completely spent, totally inoperable. They slept as if drugged.

They overslept.

The next thing they knew Decker heard a car. Naomi felt him rouse and she opened languid eyes to smile. He kissed her gently and said, "I think Rick's here. Don't attack me again."

"I wonder at your adolescent dreams!"

"Yeah. Lurid. You must have been a telepathic part of them because you knew exactly how to react."

She gasped in shock, "I?" and puffed in indignation, "I've never even *dreamed* of—"

"Shhh. They'll hear you and think you're trying to seduce me, and, Buttercup, I just can't, right now."

Naomi laughed soundlessly.

So they heard the knock on the front-door panel. That made Decker raise his eyebrows at Naomi, and they understood that Trisha hadn't allowed the sound of Rick's car to act as a heralding of his arrival. She'd waited until he had had to knock. In the back room, the lovers frowned. Trisha was going to make Rick sweat. And they heard Trisha's footsteps as she went to the door.

Rick, too, understood that Trisha was going to make him go the whole nine yards. And he was ready to comply. Whatever it took. He carried a nosegay of tiny pink roses with baby's breath and pink ribbons. The selection was to indicate that whatever the baby was, it would be acceptable to him, and he was wishy-washy with sentiment. A smile hovered on his lips.

Trisha wore a soft pastel dress of vertical panels and bone-colored slippers. She looked as cool as a man's vision. She was beautiful. She said, "Rick!" as if she hadn't written him the note inviting him there and was surprised by seeing him.

He said, "It's good to see you, Trish."

"Won't you come in? I have tea."

"Thank you." He handed her the nosegay.

"Why, how lovely. Thank you."

"I want to kiss you."

"Why?"

"Trisha, don't make this difficult."

She gave him a distant stare and declared, "I wouldn't think of doing anything like that."

"I want you to know that even if the baby wasn't mine, I would want—"

"What?" she asked in a stilted voice. "What did you say?"

"I said that I would want your baby even if it wasn't mine."

"'My baby.'"

"Trisha, don't go difficult on me."

"I've never been difficult."

"You've been a handful ever since I first set eyes on you and..." He realized he was botching everything. "Trisha..."

"I think you should leave. Here. Take the flowers. And the basket. I have no use for them. *MY CHILD* and I have no need for anyone. We will get along by ourselves. Go away." She said it low and serious and mean.

He looked at her for a while and his face got red. "It's just a good thing you're in a delicate condition or I would turn you over my knee and give you your first spanking that you should have had twenty years ago. Trisha, you are acting. You are being The Betrayed Woman. Don't you forget that you ran out on me. You never called or wrote to me. I searched everywhere and here you were just sitting around waiting for me to come get you. I'm here. You are acting—"

"I don't know of any reason to take any more abuse from you. Will you leave or shall I call the houseman?"

In the back room, the conversation by the front door had become quite audible. At "houseman" Decker put his finger to his chest and gave Naomi a questioning look. He hissed, "Should I get dressed?"

Naomi shrugged.

In the front hall, Rick said, "I'm not leaving."

"Oh, yes, you are, or I shall scream. I cannot tolerate your calling me a whore."

"What?" He was furiously indignant.

"You said—"

"That was the other day. This is now. I didn't mean that. You surprised me. And when I asked you, all those months ago, you *did say* that you were all right at that time."

"I thought you meant in taking care of Naomi. Who could think about details at a time like that?"

"Well, *some*body should have been."

"But not you. Will you leave?"

"Trisha, if this baby was another man's—" he began again earnestly.

But Trisha put her hands to her head and screamed.

Dressed, Decker and Naomi came into the hall and stood in the doorway.

Trisha flung an arm out to point at Rick. "Remove him."

"Hi, Rick."

"Decker, isn't it?" The two shook hands. "Naomi, are you okay?"

She replied, "Yes, thank you."

"Get him *out* of here!" Trisha demanded.

Decker said, "How about going out on the porch?"

"I need to talk to her."

Decker nodded. "She's particularly hostile right now. Why don't you go out on the porch until she cools off a little."

Trisha turned and said, "Naomi, this *is* the kind of

man that Decker is, do you understand? Pay attention. Any *real* man would have thrown Rick out on his ear for all those accusations about me being a whore."

"I never said that!" Rick protested.

"Oh, yes, you did!" Trisha accused. "And you said that you were ashamed of me!"

"God dang woman!" Rick's words exploded. "You took me by—"

Decker interrupted, "The porch. Neutral territory."

"I hate to give up this beachhead. She is so damned stubborn and difficult—"

"I am nothing of the kind!"

"—and loud."

"Get him out of here!"

Naomi coaxed, "To the porch. Just to the porch. Trisha is feeling crowded."

And Decker looked over at Trisha's stomach, but he looked at her face and he didn't say what he almost did. Instead he said, "Go upstairs and calm down."

Trisha took a deep breath—

Rick said, "Be careful how you talk to her."

Decker turned his back on Trisha and looked at Rick. He gave Rick a broad wink and said, "It's the only way to treat such a stubborn, unfair woman."

Rick said, "Come outside while I explain manners to you." He took Decker's elbow and started for the door.

Trisha said, "Decker, hit him one for me."

And Rick got indignant. He let go of Decker's arm and turned, opened his mouth, but Decker jerked him through the door.

CHAPTER FIFTEEN

THE NEXT FEW DAYS WERE A LITTLE STRANGE at Naomi's house. Rick Thomas had set up housekeeping on the front porch, and Trisha paced from window to window keeping track of him, ordering him to leave. But when Rick went to Decker's store to shower or to use the privy or the public phone, Trisha would become anxious and ask, "Isn't he there? He didn't leave, did he?"

Of course, in that first day, everyone in Sawbuck knew Trisha's lover was there, living on Naomi's porch, and that Trisha had spurned him. The town took sides right down the gender line.

By osmosis, the commuters found out. "What's that car doing down at Naomi's?" the doughnut/coffee buyers inquired. And gradually the word spread. "How's it going with Romeo? Tell him to give her flowers." "He might try serenading her. He *can* sing, can't he?"

Decker explained it all to Magdalena who laughed so hard that she began coughing, and Decker had to leave so that she could stop laughing.

With Rick as porch watchdog for Trisha's safety, Naomi and Decker went to San Antonio where she

bought a video camera. When they returned to Sawbuck, they took pictures of all of Sawbuck. They got
the suggested one of Magdalena futilely turning on
the spigot in the sink. She arranged all her wrinkles
into lines of despair. It was clear that ancient lady beat
even Trisha in drama. Magdalena was brilliant.

Decker borrowed Buzz's color TV, took it and his
own VCR to Magdalena's, and showed her that seg-
ment. She was smug. They would have shown her the
rest, but she coughed so hard that again they had to
leave. Decker told her granddaughter, "Magdalena
should see a doctor."

The granddaughter, who was only sixty-two, replied, "It's just a cough. She coughs all the time. She
just needs some more peppermints."

So they bought her peppermints.

And Decker went to see his uncle.

Hostile, with a Cuban cigar clamped between his
teeth and his hands clasped behind his back, Uncle
Gimme stood like a bulldog, blocking his front door.
"You're a big disappointment to me, boy. I thought
blood was thicker than sex."

"Careful."

"It's you who oughtta be careful or you'll find you
stick in my craw. That could be chancy for you."

"You order the dam destroyed?" Decker swore
Frank's instant expression of surprise was genuine.

"What dam. You building a goddamned *dam* for
those squatters?"

"How could you call them 'squatters' when they've
been there so much longer than you've been here?"

"Tell me about that dam."

Decker obliged. "Since Sawbuck is denied water, by
you, this is one solution."

"They can't dam the creek."

"I understand that before you began water spraying so extensively and between irrigation floodings, the wash ran sweet water from the aquifer."

"I got as much right to water as the next man."

"You take more than your share. You're robbing them of their livelihood."

"Who you backing?" His voice was murderously soft.

"Sawbuck."

"You damned traitor."

"I am your kinsman so I'm obligated to be courteous, but I can think of the kind of man that you are. Why are you so greedy?"

"Get off my property! I don't ever want to see your face again. To me, you're dead!"

"Good-bye, Uncle."

"Go to hell."

Decker turned away, and Elise ran out of the house to Frank. She was highly distressed and said, "No, Frank! Stop this!"

Cynically, Decker said, "Good-bye, Auntie." He smiled before going toward the truck.

His uncle said, "Don't you touch that truck, it's mine!"

Decker halted in surprise. "How can you speak to me? You just said I was dead."

"You heard me, you bastard, I—"

Very dangerously Decker turned back. "What are you calling my mother?"

Frank was joggled. "I didn't mean nothing about her. Only you must've been switched at the hospital, because you could never have been born of that lady."

"Frank, you do amaze me. When you can calm down, we'll talk about saving Sawbuck."

Frank spit the cigar out of his mouth and turned purple. Decker got into the disputed pickup and drove out, watching in the rearview mirror as Elise soothed her irate husband . . . while looking anxiously after Decker.

But it was still a surprise to Decker when Elise came into Sawbuck the next day. It was early on Friday that she *got off the bus,* and she *had* tried to look ordinary. Decker smiled inwardly at such a futile attempt as he sat among the other idle men who had nothing to do.

Since the Jones men had dismantled the dam for them, they'd had a couple of days rest while Ned searched for another flood gate and some replacement sewer pipes. So they were all there to witness Elise's first visit to Sawbuck. Decker watched Elise stand on the sidewalk, as the bus disappeared off down the road.

She had already cased the town and the visible occupants, so she slowly turned her head and set her eyes on . . . Decker.

He thought: Oh, hell. Every man jack there in Sawbuck knew Elise was Frank Jones's wife. She had never "seen" any of them, but even Buzz said he wanted to see Frank Jones as he slept next to that young wife of his. Especially some women never appear to realize how visible they are. If they aren't aware of people, they think of themselves as unseen, unnoticed. Elise was just such a one.

Decker saw that she tried to walk unprovocatively, which was just plain silly. How could she do something so ordinary as just . . . walk? Her body was made for

men to watch and want, and even her stiffened movements couldn't disguise that fact.

Being a canine gentleman and uninhibited by conscience or fraud, Wellington met Elise with courteous
greetings for his bath attendant. She absently touched
his dirty head.

No witnessing man moved. They were paralyzed,
waiting for her to come to them, their fantasies longing to be the target of her approach. She never looked
away from Decker, but he didn't rise from his chair.

"Sir," Elise addressed Decker. "I need to discuss a
problem with you."

She had come there for a last attempt at laying him.
He knew that. He stood up, "Ma'am, I'm new in Sawbuck, perhaps one of these other gentlemen can assist
you."

She didn't even look aside. She formed the word
with those soft, maddening lips. "No."

"Then would you step down the way, away, so that
we can be private?"

There were snickers and snorts of envious humor
from the watchers.

In avid silence, the two walked down the cracked
walk under that tin overhang, and Decker's spurs
were the only sounds. At the last of the stores, he
stepped down from the last of the walk and turned
to offer her a hand. Even as he made the gesture, he
knew he risked having her throw herself on him and
embarrassing him scarlet. Her just *being* there would
mean complex explanations due to Naomi who was
improbably watching from her attic window, over the
roof of the stores across the street. Naomi would have
no reason to be watching, but Decker seemed to feel
her stare. His ears turned red.

Elise shunned his proffered hand, stepped down onto the ground with no problem, and advanced with him under the spreading oak that was alongside his store.

"Now, Auntie, you've put me in one hell of a bind? You do understand that. What in blue blazes made you come over here in broad daylight to see me. You've got to know everybody in this town has stuck pins in wax dolls of you and—"

She looked startled.

"Didn't you know they all know who you are?"

"No."

"Why are you here." It was a statement to begin her explanation. Which had better be good.

She didn't speak at first. Decker stayed clear of her so that she couldn't touch him. He was anxious only that she leave . . . how? She'd come to Sawbuck on the bus. He would have to take her home. Good God Almighty. He resettled his Stetson and moved so that his spurs clinked.

Elise said, "Your visit was very upsetting to Frank. How important is this dam?"

"Vital to the town. They have no water but that one pump." He gestured to the one by the fence. "The whole town drinks water that's held stored in oil barrels."

"Why?"

"We're on the bottom edge of the Edwards Aquifer. That's a miracle underground river that's been there forever. First San Antonio's million people, then Frank using it for spraying crops, sucks up all the dwindling supply of water. Before it's used up entirely, he ought to begin reverting to crops that need no irrigation. If he doesn't change crops in these times of plenty, he'll go broke."

"There's nothing else for these people?"

"They have only enough land for truck farming. They can't commercially grow milo or sunflowers or cotton. Most of the people are descendants of those who were here since this land belonged to Mexico. It's their home."

"I see."

"We need water."

"You are one of this town?"

"Yes."

"Decker, I love Frank."

Sneering, he elaborated, "The faithful wife."

Elise didn't take offense. She accepted his statement as of no consequence, but she replied to it. "Yes. We can't get pregnant. He won't admit to a problem. He won't be tested. You are so like him. Would you go to this clinic and donate sperm for us?"

"Good Lord."

She began silently to cry. She did that beautifully with only a spilling of tears which oddly seemed to annoy her. She ignored them. "You would be kin. It wouldn't be a stranger. You are of Frank's blood. He admires you—"

"Not lately."

"Once he said something about you being the most like him. That's why he asked you down here."

"So that you could screw me?" His voice was sour and scoffing.

"There was some 'joking' talk," she admitted. "I was led to believe he wouldn't mind. He allowed us to be together. You know that."

"I could never believe it."

"We are collecting his sperm for concentrated tries. If you donate some, no one would know for sure if the baby wasn't Frank's, if it works. Please." She stepped over to him and put the slip of paper in his shirt pocket. She did that without touching his body even with the tips of her fingers. Again she asked intensely, "Please."

"I've never heard of anything so outlandish, Elise. What are you trying to do to me?"

"We need your help. Think of us. I truly love Frank."

"—his money."

"I have my own. I signed a prenuptial agreement. It is generous but there is nothing in it for a child. That is part of our pact. If I have a child, it is mine. Decker. I really love Frank."

"So you want my baby?"

"A baby," she corrected.

"Yeah."

"He won't adopt."

"Why not any of the eager studs on the place?"

"Don't be insulting."

"You've propositioned me. Why not them?"

"I have no desire for another man."

He chuffed a disbelieving laugh. "Yeah. And you were on my bed, naked, by mistake? You lost your way in your own house?"

"I thought I could do this more easily. If you will recall, I told you it was the right time?"

He watched her, remembering. "'A good time.' I thought you were offering fun and games."

"You are so like him."

"I'm getting tired of that insult."

"He's just frustrated. If he had someone to plan

for, a child, he would be more like you. Help me. Please. Think of your uncle. Help us."

"There is no way—"

"Think on it, first. The sperm can be frozen. You'll never have to see us again. Just give us this."

"If it was my kid, I wouldn't want him under Frank's influence."

"Frank is a good man."

"He's a sleazy wheeler-dealer."

"He's frustrated."

"I believe he's killed a couple of men."

"And you? Haven't you? Not him. There was an accidental shooting that he covered. And there was a murder. An appropriate one."

"He's judge and jury?"

"If the truth had come out, too many innocent people would have suffered needlessly."

"I can't swallow that."

"You don't have to." She dismissed the need and continued: "You have my word. I investigated him before I married him. I knew his reputation. I saw all those old news clips."

"And you saw his bank account."

"Do you know my family?"

"No."

She countered, "I know yours, and I know why you were beaten and where you were at that time."

"How did you find out?"

"And I know about Anne."

"My God," he groaned. "Frank has no knowledge of that, I'm sure of it. How do you know?"

"I tell you those things to show you that I truly investigated Frank. Do you believe me?"

"I may have to."

"Then give us the benefit of your doubt. Help us."

"I'll consider it. But I doubt it."

"Please."

And Decker finally saw her as a woman instead of a teasing poster. He stared at her. "You're real."

She didn't respond at all.

"Do you want me to take you home?"

"No."

"How are you going to get there?"

"Chico is coming by for gas almost right away, and I'll bum a ride."

"Since you're the brains in this outfit, what am I to tell the salivating mob as to why you're here?"

She slid her eyes sideways toward the town and saw some of the men standing tensely out in the street, watching. She lifted incredible, undarkened eyelashes and looked fully at Decker. "Tell them I asked you to breed me. They'll scoff and laugh and never believe it for a minute. And your reputation for honesty will not be smirched."

He laughed and relaxed.

Slowly, not talking, he walked with her back down the sidewalk, past the hastily reseated, silent men, and escorted her to the filling station. Buzz was there. He was filling Chico's gas tank. Chico didn't "see" Decker. Buzz just watched Elise. Elise was the only woman Decker had ever seen ignore Buzz. She didn't even know he was there.

Decker tipped his hat to her and went back up the walk. The men were like dogs getting ready for a hunt. They almost visibly wiggled in anticipation. Decker sat down on his chair and faced them calmly.

"What'd she want?"

They didn't ask who she was, they knew. And

Decker gave a long, put-upon sigh before he replied, "She heard about me being here, and knew my reputation, so she petitioned me to breed her."

They fell off their chairs laughing.

Then the men leaned back and relaxed, but when they began speculating on how it would be to breed Elise, Decker chided them as ungentlemanly. He wouldn't allow her name to be bandied. So the men figured it had been a serious confrontation, that sex had had nothing to do with it.

"She asked how important the dam was to the town."

That stymied them all. They mulled over the fact that she might be different from what they'd thought. But could she, or would she help them? Maybe they could get her to slip a sharp knife between Jones's ribs while he slept? Decker doubted that.

So with the men, explaining Elise's visit was easy. But Decker knew that Naomi would be another matter entirely.

In the heat of the August day, Decker clinked down to Naomi's, and an unshaven Rick greeted him from the glider. "Who was she?"

"Frank Jones's wife."

"Wow."

"Why 'wow'? You didn't see her."

"I heard about her."

"You're too useless sitting here on the porch with nothing to do," Decker observed.

"One of the commuters gave me a guitar and an instruction book. I've been practicing."

Decker nodded. "For serenading."

"Yeah. I'm driving Trisha crazy," he said with

pleased comfort. "She'll give in just to get me to quit practicing."

With real interest, Decker inquired, "Who's running your office?"

"My dad. He and Arlene, my mother, have been traveling and sightseeing for several years, and he leaped at the chance to get back in harness."

Decker could see that. But he dawdled, wasting time, waiting for Naomi to acknowledge he was there. She came to the door.

"I thought I heard your voice. I've heard Rick's all day, and it was such a pleasure to hear someone else's."

"She isn't a very good hostess," Rick mentioned.

"Oh?" Decker turned to survey his love.

Rick complained, "She wants the porch tidy. She wanted me on the side porch, and it is screened, but this is more comfortable and I get to greet the visitors and hear the gossip."

Still standing on the porch, Decker looked around, considering Rick's telling words. Naomi hadn't tried to run Rick off, she just wanted him tidy. He was not. The table was piled with books, folders, and loose papers weighted down with rocks. There was excess clothing and a spare pair of shoes someone had supplied. There were sheets and a blanket and a pillow. There were empty glasses and used dishes.

Decker commented, "You do appear to make yourself at home."

"Well, with Trisha about to deliver *our* baby"—Rick said the last two words at the window—"I thought I ought to be handy." He stated that in the manner of a man who accepts his nobility as his burden. "She won't go home with me."

"She spoken to you yet?" Decker inquired.

"Not kindly."

Naomi said placidly, "We're rather sick of him."

Decker smiled at his love.

But she just allowed her gaze to rest on him in a neutral way. It made Decker smug that Naomi might be hostile about another woman. He guessed, "You're waiting to hear what Frank Jones's wife wanted with me."

"Who?"

She didn't change expression, and he laughed. Rick was an interested observer as Decker explained to Naomi, "She asked how important the dam is to the town of Sawbuck."

"Why."

"Apparently Frank's apoplectic over our building the dam, and she loves him and is alarmed by his distress."

"How precious," she observed insincerely.

That made Rick laugh, too.

Decker chided, "A good Christian woman would be compassionate."

Naomi shot him a side look that should have shaken him. "How come she had to wiggle her tush over here on the bus?"

"She came incognito."

Rick laughed immoderately, and there was an indignant sound from inside the house by the window.

Naomi contributed: "You must be making a try at humor. She would still be noticeable with a sack over her head."

"When did you see her?" Decker watched as Naomi glanced in jerks at everything but him. He told her gently, "She's nothing but a rag, a bone, and a hank of hair."

Naomi almost smiled.

"She's got eyelashes you wouldn't believe."

Naomi stiffened.

"She likes little kids."

Naomi gazed out over the wash.

"But I don't believe she'd ever fight fire demons." Mentally he apologized to that brave woman. Elise was fighting for Frank, who was worse than any fire demon, but Elise loved him.

Naomi looked back at Decker very solemnly.

"She can't hold a candle to you, Mouse."

"Mouse?" Rick frowned.

Decker looked over at Rick. "Don't you have a home of your own?"

"You're standing in it."

"Good gravy, Naomi, you don't have any taste at all in people. First Trisha who is such a testy woman, and now this yahoo."

From the inside by the window, Trisha's voice said, "Knock him off the porch, Rick."

Rick replied, "I have a sprained wrist."

Trisha exclaimed, "Sprained *wrist*? How did you sprain your wrist?"

"Trying to play that damned guitar for you."

"The reason you can't play," Trisha told him succinctly, "is because you have no ear."

"I play with my fingers and thumbs," he replied loftily. "Not my ear."

Decker asked Naomi, "Do you hear this stuff all day?"

"All day and half the night."

"Let's go skinny-dipping."

Rick sat up. "Me, too?"

"No," Decker replied.

Naomi said with exaggerated patience, "You are supposed to ask me to go swimming. You don't specify what we'll wear. How can I agree to go skinny-dipping with you in front of all these people?"

He looked around and saw that Buzz had one foot on the bottom step and stood with his hands hanging by their thumbs from his jeans pockets. He was smiling. With Decker's eyes on him, he said, "Me, too," and looked over at Naomi.

"What are you doing here?" Decker's tone wasn't cordial.

"Idle. Somebody tore down the dam, we can't find a flood gate, and there's nothing to do."

"Well, you're not going swimming with us, that's for certain."

Buzz coaxed, "Naomi, you want me along, right?"

"You can go with Decker. I'm going into town."

"It's going to rain," Buzz told her.

"How do you know that?" Naomi looked up at the overcast sky that was white and not dark or threatening.

"My Indian heritage," Buzz responded.

"Oh." Naomi looked at him seriously.

"And the forecast on the radio at the filling station."

"Semi-Indians bend the truth," Decker warned Naomi. "Real Indians don't speak with the forked tongue."

Buzz sighed with patience. Then he told them: "There's going to be a gully washer west of here. We might get a real volume of runoff."

Naomi looked over at the wash in panic. "And the dam is gone."

With his usual spur clink, Decker walked over to that side of the porch and looked out over the empty basin. "You know, if we blocked that end, somehow, we could empty it in the spring, fix the dam, and get the next runoff."

"How're we going to do that?" Buzz was next to him on the porch.

Rick stood up. "You're going to build a dam? Where? Let me help."

"Rick!" said the empty window.

"You'll be fine here, honey. I'm going out of my mind not doing anything but practicing the guitar. We'll all come back after the dam's built and sing to you . . . uh-h-h-h, how big *is* this dam?"

"It's more than a day's work," promised Buzz.

"We need a front-load tractor," Decker decided. "Does anyone have such around here?"

"Hernandez," Buzz didn't hesitate to reply. "I'll go find out if we can borrow it." Buzz turned back on the stairs. "He might want rent."

"A case of beer?"

"We need to flag Ned down and ask his advice." Buzz waited for confirmation.

Decker agreed, "Yes. See if we can get some commuter volunteers. Are Joe and Ann doing the dinners tonight? Good. Tell them to spread the word. We need pickups. They'll need gloves. We'll see what we can do."

But Ned didn't come through Sawbuck, so they made their own decisions and it was John who took control. The Hernandez tractor didn't have a front loader. So Decker went to the pay phone and called Elise. "We need a front-loading tractor for the dam. What are our chances?"

"Zero. I would do about anything for you, Decker, in a swap, but I can't go against Frank in this way. However, you might see Mr. Farrino Jenkins who lives beyond Sawbuck about five miles. He would be fascinated."

"How will I know his place?"

"There's a crossbar over the entrance trace with Farrino Jen—"

"—kins on it. Right."

"If he does help you, will this count in my favor?"

"Elise, let up."

"Think hard on this."

"Yeah. Thanks." Decker hung up and turned from the booth, looking around. He saw Buzz down the road and gave a sharp whistle.

Buzz looked back, and Decker signaled him to wait. They met at a trot. "Do you know Farrino—"

"Jenkins! Yeah. Good thinking. Who'd you call?"

"Elise Jones. She wouldn't lend us theirs but she suggested Farrino."

"Let's go."

CHAPTER SIXTEEN

MR. FARRINO JENKINS WAS A SPARE, A-TYPICAL Texan. He worked at it. Somewhat past the full flower—however sparse—of his middle age, his Stetson was tall and the boots and jeans were worn. The cuffs of his blue shirt were buttoned, and the work gloves were stuffed into his hip pocket with the fingers outward so that they looked a little like an off-center rooster's tail.

His clothing looked very like those worn by Decker as he had gotten off the bus that first day. By the Jenkins's front fence, the two fakes smiled at each other.

"You Paul Jones's boy?"

"Yep."

With his arms crossed on his chest, Buzz was listening intently as he lounged indifferently against the pickup's fender.

Then Mr. Jenkins looked over at Buzz. "Who's your daddy, boy?"

Buzz shrugged.

Mr. Jenkins looked at him shrewdly. "I know you. You've been gone from here for a while, but your daddy put his stamp on you. Now don't you try to fun me, child, I know both your momma and daddy. They're good people. You still rebelling?"

"Not me."

Mr. Jenkins laughed. "What can I do for you children?"

Decker inquired, "Do you favor Frank Jones?"

"From that wordage, you must not."

Decker resettled his hat. "He's stolen the water from the town of Sawbuck."

"That is a problem. He's got a big operation going over there. You give him any chance to correct that?"

"He had a deep well dug by his fence."

"Ah." Mr. Jenkins lifted his chin and looked at the two visitors from under the brim of his Stetson. "What are you planning to do?"

"Buzz says west of here there's a cloudburst about to commence. We intend to dam the wash and collect us some water. And we need a front-loader tractor to hurry the job."

Mr. Jenkins walked several paces over and back. "I see," he said. "Yes. I'll lend you the tractor, if I can come watch. I may have a suggestion or two to help?" He asked permission.

"We'd appreciate it. But you need to know that Frank Jones's boys tore down our half-built dam. There could be trouble."

Farrino Jenkins bobbed his head slightly in an agreeing tremor, then he commented, "I've noticed the paint job on the town. It jarred a little at first, but I find it real cheerful."

"You ought to stop and try the doughnuts in the morning."

"You all selling doughnuts?"

"—and coffee."

"Nice. I'll look it over. When do you want the tractor?"

"Now."

"Of course. Just let me explain to my wife. She likes to know where I'll be."

Decker smiled. "I hate a bragging man."

That pleased Mr. Jenkins and he grinned. "I ought to call Frank and tell him he's missing all the fun."

Decker demurred, "Best not."

Mr. Jenkins laughed in a thoroughly amused way. "He'll never hear the end of this."

"I hope he never hears of it a-tall.".

Mr. Jenkins coaxed, "Now, if I lend you the tractor, you got to let me needle him."

"After we're solid," Decker said. "I don't want any trouble for the town."

"Looks to me like you're doing some solving."

"We are trying," Decker agreed.

"I'd be proud to help out."

Decker said, "Thanks."

"You're welcome. Come this way. Can you drive a tractor?"

"I can," Buzz said.

"Now where did you learn to do that?" Mr. Jenkins was curious.

"In Honduras."

"Ohhh. You got mixed up in that?"

"Very easily."

"'Easily.'" Mr. Jenkins liked picking out that word. It wasn't one that Buzz would ordinarily say.

Buzz explained lazily, "'Easily' was a word everybody down there used for everything."

"I'll bet that's true," Mr. Jenkins said, no longer teasing. "Here's the keys. The tractor's over in that shed. I'll whistle the dogs in before you go through the fence."

"I'd appreciate that."

Mr. Jenkins really laughed and slapped Buzz on the shoulder. "Watch."

He put his fingers to his mouth and gave a shrill sound. Two tiny, yapping Pekingese came bobbing across the unkempt, utilitarian grounds.

Buzz and Decker shook their heads, exchanged a glance, and agreed, "A comedian."

"Well, a man has to have his little jokes." Mr. Jenkins then whistled in a different way and two Great Danes came bounding out. Mr. Jenkins laughed as he went through the fence, calling to his wife. When she came out on their porch, he put the dogs inside the picket fence in the neat house yard. "I'm going to go to Sawbuck to build a dam? That's Buzz and this here is Decker." The two men touched their hat brims. Mr. Jenkins continued to his wife, "You might like to pack up a basket of sandwiches and a thermos of coffee and come on over?" That was a do-you-agree.

"Sounds good. He must be Paul's boy."

"You got a good eye, Polly. See you later." Then he said to Buzz, "The way's clear. Want us to follow you?"

"No problem. I'll go overland. It'll be quicker. Go to the lip?"

Decker suggested, "How about stopping at Hernandez's place and taking along a scoop of sand?"

"Right."

The two men watched Buzz jog over to the shed and the dogs barked questioningly at Mr. Jenkins. "It's okay, boys," he told the dogs. "Settle down."

"How do you know my daddy?"

"That's not the interesting question. The real interesting one is do the Sawbuck folks know you're Frank's nephew?" He pointed his chin toward Buzz's diminishing figure.

"No."

"Somehow that doesn't surprise me," Mr. Jenkins said. "How'd you end up in Sawbuck? You been changing sides?"

"Yep." Decker gave Mr. Jenkins a level look.

"With Frank, that's easy."

"Do you know Elise?"

Mr. Jenkins nodded. "She takes some getting used to."

"Do you know I do believe that she has a brain and that she really loves Frank?"

"Glory be." Mr. Jenkins resettled his Stetson.

Decker agreed, "That takes a little getting used to, too."

"I can see where it would."

They opened the gate as Buzz drove the tractor back through. He paused, and over the sound of the tractor's motor Mr. Jenkins yelled, "Go to the road, you'll see a dirt cutoff to the left, down the way, that we use to get to the cane fields? Take it alongside the fields to the top of the wash and cross there."

Buzz raised a hand to acknowledge that.

They watched Buzz go past, and Mr. Jenkins closed the gate as he said, "He plays the Indian role especially well. He's Harvard, you know."

"No, is that right?"

Mr. Jenkins laughed. "It really is! He's a big surprise. What's he doing back around these parts?"

"Loafing, as far as I can tell."

"I wonder if it's him that's putting out the Eye of God."

"Ahhh," Decker said in recognition. "You've seen it?"

"More than one. Somebody's out there shifting them around nights."

"Why are those signs out there?" Decker asked.

"I don't know, but I suspect they're there to discourage drug trafficking." They went to Decker's pickup and got in. Decker started it, and Mr. Jenkins said, "Nice motor." He grinned with sparkling eyes.

"It's a good truck." Decker agreed. Then he said, "I haven't heard anything about drugs. I've been in Sawbuck for two months, and there's been no indication that's around. What does the Eye of God have to do with drug trafficking?"

"I don't know," Mr. Jenkins said again. "I believe the signs are put out there to remind the runners that God is watching them. The Eye of God is in a lot of churches in South Texas and across the border."

"Anyone who traffics in drugs can't believe in God." Decker was sure.

"Now, how can you say that when the Mafia are good Catholics?"

"Yeah." Decker's voice was sour.

"Are you disillusioned with life?" Mr. Jenkins had one arm along the windowsill and was lounged back with the other arm along the back of the seat, comfortably settled to inform himself about this child of Paul Jones who was battling his own uncle. Life was fascinating.

"Life? No. Some aspects of it, yes."

"And you've decided to take a hand in Sawbuck's future. How did that come about?"

"I have to remind you that I'd be drawn and quartered if the town finds out I'm kin to Frank?"

Mr. Jenkins gave one nod. "Right. My lips are sealed."

"Thank you. He sent me over there to run them out of town so's he can straighten his borders."

"That sounds like Frank."

"Do you know any of the Sawbuckers?" Decker inquired.

"I used to know the Conners. I grieved we lost Brad."

"What was he like?"

"A superior man."

"Damn."

"Oh? Now, why does that bother you?" And Mr. Jenkins smiled in anticipation.

"We're almost there. We need to stop and tell the ladies that your wife will be along so they can look for her."

"That's considerate. Thank you."

They stopped along the street, and Decker introduced Mr. Jenkins to the ragtail mob. He was charming. One of the boys. It was his suggestion that since time was of the essence, they get a crepe myrtle tree and put it bole first into the gap. It was peculiarly appropriate for their purpose because it was a condensed tree, not tall but compact, with dense twigging. Its myriad branches would support the temporary fill for the dam. "A tree like . . . Mrs. Billmont's?" John asked.

"Is she still alive?" Mr. Jenkins exclaimed. "My goodness, she has a year or two on my daddy."

Decker watched Mr. Jenkins. "Will you talk to Mrs.

Billmont? She's not really in touch. And refuse any raspberry tarts."

"She used to make perfect ones. Is she slipping?"

Decker nodded. "She's slipped a cog. She hunts raspberry tarts all over the—"

"Misplaces them?"

"—in drawers, under tables..."

"Oh. Well, let's give it a try. There isn't another crepe myrtle, is there?"

John reminded them, "She has three."

But it was Decker who made Mrs. Billmont understand. He drew a picture of the dam in the dirt by her door. She said, "I see. Yes, we need the basin filled with water." So when she gave permission, she did understand.

She watched as they cut down the tree, and saw it lifted by a pack of men onto a pickup, then she rode with Decker to the dam site and watched as the men wrestled the tree into the slot, laying it trunk first into the slit. At that time, she did understand. In fact, she promised them all raspberry tarts when they'd finished the job, and she stood with Farrino Jenkins as her guide and protector, to watch as the men worked on the dam.

Buzz arrived with the front scoop. He dumped the sand load back from the rock lip of the dam site, then drove the tractor around until he could go down into the dry streambed and drive back to the dam. There, the men gathered rocks and put them into the scoop.

Buzz eased the tractor up to the bottom of the slot, the men lined up to hand the rocks along, and they were placed around the trunk with care as solidly as the men could manage.

Mr. Jenkins mentioned to John that slabs of rock

should be taken by the tractor to be placed along the basin groove to slow and divert the water from its usual straight run, and send the flood out into the basin. The unrestricted force of the flooding could tear through the dam unless there were a series of delays implemented with the slabs. Mr. Jenkins advised, they should be piled here, and there, and over yonder.

The men discussed the wisdom of the suggestion, and agreed. So a crew was set to do it.

Then Ned arrived. "Just what the bloody hell are you guys doing?"

They explained. He was appalled. But he could see the reasoning and he helped. He was especially helpful in rigging ways to lift slabs and balance the tractor without the weights of the slabs floundering it.

Mr. Jenkins drove into San Antonio for more work gloves. He took Mrs. Billmont along, because no one dared to allow her to be unsupervised. She appeared to enjoy the ride. She spoke only once and that was to inquire with curiosity, "Are we running away together?" And Mr. Jenkins explained about his wife.

So when they returned to Sawbuck, Mr. Jenkins took Mrs. Billmont to Naomi's and introduced Mrs. Billmont to his wife, and left her there as he went back to the dam site.

Mrs. Billmont told Mrs. Jenkins, "I wouldn't run away with him."

"Thank you," Polly Jenkins replied kindly.

"I made him bring me back."

"Good for you."

And Naomi had Mrs. Billmont sort real raspberries for tarts.

Since Naomi's house was closest to the dam site, it

had become information, food dispersal center and first-aid station.

It was with avid curiosity that the onslaught of Saw-buckers and eventually the commuter volunteers looked at Rick's porch-living quarters and smiled as they exchanged glances. The men especially stared at Naomi. They had always looked on her as an un-touchable woman, but they knew that Decker had pegged her as his. That made them look on her as a mortal woman, and one a man had . . . touched.

The edge of the basin became as busy as a mouse run. There was purpose. It was a community effort, and they really worked hard. Women and children began to gather the smaller stones. They piled them up on burlap sacks and went for more. None was smaller than a man's fist.

It was then that Naomi understood what Decker had meant when he'd said that it wouldn't be her town or her suggestions that would guide the town. The people would take over and do things for themselves in their own way, and she might not always approve. It was true. They had taken a firm step in controlling their environment.

Even in her house, there were strong women who were directing the supplies. "Naomi, do you have a cotton sheet? We need some bandaging that's tough."

"Yes." Naomi sacrificed a cotton sheet.

Someone else said, "I think we ought to take the coffee and sandwiches to them. They don't need any more exercise. Juanita, you and Marie go scout for a place to put a couple of card tables that are close enough without being in the way. Ask Mr. Jenkins. Carry the tables with you. Then come and help with carrying the food. Don't stop to flirt. Naomi, is it all right if they take the porch table? Do you have a card table? Fine. Girls, get them."

Naomi watched her sheet and tables carried away. She was no longer the director, not even the background manipulator. And it was a relief. She'd never been so firm and sure as the women were now, working together.

But it was still Decker's leadership that was the impetus for the men. Decker. And he belonged to her.

Then Rual, the Big Dog, came along in his uniform. "What's going on here?" He opened the screen door and came uninvited into the house. There were only women. If there'd been even one man there, he would have knocked—with his nightstick.

No one else would reply to him, no one knew which side he'd take about the dam, so Naomi said, "There's the possibility of a gully washer. We're preparing for it."

Rual looked around in his Big Dog manner. "With coffee and sandwiches? You evacuating? What's going on here, Naomi?" It was the first time he'd said her name out loud to her, and he felt stronger and more in control than he ever had.

"The men are working to stop the water." All of which was true.

"I see." No one said anything. No one moved. He said jocularly, "How about some of that coffee?"

It was telling that he'd had to ask for some. Naomi didn't move. One of the women signaled another who poured it for him, then she handed it to him.

He sipped the coffee cautiously, not thanking her or commenting on it. He looked around Naomi's house, fitting himself into that place, and he felt himself grow to fit his image.

The Big Dog walked along in his tap-heeled boots on the polished wood floors and sampled the sandwiches as he looked at the remarkable paintings on the walls. He thought it was a house that was made for him. He tried to stand by Naomi, but she kept disappearing. When even he could stay no longer, and the awed women still didn't move or speak, he finally made his impressive departure and went out on the porch. Alone.

Rual looked around at the evidence that someone was camping out on Naomi's porch, and he frowned. But he had left the house and the women were still silent. He couldn't go back inside and ask who was living on the porch, or he would lose face. When he'd arrived he had been so intent on seizing the opportunity to go inside Naomi's house, that he hadn't looked at the porch. Who was camping out there? Buzz? Decker? Maybe Naomi wasn't so untouchable after all. The Big Dog smiled.

Naomi helped Mrs. Billmont carry her freshly baked raspberry tarts out to the dam site, and she watched the contentment on the old lady's face as the men took the tarts and thanked her. She smiled at Naomi, and having forgotten, she asked, "What are they doing?"

"They're building the dam. When it rains, the basin will fill with water."

"That's nice. It will be a nice size."

Naomi agreed. "About two blocks by three or so. A nice little lake."

"Yes."

Mr. Jenkins took one of the trucks and brought

Magdalena back so that she could see what was going on. Buzz carried her to the lip so that she could really see. She was avidly interested, but she wasn't strong, and Mr. Jenkins readied her to go back home. But Magdalena said that Mrs. Billmont was tired, and she also should be returned safely to her house. In their own excitement over the growing dam, no one else had noticed how frayed Mrs. Billmont was.

The men had to quit about ten that night. Their struggle had been prodigious. While several men had labored, placing the diverting slabs on the funnel run of the basin, the rest had built the dam higher than half. They sweated the gathering storm out west of them. If the storm held off until the next day, the dam might be completed. But the men were staggering. They separated to sleep.

Naomi helped Decker shower, and Trisha allowed Rick inside to use the bath downstairs. He shared his extra T-shirts and boxer shorts with Decker and, clean, the men collapsed and slept unmoving. Decker was in Naomi's bed. Without any real reconciliation between the estranged lovers, Rick was in Trisha's bed. The women were in another bedroom.

In the night the women in Sawbuck heard the rain begin. They looked on sleeping men and decided not to mention it. It was a gentle rain. No one had bothered to listen to the radio and learn of the torrent of water that was pelting the land far to the west. So the men did rest.

But then the rumble of distant thunder shivered the houses and the men stirred. Again the houses trembled, and the sound penetrated the sleep-soaked brains. Eyes opened wide, and the men were trig-

gered. "It's raining west of here!" Versions of that
were said by men in all their houses. And in the houses
of some of the commuters.

They dragged on clothing and new gloves and went
out into the rain. The air felt different. Heavy. The
clouds were blacker, lower, moving somewhat slug-
gishly. The sounds were hushed in an odd, attention-
getting way and the birds were silent.

It was interesting to see that as the men trudged or
drove to the dam site, they stopped and picked up
rocks. Those walking pitched the rocks into passing
pickups. They walked in order to loosen stiff muscles
before they began to work again.

At Naomi's, the two overnighters drank a hasty cup
of coffee and kissed the two hovering women before
they left. Rick could hardly let go of Trisha. "I've
missed you so much," he told her. "Don't ever leave
me again."

"I won't."

As the men left, Naomi told her friend, "Have you
ever heard the saying that ' 'tis an ill wind indeed that
bodes no good.'"

"Yes."

"The ill wind out west of here helped you accept
Rick's apology."

"I just accepted him. He never did apologize."
Trisha was a stickler at times.

"He will. He may not say the words but he already
has apologized with the roses and camping on the
porch."

"I know."

"You were difficult," Naomi prodded.

"I know that. You don't have to tell me."

"He probably won't mention it, so I thought you ought to know it from somebody."

"And you volunteered." Trisha gave her friend a tolerantly irritated look.

Naomi laughed and said, "With some pleasure."

"I honestly don't know what I would do without you, Naomi."

"It has worked both ways. I'll owe you forever."

"Remember that."

It rather surprised the men to see a trickle running in the wash. It was a goad, and they really worked, straining, their movements quick. Mr. Jenkins came and ordered their pacing. "You'll do better in the long run. You still have a way to go. Pace yourselves, or you'll collapse."

So he stood on the bank after that, watching, whistling to get attention before calling, "Slow down, there on the tractor," to a man who was unloading rock. Or he'd call, "Slow down, there by the bank." He took the responsibility of seeing to it that the men didn't tire too quickly. "You there, you need to sit down for a few minutes. Come have a drink of water and talk to me for a while."

The trickle became a nice run, and the men sloshed around in it, making an arrow of diverting rocks ahead of the dam, reinforcing the slabs laid for that purpose.

At Naomi's house, Trisha had the first contraction.

"You never can stand for attention to be diverted from you, can you," Naomi teased as her own stomach gripped in sympathy.

"I'm sure it's false. I've been upset by Rick and all this excitement, and I'm a little tired."

There was more diversion work in the basin, as the

men actually saw the need for it. The water increased
its run and puddled at the dam. That water lapping
at the base of their dam was very satisfying and exciting for the workers.

The rain came heavier. The men's footing and the
rocks were slippery, and everything was harder to do.
A canvas had been rigged over the food and coffee
so that it was reasonably dry. The men no longer
thought about trying to stay dry and just reached
under the cover and were handed food that they ate
or coffee that they drank while standing in the rain.

Their bodies steamed.

Ned explained, "We need to get the rocks and filler
packed to the top. With leakage and evaporation we'll
lose water. That can't be helped. You men are doing
a fine job of building this dam, I'm proud of you. The
sizes of rocks are excellent. The dam won't be water-
proof, but we can keep the basin in water for a long,
long time. Keep at it. We're going to win."

It was a needed pep talk. They'd been thinking,
half a basin of water was better than none.

The rain increased to a downpour and the backup
at the dam was exciting. The men grinned as they
saw the water stopped. It gave them impetus and renewed their muscles. Now they had to scrounge for
fill farther away. They went out in teams on pickups
and hurried back in relays.

At Naomi's the ladies also worked to keep the men
supplied. And they discussed the fact that Trisha was
probably going to have her baby. With the contractions becoming regular, Naomi began to pay closer
attention, and she saw that Trisha was more uncomfortable than she had allowed them to know. That set
Naomi into motion. She told two men, "Tell Rick and

Decker that I'm taking Trisha to the hospital. We think the baby may be ready, but with the first, I understand it takes a while." She turned to Trisha, "Shall I ask Rick to come now?"

"If it's really serious, we can get word to him, then he can come. This is a big adventure for him, to build a dam."

"So's having a baby."

"He can be there in twenty minutes."

"Okay," Naomi agreed. Then she told the two messengers, "Tell them we'll be in touch."

The men smiled and said to Trisha, "Good luck."

Trisha replied, "Get the dam finished."

"We will."

CHAPTER SEVENTEEN

THE TWO MALE INFORMANTS, CARRYING NA-
omi's message, found Decker and said, "Naomi said
they'll call you if anything develops."

Distracted, Decker asked, "Huh?"

"She's taking Trisha to the hospital."

"Trish okay?"

"Yeah. She was standing up and walking, and she
said we're to get the dam done."

"Okay. Be sure to tell Rick."

"Where is he?"

"Down the wash a way. Find him and tell him before
you do anything else."

But things don't always happen the way one in-
tends. The two were separated and snared into helping almost right away. Each thought the other would
find Rick. They mentioned Trisha, and they got nods
from men who hadn't heard them, not really.

So Rick wasn't told.

It rained and the wind blew so hard that the men
finally had to retreat to the dam and just try to build
it high enough. The backed-up water was swirling into
the dam and creeping higher. It was thrilling to them
that none of the water appeared to be leaking

through. They couldn't actually tell if that was true
because the rain fell so hard everywhere.

A state cop came in with his siren wailing and said,
"Get to higher ground, there's a flood coming! Be
sure everyone is warned!" And he went his perilous
way with siren wailing into the torrents of downpour
that was making its own flood.

With the rainfall the week before, the ground was
sodden. So the new downpour ran off. It fed all the
low-lying areas and it rushed along a feeder tunnel
that was never noticed, until then. With the normal
runoff through the wash temporarily stopped, the
feeder tunnel ran rampantly along, running wild and
free, and it spewed across the dip in the road between
Sawbuck and San Antonio.

Driving Trisha to the hospital, Naomi hesitated at
the road dip, giving the windshield wipers time to
catch up. She eyed the curling waters that covered
the road before she glanced with calculated calm over
at Trisha, who had her eyes closed and was biting her
lip.

Pickups can go through anything as long as the
exhaust is clear. Her truck would make it, Naomi
thought. And it almost did. She hadn't expected the
push against the tires, and she couldn't see the edges
of the road. She went onto the left shoulder, thinking
that she was still on the right-hand side of the road,
and her truck began to tilt.

She turned the wheels into the tilt, and they were
on the tree-lined, rock-bottomed streambed, in
deeper water. The pickup's motor sputtered, and they
were half floating. Naomi started to sweat.

"New way?" Trisha inquired in a normal voice.

"Yeah."

Among the trees to her left, Naomi saw the shed. It sat out of the main run of the flooding, and she aimed for it. She knew the wash deepened below there. She used the last of her motor to gun the car over to that side of the stream and came to a rest, parked against the shed.

In the deepening flood, the shed roof was higher than the surrounding land. If the shed held firm, the roof shouldn't be flooded. She said to Trisha, "We'll climb onto the hood, to the top of the cab, and up onto the shed."

"Fine."

It was not easy. Trisha was awkward, protecting her stomach. Naomi made them move slowly and carefully. They did make it to the shed roof as the truck began to rock in the deepening water. With Trisha safely on the roof, Naomi went back down to the pickup for the first-aid kit, and she scooped up a woolen blanket and a rope.

There was a giant oak hovering over the shed. Its branches spread far out. Naomi thought that from the shed roof, they might be able to get into the branches.

Trisha sat at the peak of the shed's mildly tilted tin roof. "I never realized this was here. I'm glad that it is."

They watched the pickup float a bit and move from the shed. The flood rose higher. The current was swifter.

"I wonder if the dam will hold." Trisha's thought was mild.

Naomi was firm. "Yes. It will."

The rain poured down, but it helped that the ref-

ugees were under the oak's umbrella of tiny hard
leaves. They saw the first snake.

Naomi wrapped Trisha in the woolen blanket. Even
wet, wool keeps one warm. Naomi then took up the
rope and held the coils in one hand with the free end
to use as a whip. Snakes might want to share their
refuge.

She eyed the tree limbs above their heads, and in
that sodden weather Trisha commented dryly, "I cannot climb a rope. Forget it."

"Trisha, I have to get help. I should never have
tried that stretch of the road when I saw that it was
underwater. I had no idea it ever was—"

"I doubt that it has been, in years and years. It isn't
your fault that we're here. We could have turned over
when we slid off the road. I thought we would. You
spotted this shed, and we're safe on top of it. If the
baby decides to see what's happening, so be it."

"While you're holding to this good attitude, I should
go for help. We'll never get a helicopter in this downpour, but we might find someone who knows more
than I." She used the knife in the first-aid kit to saw
through a portion of the rope. "Use this rope like a
whip if a—anything should come up on the roof. Are
you all right?"

"This child will hear this tale forever and get heartily sick of it."

"I'll help perpetrate that. Let's see if I can do this."

Fortunately, Naomi was in jeans. She tried several
times to throw the rope over the lowest limb, but she
wasn't successful. She told Trisha rather airily, "I
could stand on your shoulders and knot this."

"Try something else first."

So Naomi made about six knots on top of each other

at the end of the rope. With the additional weight, she flung the knot precisely over the branch she wanted. She pulled it down, unsure of what to do next.

Trisha suggested, "Make knots at eighteen-inch intervals, then shinny up it."

"Good thinking." She did that and had a time getting up the rope. After the failure of the first attempt, she told Trisha, "Better scoot out of the way." Climbing ropes wasn't a skill Naomi possessed, but she was determined, so she did make it. From the branch, she looked back. "I won't be long. Be brave."

"Don't dally."

From the way Trisha's voice sounded, she was having a hard contraction. Naomi turned and surveyed her tree route. The branches were rough, but the rain had made them tricky, so she was careful.

Left to themselves, oak trees are umbrellas. Their branches grow down to the ground all around. So getting over to the bank was not impossible, and Naomi finally stepped over onto the ground and looked back. Trisha wasn't watching her, she was watching a snake.

Naomi fled. The sooner gone, the sooner returned. Then her guardian angel, or Trisha's, made Naomi go back and tie her shirt on a branch so that she could find the tree again without blundering. She ran until her lungs seared and she couldn't catch her breath. She screamed, "Decker!" in a heartrending wail.

Toward the dam site, a man came from the trees to the roadside. He watched her with caution. She didn't recognize him and called, "Have you seen Decker?"

"Decker. *Sí*."

It was one of the new, non-English–speaking arrivals in Sawbuck. She said intensely, "Find Decker."
She turned and pointed the way she'd come. "Baby.
Bambino." She rocked a pretend baby in her arms.
"Decker. Bring Decker there." She pointed again.

Another man emerged from the trees. He was staring at her, and she realized she was not completely
dressed. She stood in bra and jeans and Nikes. She
said, "Decker. Get Decker. Hurry. Vamoose—is that
the word?"

They nodded. "Decker."

"Yes! Trisha's bambino."

"Bambino."

"Decker. Get Decker." She put back her head and
howled, "Decker!" But the rain seemed to beat the
sound back down.

"Please," she said to the two men. "Get Decker."
She realized she was close to babbling. She went beyond them. There was no one else around. She knew
no one would be in town and it was too long to leave
Trisha alone to try for the dam site itself or her own
house where there were women aplenty. She asked
one last time. "Go, vamoose, get Decker." She pushed
them with her hands. "Bring him there," and she
pointed yet again. "Naomi."

"*Sí.* Naomi."

"Baby."

They looked at her body again.

"Trisha's baby."

"Trisha's baby."

"Hurry!" Praying wordlessly, she turned back and
ran down the road and back to Trisha. When she
turned toward the oak, she looked back and saw one

of the men watching. She pointed elaborately to where she was going. And he waved.

Going to the tree, Naomi thought she should have just brought them back. They could at least keep the wildlife from sharing their perch. She almost passed her shirt and stopped to spread it out more fully. Then, with great trepidation, she peered through the tree branches, and Trisha was still there. "I'm back."

"I'm so glad."

"I know, honey. Everything will be all right. I found someone to find Decker." No need to tell her that could prove futile. With difficulty, her heart in her mouth, she regained the shed roof. She was trembling. "How's it going?"

"My water broke."

"Oh." Naomi couldn't think of anything else for a minute, then she said pragmatically, "So you're going through with this." She hadn't intended being funny.

Trisha almost could laugh.

Naomi eyed a swimming 'possum and stamped her feet on the metal roof.

"What *is* it?" Trisha panicked.

"No, no, it was just a 'possum."

Trisha had turned pale and appeared faint.

"Everything is all right. I'm here, and I'll stay with you. Decker will be here as soon as he can. Don't worry about anything."

Trisha smiled and slowly shook her head. "You took Coping With Hysteria 101."

"The one hundreds are all slapping. I just quoted two-hundredth-level Reasoning."

"I see. How far did you go with hysteria?"

Naomi looked around distractedly but her voice was calm. "I did independent study."

"You may need everything you've learned."

As Naverro sought Decker, people tried to waylay him and give him things to do in their frantic fight to finish the dam under such circumstances. Each time, he said, "Decker? Decker." And he waited expectantly.

He found an almost unrecognizably muddy Buzz and took his arm. In Spanish he said intensely, "Give me aid in discovering Decker. His woman, Naomi, was running on the road and seeks him urgently."

"Where is she?"

"She ran back down the road."

Buzz straightened, alert. "No truck?"

"No. And without the shirt. 'Trisha's baby,'" he repeated carefully.

"Now what the hell..." But his attention was riveted. He did recognize that something had gone wrong. He bellowed, "Decker!"

"He's gone for sand."

"Where?"

"Hernandez's."

"Come with me, Sammy. You can handle a tractor. We've got to find Decker, and we'll need you to bring back the tractor." He turned to Naverro and said in Spanish, "Come along. You need to tell Decker." Then he called to Jenkins, "We have an emergency with Naomi. We must leave. Sam will bring back the tractor."

Mr. Jenkins lifted an acknowledging hand.

The three muddy men appropriated a truck and drove to Hernandez's where they did find Decker.

Getting out of the truck and indifferent to the thudding rain, Buzz said, "Naverro says Naomi was running on the road without her shirt. She told him to find you. And she said, 'Trisha's baby.'"

In Spanish, Decker tensely questioned Naverro, "Did she say where?"

"She returned where she came. Ramon watches the way."

"Good, thanks, let's go." He whistled for his dog and slapped the back of the pickup indicating to Wellington that he was to jump up in the back. He said, "Sam, take that load to the dam site?"

"Sure. Go on. Hurry."

In the truck, driving along the road, the windshield wipers almost useless, Naverro said, "She wept."

His Naomi crying? "Wept?"

"Yes."

Decker groaned and was silent. Then he speculated, "They must have gone off the road. Naverro, was it down where the road crosses the wash?"

"Possibly."

"Look for Ramon."

They found him waiting almost at the crossing. He stayed carefully to the side in case they didn't see him in the downpour. But he yelled and waved his arms. The men got out and judged the sand along the side of the road, and decided to risk the truck getting stuck.

Naverro advised, "Look for the shirt. She had none. She may have used it as a signal to find her way back to her friend." Naverro felt important with his advice.

Decker said, "Good."

They almost missed the wet shirt. But they got out of the truck. In Spanish so that the two could also understand, Buzz said, "The shed. I hope they're on top of it."

Decker automatically replied in the same language, "If it was possible, Naomi got her up there."

"There will be snakes."

That silenced the men.

The heavy rain was making the mud drip from the men who went cautiously to the edge of the bank, careful not to start a landslide. They peeked over the edge. The two women were watching a bobcat who was deciding whether to land on the roof. Naomi was standing close to the edge of the roof with the piece of rope that could be used as a whip. She was being very brave.

Buzz picked up a rock, his hands noting it was perfect for filler at the dam, and without hesitating, he chunked it at the bobcat. It veered away as the women jerked around.

"Decker." Naomi breathed his name. Then she looked at Naverro and Ramon and said, "Thank you."

They smiled, very pleased with themselves.

Trisha asked, "Rick?"

The men had forgotten Rick. Decker said, "He's on his way." Then he growled very low at Buzz, "Get him here. You'll have to run. We might can use the truck so we don't dare let it go."

"I'm gone."

"Take these two with you and see if you can rustle up an army vehicle, an all-purpose one that can get us across that road to a hospital."

"We'll do our damnedest. Will you be okay here? I know how to do this kind of thing... Honduras." He shrugged over what had been necessary at one time.

"If you can't find anything certified in this kind of

job, come back. But find Rick as soon as you can."

"Don't worry."

"I will be waiting for you with great intensity."

Buzz grinned.

He translated it all into Spanish and the two new-comers laughed.

Naomi said, "It's so nice you find this amusing."

She sounded just a little testy. He took her shirt off the oak and put his own there as a beacon. Then he put a rope from the truck around Wellington and led him from the bank up and along the wide oak branches.

From the shed top, Naomi inquired in a very patient way, "What are you doing with that dog?"

"Now, I know that you think Wellington's gonna climb down that rope, right? Well, he can't . . . yet. He's still working on learning. However, he's the best snake dog you'll ever meet." Decker adjusted the rope hitch around Wellington, who stood still for it, and Decker carefully lowered the dog to the shed roof.

The women watched that without any show of ap-preciation at all.

The hitch was such that as the dog landed, Decker looped the rope, and Wellington expected that be-cause he knew to step from inside the rope and stand free. Then Decker laid his own rope loosely over the tree branch and skimmed down Naomi's knotted rope.

He set his feet down and released his hold as he smiled at Naomi. "Glad to see me?"

She nodded and looked at him. It was then he knew how very scared she was. He explained, "I only look like Trisha's guardian angel. I'm only a human person and not at all magical." He grinned at Trisha.

She was in labor.

He said enthusiastically, "Look at this rain-scrubbed, gently tilted roof. A perfect delivery table."

"Now?" Naomi whispered.

"Pretty soon, now. How's it going, Trish?"

"Hard."

"Ummm. Don't rush. We have to get Rick here for the grand entrance."

"It's going to be here?" She groaned and lay back. "My God."

"Tell me," Decker requested.

"The kid's moving around."

"I'm going to put my hands on your stomach. Okay?"

She was opening and closing her mouth.

"Relax. It's just getting ready. I think it was wrong side down."

"That's what the doctor said."

"Well, the kid figured that out, and it's turning around."

"My God!"

Her stomach undulated and shifted rather remarkably. She panted with tension.

"Be calm. It's a natural business, and you can do this. That's what males always tell females, with perfect confidence, since they don't have any idea what it's like."

Trisha gasped, "Interesting."

"Atta girl."

"—woman."

"Atta woman. Think how curious the kid is with all this flooding and you on a shed roof. There's a lot going on and he can hear us, you know. He wants to see for himself. He could have seen his first bobcat if he'd been out by then."

"I certainly wouldn't want her to miss anything."

"See? Your old snappy self. This'll be an experience. We might get you written up in *People*. I left my camera at home. Well, shucks."

"Are you going to deliver her?"

"It'll be a boy. I can tell by the handy way he turned around at the last minute. Shows good reflexes. Probably be a hell of a basketball player. And I believe I shall aid you in this undertaking."

"Do you know how?"

"I had a dog—"

"So did Naomi."

"Did you! You deliver her? I shall welcome a colleague."

"You're on your own. My dog did it by herself."

Trisha scoffed, "Naomi just clapped her hands and bragged."

"You know how to do that? We need a hand-clapping bragger."

"You got it."

He smiled tenderly at his love. He was trying to calm them both. He wasn't at all calm. Where the *hell* were Buzz and Rick?

Trisha asked, "Are you ignoring my inquiry about your license to practice?"

"I've taken part in lots of birthings. It's no big deal. I've delivered lambs, pigs, and puppies and you're a mammal. Babies can't be that different. You're in good hands." Where was Buzz?

With the baby in position, it was quiet. They both rested. Wellington patrolled the perimeter efficiently. Naomi was in a daze of nerves. She'd run out of bravery now that Decker was there. She didn't panic or cry, she was numb. She knew that one problem was past, the baby had turned. How to warn Decker without alarming—

"I tend to bleed," Trisha mentioned the real problem.

"Oh? I know all the pressure points, and Naomi is here to take care of the baby—what're you going to name him?"

"Priscilla."

"Now you know that will cause him all sorts of problems?"

"She won't mind."

Decker stood up and held his hands to the rain to clean them. He set his Stetson on the roof and allowed that, too, to be washed. He was shirtless and he looked magnificent and calm to Naomi. He kept track of the area. Then he went and lay along the slight downward edge of the tin roof, looked under it to be sure nothing was harbored there, then allowed the rain runoff to clean his hands better. He washed his face and worked at his fingernails. He was trying to remember pressure points. He was trying to assimilate that it would probably be he who must help Trisha through this, and he prayed God to guide him and sustain her.

The baby was still resting. Naomi didn't move. She sat by Trisha, but she didn't say or do anything. She'd turned this problem over to Decker. Trisha had been the second most important person in her life. Brad had been first. Now here was Trisha in this unusual circumstance that could . . .

She glanced down at Trish who had her eyes closed against the rain. She said to Trisha, "I thought you were a terribly pushy child, when we first met, do you remember that?"

Musingly, Trish replied, "I've always had to fight to get my share."

"Your fighting wasn't to get your share, you just wanted to be sure that your share wasn't littler than what everyone else had."

Trish considered Naomi's evaluation. "That's true. I never thought of it that way, but that is true. You know me very well."

"I love you, Trish."

"Good God, don't get mushy. I'm hanging on to my hysteria by my fingernails. Don't jar me loose or I'll come apart."

"You're the bravest woman I know. Do you remember the rattler in our cabin?"

"It was so beautifully dangerous. The only thing that rattled was Trudie's bones. She about jumped out of her skin. I'd never realized she could understand the world beyond her own wants, up until then."

"You saved her life."

"I just covered up the snake."

"You have a lot of Brownie points piled up. It's your turn to get them redeemed."

"Is that the way it works?"

"Yes."

Her lips pale, her eyes closed, Trisha said quietly, "Are you listening, God? Take care of my baby."

It wasn't the "kid" anymore, it was the baby.

They heard the truck. Even in the pelting rain, they heard the truck because they were honking the horn the whole way.

Trisha opened her eyes and looked up at Naomi. "Rick?"

"It should be."

And her labor began again. By the time Buzz and Rick got to the ropes, Trisha was panting. Rick wasn't paying attention to his feet on the branch, he was yelling, "Wait for me, honey, I'm coming!"

But Buzz had a firm grip on Rick and he commanded, "Decker, watch out for him!"

"Got him." Decker moved beneath them, and at the ropes, he reached up and steadied Rick's feet and body as he came down. Rick went to Trisha and took her hand. "You have never been conventional," he chided tenderly.

"But I do come through. I'm glad you're here."

Buzz dropped down lightly onto the roof and went to Trish. "How's it going, beautiful?"

Rick said, "Hey, don't talk to her that way?"

"All doctors talk that way to their OB patients. I'm her doctor, if nobody else shows up."

"You?" Rick's mouth was appalled.

"Be calm, you're looking at an experienced man."

Trisha panted, "What *sort* of experience?"

"Picky, picky." Buzz moved so that his Stetson covered her face and she could open her eyes. "I've got everything under control, as usual, and you don't have a thing to worry about. Just do as I tell you. Now relax. I need to feel your stomach. Did he turn?"

"She realized she was upside down, uh, bottom first and she turned around."

"What a bright child!" He grinned at Trisha. "You going to name him after me?"

"Buzzie?"

"I won't hold you to it. How long since the last one?"

Naomi looked at Decker.

Trisha replied, "Just as you two arrived, it began

again. After the baby turned, she rested."

"Good," Buzz complimented. "He's a smart kid, we're in luck. Some kids have no sense at all. But this one will help. So will we, Trish. Don't worry."

"I'm bordering hysterical."

"Why?" He seemed honestly surprised.

"Well, look where we are!"

As Decker had, Buzz looked around at the sheltering tree, the rushing water, the rain-filled day. "A nice rain, good clean roof, friends, what more do you want?"

"Two aspirin?"

Buzz told Rick, "You've got a spoiled woman here."

"She's mine."

Trisha smiled.

Buzz said, "Give her your hat."

"My *hat?* What's she want with a hat at a time like this?"

"She's lying almost flat, the rain goes into her eyes. I need to move my head, and I don't need rain running down into my eyes right now. I keep my hat. She needs one. You don't."

Rick had already taken his off and was propping it on Trish's head so that she could see and yet be shielded. "I wasn't thinking. Sorry, honey."

"Hold my hand."

"Oh, Trisha."

CHAPTER EIGHTEEN

WITH WELLINGTON PATROLLING THE EDGES OF the shed roof, Decker loosened the damp blanket that was bunched around Trisha, and cut a square from it. He replaced the lessened end around Trisha, then wrapped the cut piece around his bare upper body, and tucked the lower edges into the top of his trousers.

Trisha was between contractions, and Buzz rose, leaving the lovers murmuring together there on the gently slanting shed roof. Buzz watched Decker's actions, frowning. Then Buzz smiled a little and said, "For the bambino?"

Decker nodded. He'd put the wool on his body in order to warm it, and Buzz gave him a pat on the back. "If I was ever in a tight fix, I would want you along."

Decker's quick glance was sharp. "Are you now?"

As Decker had, Buzz was using the rain to wash his hands and face. "Not yet."

That's when Decker really knew that Buzz was the special agent assigned to something going on in that area. "If I can help, call on me."

"I would." Buzz shifted his feet as if to pass that

subject, then he indicated Trisha as another problem. "How are you with blood?"

"I've seen a lot of it."

"I would bet you have. Mostly your own."

"Not always." Then very quietly he told Buzz, "I'm especially glad that you're here. She tends to bleed."

"Ugh." Buzz looked at the sky from under his hat and scanned the flooding wash. He saw the trees on the opposite bank greyed by the curtain of pounding rain. "No chance of a chopper in this mess."

"With the flooding, are there any army engineers nosing around? Any ATVs?" All-terrain vehicles.

"We've got the word out. How's Naomi in this situation?"

"She's a lion. Look at her. She's calm and terrified. But she loves Trisha, and she'll hold up and be brave."

"Yes. Help her. I'll let you know if I need you. Keep that blanket warm. I figure we have about half an hour."

Buzz went back to squat down by Trisha and a soothing Rick. Rick looked up and said, "She didn't let me know in time to take the prenatal birthing lessons. Do you know what I should do?"

"You're doing very well, right now." He laid his hand on the bulge in a professional, judging way, then smiled at Trisha and said, "So are you, doing very well. Keep your breathing normal, pant through the contraction's climax, relax."

"I'm glad you're here." Trisha was solemn.

"Me, too," Buzz told her. "Births are a miracle."

Trisha smiled ethereally, and Rick was almost unmanned.

On over a way, on the slanting shed roof, Decker squatted down by Naomi and took her cold little hands in his hot ones, holding them sandwiched between his. She asked coldly, "Are you warmer with the blanket?"

"It's for the baby," he explained kindly.

Her eyelids closed down and her head bowed. "I'm sorry."

He tilted up her chin. "You don't know me well enough, yet, but you surely will, although it could take you the rest of your life."

Buzz said, "Listen!" He stood up in alarm.

"What?" Decker, too, stood.

"A surge, get the women up on the branch! The dog—"

"What?" "What is it?" Rick and the women demanded.

Buzz eyed the distance the water was from the roof. "We should be all right after the first surge! Hurry!"

Decker threw Naomi up onto the branch. "Stay there!" Then with difficulty, he lifted Wellington up. "Stay!" The three men stood Trisha up, jammed Rick's hat down on her head, and the other two pulled theirs down just as firmly. The three men put their bodies at various heights between Trisha and the force of the expected wave, and they clung to the doubled ropes and each other.

The wave roared down the channel looking as if it would cover the earth. Buzz yelled, "Pray God there's no debris."

And it hit.

The shed was to one side on the bank of the channel, not in the main stream of the surge, so they didn't get the full impact. There were some minor glancing blows from debris. The shed moved on its foundation with a grating they couldn't hear over the water, but which they could feel through their feet. They bent with the force of the water and swung on the ropes, but they survived.

Decker scrubbed the water from his eyes and looked up—into Naomi's widely scared eyes. "You okay?"

"Yes." Her breath trembled.

His head jerked to Trisha, then to the men before his sharp glance hit the dog. Wellington was standing on the limb awkwardly bent over, not liking what was going on and being brave about it all.

Trisha was panting.

Buzz helped Rick to lay her down on the miraculously surviving roof. There were now a few curled-back edges in the tin sheeting, witness to the force behind the surge. And the higher water swirled over the lower half of the roof. Their island was diminished, they were all dripping water, but they were still above the flood.

Buzz told Trisha, "You have to appreciate what we will do to distract you?"

Trisha put her hands to her face and shuddered between laughter and crying.

Decker went up the rope to retrieve the dog, who then ventured sloshingly into the remembered territory that he was guarding. Decker then turned to Naomi. She was shivering and deliberately in control. He talked to her, putting the baby blanket around her.

She said, "I don't think I can grip the rope."

"There's no need. I'll get you down. Unless you want to go to the truck and warm up?"

"No, I'll go down on the shed roof." Her voice shivered.

"You're very brave."

"So is Trisha."

"Yes."

"So are you." She looked into Decker's eyes.

The words were like a soothing balm to the deepest, most bruised of all his parts.

The pair saw that Rick calmed way down. He took Trisha's soothing over with efficient easiness. He talked to her normally and held her hand and allowed her to pretend that everything was under control.

To Decker, Naomi mentioned almost idly, "My truck is gone."

"It's probably under there somewhere. I'm just glad you're up here. Trisha was lucky to be with you. You are brilliant under stress."

"No."

"If it hadn't been for you, she would be in that truck."

That was true. She admitted, "I didn't think it out."

"Instinct. You just went ahead and did what had to be done."

"Will we be here all night?" Naomi looked around with worry.

"No. The baby will be here soon."

"When I can, I'm going to cry about all this."

"Maybe." He smiled at her and put her wet hair behind her ear. Then he put his hat on her head. "I would have given it to you sooner, but it's too big for you and I suspected the western flood wave was coming. If you'd been wearing the hat, it would have been lost. That's why I took that piece of blanket so soon."

"Not just to get it warm?"

"No, to have it."

"Buzz saved the rest."

"Yes."

"He really comes through in a pinch, doesn't he? I thought he was only a womanizer."

Trisha made urgent sounds.

Decker lowered Naomi to the shed roof, followed her down, and they stood, helplessly watching.

Buzz was saying, "Good. Good. Easy now. With the next one, take three deep breaths and hold the fourth and push. Okay? He's just about ready. You're doing great. Easy. Easy. Just a little push with this one. Let the kid know you understand what he's doing and that you'll help him. It's the first indication that he won't be alone when he gets out. Easy. Take another breath, now push. Not so hard. Now he's ready. With this next one—it's starting, now—when it feels like it's full blown, take that breath and push. There you go, ahhh, here he comes, smooth as glass.

"And...he's fine. All the proper equipment needed. I'll just clean his nose. He's breathing good, looking around, wondering why you chose this particular place. You'll have some explaining to do. Now, I'll just put him on your stomach for a minute, there's a final surge of nourishment through the umbilical that he can use. Gimme the blanket, Decker. Good. Nice and warm. There we go.

"Here Rick, saw through that. There's no nerves in it and it won't hurt either of them. Good. I'll tie this. There we go. We need the afterbirth. Feeling a little battered? You'll be fine. No, don't help, I can do that for you. Here, Naomi, you and Decker can handle the baby. Wrap him in that blanket. Fine. We'll do the afterbirth like my people did." He took it over to the water, lifted it high and offered it as sacrifice. Then he leaned down and released it into the water.

What else was he to do with it in those circumstances? He had to get rid of it. And it pleased him to make a ceremony of it.

Decker was better with the baby than Naomi. She was awed. "Look at him. Oh, Trisha, he's beautiful. Perfect."

Decker wrapped the baby in the strip of wool.

Holding Trisha's hand, watching his son, Rick let go of Trisha and stood up, opening his shirt. He pulled down the neck of his undershirt and said, "Put him in here. Let me carry him now."

And Decker did that.

Buzz was back with Trisha. He'd ripped off a length of the blanket and pressed it gently to the birth wound. "You're doing fine. No unusual bleeding. You're all right. And it's over, Trisha. You were just great."

"A boy?" she asked not Buzz, but Rick.

"Yes." Rick was crying over a very large and tender smile.

"Is he all right?"

"Perfect. Oh, Trisha. We'll have a girl next time, darling."

"Where?" she asked cautiously.

And there were watery laughs.

The other two men then began figuring how to get Trisha up the tree and to the truck to get her back to Sawbuck.

But a national guardsman said from the bank and down a way, "You people looking for a doctor?"

"Yes!"

"We have one for you. Do you need help getting off that roof?"

Rather dryly, Decker said, "We could use some

help. But the doctor should see the new mother first and supervise her transport."

"Right, sir. Right away."

The guardsmen very calmly rigged a pulley with a sliding bucket seat. The doctor came down in it, effortlessly, saw to Trisha and checked the baby, as the others were evacuated. Two of the guardsmen came over onto the roof and helped get Trisha back on the bank.

Beyond the streambank, they eased Trisha onto a stretcher, then put her and Rick with the new baby in the ATV. They drove routinely across the road, then into the flooded stream and across it. There was an ambulance on the other side. The couple and their new baby were transferred to that vehicle, which took off for San Antonio.

Those left behind had been put into rescue jackets and given hot coffee. The captain of the guardsmen said, "We understand you're building a dam? Where is that?"

So they showed them. "No problem," the captain said. "We have some backup."

After a time, the army engineers came and surveyed the dam attempt. "Not bad," one engineer said. Ned beamed. "The tree was an excellent solution." Mr. Jenkins beamed. "This dam probably saved a lot of damage downstream. You only need a little more fill to hold the water. But you know that it'll have to be torn out, and a proper gate installed so that you don't impede the flow of the stream."

"There is no flow," Decker put in. "That's the problem. There is too much spray farming and irrigation. The overdraw of water from the aquifer has robbed the streams and the wells of the folks around here."

"We can't solve that. That's civilian. Right now we can get some fill in for you. There's more rain coming. We'll certify that we needed this to help slow down the stream. With your dam, some of the overflow will be guided onto that seep, yonder, and that will make the environmentalists happy. It's a protected wetland, but it's been drying out."

"So have Sawbuck wells."

"You ought to get together with the other little towns and independents, along here, and do something for yourselves. All I can do is okay a temporary fill for your dam." He smiled. "Once done, it takes a lot of litigation to get it undone. But you have to know that without the gate, the basin will eventually fill with silt."

"Yeah."

After the captain left, issuing orders and writing notes, Decker, Buzz, and Naomi found out what damage the wave had done above where they'd been. They said her house upstream was okay. Its stilts were just right because the water hadn't funneled, but had spewed out over the basin. Whoever had built that house had known how to do it correctly.

Two of the men working on the dam had been swept away and found downstream in trees. One had a broken arm. The men were all exhausted, and night was coming on, but Mr. Jenkins seemed to thrive on it all. "Polly is having such a fine time helping the ladies. I do hear that one of the ladies is missing."

"Missing? Who?"

"Mrs. Billmont. The lady who donated her crepe myrtle to the dam? She went out to get more raspberries."

There was no discussion about how tired they were,

they all searched, and it was John who found her upstream. The wave had caught and flung her. She'd sustained a hard blow to her poor empty head, and she'd been mercifully, quickly killed. They carried her back to her little house.

The ladies washed and dressed her. They laid her on her bed and covered her with a quilt. There was no way to get her to the funeral home until the water went down. The ladies volunteered to take charge of the wake, bringing food and drink for those keeping watch, and everyone was quiet in their talk and a little saddened. The mourners included some of the commuters who hadn't gone to work that day, in the city, but had joined those working on the dam in Sawbuck.

One said, "I think I'll buy Mrs. Billmont's house. I like this town."

Ned said, "I was thinking about that."

"I said it first."

"I might build one here." That was Dick. "With the basin filled, there'll be fishing. I could come home nights and swim for a while before supper at Joe and Ann's store. Then I could fish until bedtime."

"There won't be any fish for a while."

"I don't mind. We could stock it. Some catfish, some perch. We ought not to have motor boats. Too noisy. Just paddles or oars."

"That's right."

"The town'll have to vote on it," Joe put in.

"We need a mayor," one commuter decided.

"How about Jenkins?"

"I was thinking about . . . me." Dick smiled.

There were scoffings.

"That little island out there in the basin with the

two trees is just the nicest thing. We ought not let anybody build on it."

"I think that's a good idea."

Decker and Naomi listened. None of those deciding the future of Sawbuck even lived there.

And an environmentalist came along and said, "You finally dammed it! It's about time. There's a seep across the way that needs the moisture for the wildlife. This was an excellent solution to that. Didn't you get our letters? They were sent to Frank Jones. Which of you is he?"

"He's the son of a bitch who took all the water," Mr. Jenkins volunteered, since no one else spoke up. So he turned out to be the quoted one. Involved for one day in Sawbuck's fate, it was he who had the clout and the connections to do something about Sawbuck. Incredible. Naomi and Decker laughed.

When the next Sawbuckers came to take their turn for Mrs. Billmont's wake, they all talked together for a while, but the first bunch left the house and went tiredly to their beds. Decker went home with Naomi.

The Conner house was there as it had always been. The ground was wetter than in years and years. The lovers slogged through the gooey mud trailed by the muddy dog. They reached the stairs where Naomi removed her shoes.

Decker took the hose and washed Wellington, well away from the porch since he would shake himself all over everything.

That done, he removed his own shoes, and they went tiredly up onto the porch, across the porch, and into the house. It was neat as a pin.

Naomi looked around and said, "I think they even dusted."

"I need something warm," Decker mentioned.

"Tea?"

"Cocoa." He thought a minute. "With marshmallows."

"I have some miniature ones."

"I can accept that."

They went into the kitchen, moving slowly. He found the cups and saucers, while she made the cocoa. They didn't have anything to say. Silently, they sat at the table, still wearing the army jackets, and they drank the hot cocoa. Then they went upstairs, stripped and showered, long and relishing. "How can more water feel so good?" she asked.

"Yeah."

And they went into Naomi's room, turned back the covers, got in, pulled the covers back over them, and lying naked in each other's arms, they simply went to sleep.

It was almost noon before they wakened. Rick called to report in. Mother, son, and father were all in excellent condition. "Thanks be to you," he said. "I have to see Buzz. He did such a good job for Trisha. And so did you two. Without you all, we never would have made it."

"We just stood around." Decker denied any credit.

Rick listed their endeavors. "Naomi saved their lives from the flood, you got there with Buzz and sent for me. I was no help at all."

Decker told Rick: "You made her think everything was in control."

"She wanted me there. She needed me." Rick accepted his part in the drama. "We've matured with this experience. We'll be different people."

"We liked the old pair." Decker smiled at the phone.

"Take care. We'll be up to see you later, if we can."

They hung up, and Decker turned to his naked love. "And how are you this noon?"

"Zapped."

"I can remember a time when you sapped me."

They smiled at each other and stretched. Every muscle, every bone, every inch of their bodies was still tired. They stretched and yawned and moved their bodies in the luxury of being able to do that.

"I like to see you stretch," he said huskily, smiling a little, his eyes hot.

"There is no way that I'm going to go a couple of romping rounds with you."

"Oh." He was surprised. "Did you think I meant to seduce you? I can't even lift a *finger*, I'm so tired."

But when she moved her shoulders and stretched her legs down to the bottom of the bed, he did slide his hand under the covers and put its rough surface on her side and run it down the length of her. "Ummm, your skin is so smooth."

She gave him a slanting, suspicious glance; he smiled like a satyr, and she laughed.

He offered in a good-citizen voice, "I can help you stretch in interesting ways and relax you."

"I'm relaxed."

He took her hand and ran it down his hairy chest until it encountered a very stiff muscle. "Then you can help me."

"Good heavens, what caused that muscle cramp?"

"You." He reached a hand to her far side and slid her across the sheet to him. "Have I told you that you were magnificent yesterday?"

"I believe I still need to sit down and just cry. I have

never been so glad to see anyone, as I was to see you come through those tree branches."

"Like Tarzan." He nodded.

"You were all the heroes."

"If no one had shown up to help, you would have done it."

"But my hair would have turned entirely white."

He was moving his hands and kissing along her shoulder. "You were perfect. In fact you still are. And I love you."

"I believe I'm becoming partial to you, too."

He pulled back. "Partial? What do you mean 'partial'? You're mad about me. Can't you tell?"

"How does a woman know?"

"I'll show you. When I touch you like this, and move my hand there, and slide my finger so, and give you my killer kiss like this—"

She did recognize that kind immediately. She helped and squirmed against his hand and breathed unevenly as the kiss deepened.

"—you do those things."

She blinked and asked, "What?"

"You squirm and help and get breathy on me."

"I was perfectly calm."

"You're just saying that so that I'll do it again. You're a shameless, greedy woman."

"And you're a pushover."

He did wish Elise could hear Naomi say that. Elise would spit fire. But he said to Naomi, "I'm a hard man to convince."

"Pah." She waggled him and and ran her fingernails lightly through his thatch and tickled him a little at his base, then she rolled over on top of him and squashed her breasts down on his sensitive chest and she wiggled.

"Hold still."

She closed her thighs around him and said, "Like this?"

"You want to get splattered again?"

"No." So she reached down and very adroitly slid him into her sheath.

"You've *attached* me!"

Lying there on top of him, she stretched, clenching her muscles to squeeze him, and then laid her hands on his chest and propped her chin on them to look at him. "Have I told you that you are a magnificent man?"

"Never."

She frowned. "I have, too."

"Not lately."

She smiled a little before she said soberly, "Without you, this town would have died."

"It isn't far from that."

"You heard the commuters. They'll move in here and change it."

"What about the people already here?" He ran his hand along her shoulder and down her back.

"With more people, who are used to dealing in a wider circle, they will get organized. They'll do as the captain suggested. They'll contact the other communities and circulate petitions and get things rolling. That nasty old Jones will be defeated. The majority will rule."

"How can you believe that?" he asked.

"Don't we?"

"If you will look at the legislation that is passed, it's

for the minorities. Sawbuck doesn't even make that category. We're a zero here."

"Why did you come to Sawbuck?" she asked softly.

"Come? Did you say that you want to come? Before I've even begun to make love to you?"

So he turned her over and laid her flat and he proceeded to show her all the ways that a man can touch a woman and how much pleasure that can give her.

She was pleasured. Her own hands caressed and petted and soothed and stimulated.

And he showed her the variety of coaxing kisses, and he demonstrated his full-out double-whammy one that involved all of both their coupled bodies and glued-together mouths. It was effective.

Her attention was diverted, and she then showed him how much she'd learned about kisses. But she never really got beyond the hello one.

She wouldn't release him so they used no protection but climbed the heights together in thrilling surrender. As they lay spent, he said, "The way I have it figured is, you'll be pregnant and *have* to marry me."

"I have an independent income—"

"From what?" he asked quickly for that had bothered him.

"My grandmother. I can take care of your baby if you are just an itinerant cowboy who will move on."

"I'm not a cowboy anymore."

"You've realized the error of trying to ride irritated horses?"

"I work for the government. I'm an agent. I was on an assignment in South America that went very, very bad. I tried to rescue some friends and was unsuccessful. I damned near didn't make it out myself."

"The beatings," she whispered, her gentle hands touching him as if he might break.

"Yes. Those are the fire demons that haunt my nights when you come and help me to be brave."

Her hands moved gently on his face, soothingly. "You are the bravest man I've ever known."

He kissed her softly and was so stirred that he again made love to her. But it was in an entirely different way. It wasn't just hungry coupling or delighted passion, it was commitment.

They were at breakfast when Mark came up in a half-track army truck.

Decker went out on the porch and stood straddle-legged with his hands on his hips. "Where did you get that?"

"I'm helping." He looked past Decker at Naomi and smiled. "Do you need rescuing?"

But it was Decker who replied, "I've handled that."

"You all and your shed top were on the news last night and this morning. I taped it for Trish and Rick. If you haven't heard, they're fine."

"Rick called." With that statement, Decker waited as if their conversation was completed and it was time for Mark to leave.

"Any extra coffee?" Mark smiled at Decker and then looked over at Naomi.

"Come in," she said as she reached out and waggled Decker's arm chidingly.

It was Decker who followed Naomi into the house, but he didn't close and lock the door in Mark's face.

Naomi went ahead of the two men into the kitchen and Mark said to Decker, "She's the one. She's the woman you were protecting. And you've got her boxed up?"

"I'm working on it. Don't interfere."

"Damn."

CHAPTER NINETEEN

MARK HAD BITTEN OFF THE WORD SO SHARPLY that Decker frowned over at him. Mark explained, "I once pegged her for later contact. She was about fifteen at the time."

"You dragged your heels a bit. Like ten or eleven years."

"She—" Mark began.

John had come up the porch steps. Decker went to the door and said, "Hi, John." Then he asked quickly, "Problems?" He opened the screen, in invitation for John to come inside.

John took off his Stetson but stayed on the porch. "The health department came to check the water, after the flooding? They found out we don't have water except from hoses, so they closed the restaurant and the drugstore."

"Ah." Decker sighed.

John inquired, "What are we going to do with all that food?"

"We'll have a thank-you party for the dam workers. Come in?"

"No. I just thought you ought to know. We are upset."

"There has to be a way around this. We'll see what can be done. Tell the others. Tell Mr. Jenkins."

"I will."

Again Decker invited, "Come inside and dry out."

"No, I am too distressed to sit."

"I'd go with you, but I can't leave my sheep woman alone with this wolf."

"I understand that. I shall tell the others what has happened."

Decker asked, "Is help needed to dig Mrs. Billmont's grave?"

"No. The Army helped."

"How'd that happen?"

"They didn't have anything to do while they watched the water. They are young and their muscles are restless."

"I remember that time," Decker said.

John laughed. "I have only one restless muscle now."

"I hate a bragging rooster."

John put his wet Stetson back on with a swagger before he went down the steps and walked back to the road.

Decker went into the kitchen, and Naomi's eyes confronted him in such a way that he stopped in his tracks.

Mark said, "I'm sorry, Decker. I let it slip. I didn't realize she didn't know."

"What." He narrowed his eyes.

"I thought Naomi knew you are Frank Jones's nephew."

Decker looked over at Naomi's frozen body and said to Mark, "I guess you managed to correct that oversight."

"Sorry. But she knows you are here to help the town. That has nothing to do with Frank. And I have some ideas about the water. Can we sit down and talk?"

Decker ignored Mark. "From the beginning, I said we were kin," he told Naomi. Her face was so still.

"Why did you come here?"

"He sent me to clear out the people of Sawbuck so that he could tidy up his boundaries."

She stared at him. "You have a strange way of doing things."

His tensed back eased a tiny bit. "Yes. I got distracted."

"Does your uncle know?"

"Yes. He said that to him I'm dead."

"Is that why his wife was over here?"

Decker was selective in his honest reply. "She asked about the dam. She's a good woman. She loves Frank, so he must have some socially redeeming factors."

Mark said, "I wouldn't have mentioned—"

"I should have told her. You aren't a man who would be that underhanded."

"In this case I might have been tempted, but I would be fair. I'd beat you another way."

Naomi frowned at Mark. "You're helping that monster across the fence, too?"

Decker snapped, "I'm not helping him." He jerked out a chair and sat down.

Mark replied to Naomi, "No. Neither am I. I've written a petition to the Board of the Edwards Aquifer. We have a million water-using people in San Antonio plus Frank Jones to contend with. San Antonio is beginning to understand that the aquifer isn't limitless and something will have to be done. That premise has been outlined and accepted, but Uvalde and those farmers at the top of the aquifer are revolting. They don't want their use of the water controlled by other people, downstream.

"We can petition. We can try to be heard. What we really need is for Frank Jones and the other farmers to go to dry farming and take their chances with the natural risks of the weather. Will they? That is the crux of our petition. We need as many of the people as we can get on this edge of the aquifer to sign the petition, to convince them to unite, and together we might at least get the wells working again."

"Why are you doing this?" Naomi asked.

Completely honest, Mark admitted: "As an excuse to see you. To impress you."

Decker shoved his chair back and began to rise. But Naomi put her hand on his arm and stopped him. She told Mark, "I love Decker."

Decker shot a look at Naomi, then he looked at Mark to see if that would shut him up.

"Well." Mark's gaze rested on her candidly. "You've loved another man as well. I could be next."

Naomi frowned in irritation.

Mark urged, "You don't know Decker. He could be flawed."

"You are not?" she asked.

"I've never been incognito. I am my own person. I'm willing to see if I can influence you."

Naomi stated: "You cannot."

"Then"—He never let her gaze drop from his—"I'll be a good citizen and help a little town."

"With a petition."

"Yes."

Naomi compared the two men. "Decker did it with

leadership. He led the men to clean up this town, and he managed to give us the dam."

Mark countered: "I might be able to get the wells again so that the people don't have to get their water through hoses and drink from oil barrels."

Decker's words gritted. "I object to your courting my woman in front of me. I find that unacceptable. I would like you to go outside with me so that we can discuss your conduct."

Mark leaned back in his chair and smiled at Decker. "I understand. Hitting me might help your temper, but I'm black belt."

"That's a start." Decker's tone was very threatening.

Mark raised his eyebrows and said, "That doesn't faze you?" He frowned. "What are you? I'd heard . . . What are you doing now?"

"I'm protecting my rights. Don't mess with me."

"That's refreshingly primitive."

"You may both leave," Naomi said in a very carefully calm voice. "I have had enough of this. I am interested in the petition. I'll help with it. But I'll be darned if I'm going to sit here and listen to the yowls of two male cats."

Decker stood up. "Let's go."

"You may find another reason to dislike me, besides my wanting to influence Naomi in my favor. I'm afraid I mentioned your relationship to Joe, I believe he's called."

"Anyone else?"

"No."

"Well, that should be your limit for this season. Why don't you take off?"

Naomi put in, "Decker, please. I asked that you both leave."

Decker turned to her and explained, "He's going.
I have to talk to you."

"Not right now."

"Naomi—"

"Please, Decker. Later."

Very civilized, Mark added, "She *said*—"

Decker snarled, "Get out of here!"

"I'll be back, Naomi, and if Decker gives you any
grief, call on me."

Decker took Mark's arm and in a low and controlled
way told him, "You can't take a hint, can you. Let me
make this clear." He took hold of Mark's belt at the
small of his back and shoved him out of the house,
banging open the screen door, hustling him off the
porch and toward the half-track. He snapped, "Stay!"
to an eagerly snarling Wellington. Then snarling sim-
ilarly, Decker said to Mark, "Don't you dare come
back."

"You're being unreasonable. I had thought you at
least had the facade of civilization. This is simply
which is the more physical man. Fighting isn't the way.
Let her decide on her own. I would like the opportunity to present myself for her consideration."

"No."

Mark smiled. "You're afraid that if she knew me,
she'd choose me."

"You'll never know."

"You're very stimulating to my dormant male competitiveness."

"Don't push me," Decker threatened through
clenched teeth.

Believing he'd made his points and not backed
down, Mark got into the half-track and skillfully ma-
neuvered it into a half circle and went away.

Wellington sat down next to Decker who was standing with his hands on his hips as he watched that. Then Decker turned and looked at Naomi's silent house. He thought she might be watching him, and he stood there for a while, waiting, uncertain.

But she *had* told Mark that she loved *him* and she had discouraged Mark's bid. Had she meant it? He called to the house, "If you intend that I serenade you, I can play the guitar a whole lot better than Rick. Healing rodeo riders have practice time."

He waited a couple of minutes, then sighed tiredly. He knew what a stray dog felt like. But she lifted back the upstairs curtain and looked down on him silently. Then without speaking, she allowed the cloth to fall back into place. He waited awhile longer, but she didn't indicate that he was to stay longer, so he trudged through the mud, back toward his store, with Wellington following.

There were two signs up at either end of the store rows: Meeting tonight—seven o'clock.

Decker was so distracted by Mark's bid for Naomi that it took a minute to see that he was being stared at by the visible citizens of Sawbuck. He nodded, and they all nodded back, but their response was that given to a stranger.

The word had spread? Now they all knew he was Frank Jones's nephew. And here came Rual, the Big Dog. That was such an appropriate labeling that Decker wouldn't have been surprised if as Rual passed a post, he'd stopped to sniff and lift a leg.

Rual's heels hit the already cracked cement of the sidewalk with ringing thuds as he approached. "You're Frank Jones's nephew. He don't want you here. Get out."

"He tell you that?"

"He threw you off his place. You get outta here."

"When I'm ready."

"Don't fool with me, shit. I can write citations on you that'd put you away permanently."

"Tell me about the Eye of God."

It had been a stab in the dark, but Decker saw the minutely involuntary flinch of shock in the flesh around Rual's eyes.

"What 'Eye of God'?"

Walking past Rual, Decker retorted, "If you don't know, you're either involved or you're a lousy cop. Which is it?"

Decker went on down to his store knowing his temper, triggered by Mark, had turned an antagonist into an enemy. So what the hell was so different? That's about all he'd dealt with in the last five years.

He went into his store, and it was like coming home after an assignment. He looked around at the clean floor, at the wall that held the two blazingly beautiful Indian paintings that Naomi had loaned him, at the renewed saddle on its block with the supple rope, and he began to relax. If the townspeople rejected him because he was kin to Frank, so be it. It was no different than being rejected because he was an American, or because he worked for the U.S. government, or because he was a white man.

He was a good man. He was on the right side of the struggle against corruption and evil, an unsolvable morass that could only be contained, never solved, because human greed and indulgence was what it was.

He began to strip off his wet clothing, rinsed himself with a cloth in a pan of water, and toweled himself dry. He stood naked, appreciating being dry. He smiled a little. Just to be dry was one of the scant gratitudes in life. For some it was bread for starving children. For some it was a growing crop. For some it was money piling up or spent in extravagant foolishness. Right now for Decker Jones it was being dry.

He took two vitamin C tablets and two aspirin, wrapped a soft cotton serape around himself, and lay down in his half-cocoon hammock. Then he smiled at the gently swinging peace, and he slept.

He was at the meeting at seven. He was clean and dry. He was rested and resigned to being ostracized. So he was a little aloof. Naomi wasn't there.

Everyone else was there, including Mark. People spoke to Decker, but they didn't smile. Joe stood by him for a while. Then Buzz came up and took Joe's place. That is what happened. It was as if Joe guarded Decker, and when he came in, Buzz assumed the role of guard. What did they think he was going to do?

Then Rual arrived. He didn't "join" them, he arrived. He stood by the door and watched. He stared so long at Decker that Decker winked at him. Rual flushed and looked away. Being dry and making Rual flush were the high points for Decker that day—

—and hearing Naomi tell Mark that she loved Decker. But had she just said that? She was for the underdog. Maybe she looked on Decker as something like the town of Sawbuck. A hopeless failure. Maybe she loved him but didn't like him. No one can control love, but liking is choice. Maybe Naomi didn't like him. Decker felt a great weight of melancholy burdening his soul.

He began to notice that the people at the meeting sneaked looks at him. He stared back. They were rejecting him. They were closing him out. There was a

religion that shunned members who didn't toe the
mark. This was another version of the same thing.
They were closing him away from their friendship.

Some of the commuters came in and greeted him
cheerfully but soon they, too, became aware of the
change in the attitude of the Sawbuckers. There were
whisperings and the commuters wore questioning
looks. Then they took careful peeks at Decker.

Hell.

He felt his burdened soul begin to weep. Then he
thought that over and decided he'd been in Spanish-
speaking places too much. No true rednecked American would have a soul that wept. He was just a little
disgruntled, that was all.

He thought about Buzz who was still standing next
to him. His guard. And how many times had Buzz
been ostracized because he was different. Times were
changing. In spite of the strivings of the sixties the
country was splitting up into ethnic groups. It wasn't
a country of Americans, people were being labeled.
The ethnic segments had their own TV stations, their
own magazines, their own rallies. In Congress there
were ethnic caucuses. "Our people," each group said.
With that attitude, what lay ahead?

Mark was speaking, talking about the Edwards
Aquifer. He had a map and showed that while the
surface rivers ran north to south, the aquifer ran under the rivers west to east. He explained how it moved
a mile a year through limestone that purified the water
better than any machine or chemical purifier that
could be made. All a man had to do was dig down a
short way and pure water endlessly bubbled forth.
Not even pumps had been needed.

Only after the terrible drought of 1957, when the

unending springs had failed, had it been made clear that the aquifer was not limitless. At the rate it was being used, it might last only another twenty years. Unless they all worked together to preserve and protect this natural resource, they would lose it.

Decker thought how familiar were the words "Preserve and protect." The Constitution. The wildlife. The aquifer. The planet.

Mark looked at Decker. "Have you anything to add?"

Decker shook his head. His part in Sawbuck was over. He would move on. Again.

John stood up and said, "We know that we are here in a town meeting and talking about our future because Decker Jones came to us. We have a beautiful lake over in the wash because Decker helped us do that. We thank this man, who is the kinsman of our enemy, who was a stranger to us, but who is now our friend."

There was applause! And cheers! Decker straightened in shock. Buzz put a big hand on Decker's shoulder and puffed the teasing words on laughter. "Our hero." But he waggled Decker's shoulder in friendship.

Decker raised disclaiming hands in front of his chest, palms down. There were commuter voices who called, "Speech! Speech!"

Decker shook his head and said, "I didn't do any more than any of you. You all know that."

They laughed, and it was very nice. Across the room, Mark caught Decker's glance and touched a finger out from his forehead in a salute. Decker acknowledged the gesture with a sober nod.

When the citizens and commuters had settled back,

Mark warned, "This will be complicated to solve. You are a small part of the overall problem. It will take work. Paperwork." He raised the petition he'd prepared without a fee. "But it is vital you make your own pleas known to the Board. You are citizens. You have rights. You need to appoint one of you as your voice. I volunteer as your advisor."

The people of Sawbuck were unsure of what that entailed, but the commuters applauded. They were more familiar with what the word ' volunteer' meant.

Suddenly Decker wondered, when had Rual left? He'd been there just before John had spoken. For some reason, Rual leaving the meeting made Decker restless. He asked Buzz, "Did you see the Big Dog leave?"

"No."

"All the sudden, I've got ants under my skin." Decker started for the door.

Buzz was right in back of him. "Let's go look."

They were the only ones outside. Rual's car was gone.

"He's gone," Decker said, his head swiveling. "Why doesn't that calm me?"

"Me, too."

Decker said tersely, "Let's check the watchers at Mrs. Billmont's wake." He was already moving in that direction.

Buzz followed. "Naomi's there. The rest wanted to be at the meeting."

"Is she alone?" Decker snapped.

"No. Maria and Sue are with her."

They tapped on the Billmont door, and Naomi came to see who was there. She didn't call through the door, she opened it in a small-town trusting.

Decker asked quickly, "Are you all right?"

Naomi smiled and gave Decker her hand. "Come in. How did it go? John said he was going to mention your work here. Did he? You are their hero. And mine. Come inside. Oh, hello, Buzz. Come in."

"Honey." Decker squeezed her hand and his eyes were intense. "Lock the doors and stay inside. Don't let Rual in, do you understand?"

Her eyes widened. "What's wrong?"

"I don't know. We're going to see. Stay inside no matter what happens. Hear me?"

"Come back."

"I will."

After she stepped back inside, the two men waited to hear the door bolt. Then they heard Naomi's quick voice talking to the other two women inside the Billmont house.

Decker's voice was low and tense. "Buzz, something's wrong."

"I feel it."

"You go that way. We'll meet on the other side."

Buzz vanished. Decker went around the back of the string of stores. There was an odd glow. Automatically, he only monitored that, it could be a distraction. He ran toward the glow carefully, but his head swiveled and he looked carefully with sharp darting glances. There was a small fire in his store! A shorted wire? Naomi's paintings were inside! The buildings were connected and the town was gathered in the one next to the drugstore!

"Fire!" he hollered. Then he kicked in his locked back door and rushed blindly inside. There was the acrid smell of fuel. Arson. Someone was there. Decker grabbed the paintings from the wall and was attacked.

He ducked automatically and kicked out in the non-Marquis of Queensberry rules for survival in the underworld. He aimed for the crotch.

Decker had kicked tellingly, and the figure hunched. Decker took the paintings and ran to the street door to meet Buzz. "Take these to safety, warn the others, start the buckets! I have a visitor inside."

But the figure was exiting through the back. It was Rual.

Decker snarled like the primitive he was, leaped after the fleeing man, and caught him. Rual, who liked to intimidate people, turned like a cornered dog. People poured from the meeting to exclaim. There were shouts and calls. Women ran to gather children. And Decker fought with a suddenly vicious Rual.

The dry unpainted inner wood of the building was tinder and with the help of the splattered fuel, it burst in roars of explosions. Flames were leaping from under the hot tin roof, endangering the oak, scorching the wall of the next empty store. The whole string could go.

But it lighted the drama taking place between the buildings and Frank Jones's fence. The fight was between two evenly matched men, and it was vicious with no holds barred.

Men ran toward them, but Decker yelled, "He's mine!"

Cloth burst with muscle strain and was torn by grabbing, clawing hands. Decker bounced off the fence, and soon the excited dogs came to run and bark along the fence, howling and snarling. Then men came from Gimme's place, but they'd already been on their way because of the fire.

Soon Decker's uncle Frank was there by the fence,

watching. In the country, fire is especially scary and
everybody works to contain it.

The towering reflection of the dancing, darting
flames was so dramatic. The fight between the two
men struggling in the fire's light and the battle to save
the tinder-box stores were played against that stunning backdrop of the conflagration.

Frank had already sent his men over the fence to
help with the bucket brigade, but he stood quietly and
watched Decker. So did Mark, who passed the buckets
handed to him, but hardly took his avid glances from
the bloody fight. So did they all.

Naomi came closer, oblivious to the heat of the raging fires. She stood there, hardly breathing, the winds
created by the fire's draft making her dress billow
gently and lifting her hair with odd tenderness. She
seemed a goddess, aloof from the chaos, caught by
her curiosity in men's affairs.

Never had she witnessed anything so brutal, but
her terror for Decker was brief. He was skilled. How
could he be so skilled? She remembered the bruises
on his body. Then she looked at the writhing flames
and remembered his nightmares.

For Decker that was exactly what was happening.
He was in the very middle of his nightmare, but he
had an adversary whom he could fight. It was real.
Then he understood his enemies had only been men,
that they, too, were not invincible. And he saw his
mouse, calmly watching. Then his timid mouse yelled,
"Get him!"

And he laughed. He laughed and was knocked
down. He was slow getting up, he was suddenly so
amused. Then Rual kicked him. That eliminated
amusement. Decker roared to his feet and smashed

Rual mercifully, for he finished the fight.

Decker stood there in front of the licking, dancing, reaching fire demons, and he was no longer afraid. He turned to his love and caught her body as she hurled herself against him. He staggered backward, for he was winded. But he kissed her, hungrily possessive, rubbing her face with his sweat and his blood, in his markings. She was his.

Buzz took charge of Rual. There were cheers for Decker that could be heard over even the booming of the great fire. And his uncle Frank was still at the fence, soberly still watching.

After that there was great confusion until Farrino Jenkins arrived. Then he directed and coordinated their efforts. He was an organizer as the town struggled to survive the fire.

Frank Jones had sent a pump and hoses to put into the new lake to spray the threatened stores and houses, to protect them from flying embers. And Jones's battery-operated searchlights were there so that the Sawbuckers could see what they were doing. Frank? Helping Sawbuck? Decker wasn't the only one astonished.

They all worked hard, but they lost the stores on that whole side of the street. It looked so sad, the charred emptiness, the singed trees, the exhausted townspeople and commuters.

"We'll rebuild it," Ned said.

The Sawbuckers just stared. There hadn't been a new building in that town in most of their memories. Magdalena said, "*Sí.*" Then carefully she said, "Yes." Magdalena was going to learn English?

Well, they said, why not rebuild? They'd never thought they'd have a lake. Why not new stores?

They all stayed late, tidying up, draining and re-rolling Jones's hoses. Helping cart the great battery lights to the trucks. The Sawbuck men were amused that the Jones crew was a little sheepish, a little too eager to be friendly. They had no idea the Sawbuckers knew who'd torn down the first dam.

It was long after midnight before the day was finished. They were all running on adrenaline by then. That and the free cold beer Decker had sent for after the fire was controlled. But eventually they drifted off. Events had been such that they were all exhausted, and that tiredness had finally caught up with them.

CHAPTER TWENTY

WALKING BESIDE NAOMI WITH WELLINGTON trailing them, Decker paused to look around the town, what was left of it. It was odd to have the string of stores missing. The gap made the town lopsided and different. Decker said pensively, "You know that I'm homeless?"

"Ah. How sad."

He nudged. "Wellington and I have no place to sleep."

Naomi gestured. "There are those two other stores across the street that are vacant."

He scowled at her. "What a heartless woman you are."

She laughed and took his hand.

"Ouch. Watch out. I'm wounded."

"Aw. Here, I'll kiss it well." She lifted his hand and kissed it gently, then put it against her soft chest. "It just so happens that I have a place you might use. And since Rick has left, Wellington can take over the porch."

"You were a little slow offering."

She laughed again and lifted her mouth for his kiss.

"That was a thank-you kind." He gave her another.

"That's Wellington's. I can't have him slobbering all over you. Speaking of slobberers, I don't know what it is about you that makes men so unreasonable."

"About me?"

He said in a cranky way, "I wonder if I have the *strength* to take on the job of keeping other men away from you."

"You're taking on that job?"

"Yeah. Since the dam's built, I don't have anything else to do, and I'm getting used to stress." She kissed his cheek, and he said, "Ouch."

"Awww. Did that nasty man hurt you?"

"He was only a man," Decker said, then he added seriously, "and the fire demons were only my bruised mind. It was just that those people outnumbered us, down there in that terrible place. They aren't invincible. Had we been evenly matched, we would have gotten away. It was just bad luck."

"You realize now that there wasn't any lack in you? Only the odds."

"Yes."

"Ah, Decker. You are such a man."

"But I would never have healed without you, Mouse. When I despaired, you were there in my subconscious and you gave me courage."

She smiled so tenderly. "You would have made it finally. But I needed you as much. I didn't know that life could go on and re-form itself, and that I can be whole again. Brad knew that. He accepted that it was so."

For the first time, Decker allowed Brad to come between them. "He was very fortunate to have had you there for him." Then, with reluctant compassion,

Decker said, "It must have wrenched his very soul to have to leave you."

"He went peacefully. He had no regrets."

"He was a braver man than I. I would tear Heaven apart to get back to you."

"I love you, Decker."

"It's just a good thing that you do—ouch, those knuckles are a little tender." He said that to distract her from any lingering thoughts of Brad. He wanted her attention on him. His hand wasn't that badly hurt.

"My poor warrior."

"Yeah."

"Come with me." She gently took his hand and led him to her house through the dark, smoky night.

A bored Wellington tagged along.

After a silence, Decker mentioned, "Uncle Frank never came over the fence."

"No. But he allowed his men to help save the rest of the town."

"That is peculiar." Decker was thoughtful.

"Funny peculiar?"

"Just downright weird. I wonder what he's up to."

On Naomi's porch were most of Decker's possessions, rescued from his burning store. Naomi's paintings were with his saddle and rope, and the cougar skin with the claw and tooth necklace—

"So." Naomi gave him a really sly smile. "You actually do have such a necklace."

"I never lie."

"I know, but you are skilled in telling the truth in such a way that you don't actually tell it all. You're selective in your choice of confidences."

He looked into her eyes and smiled faintly, then his

gaze dropped down her body in a very, very interested manner. "You'll dance for me."

She tilted her head as she considered. "Perhaps. Yes. Sometime. Maybe."

"That's not very specific. Not now?"

"You'd go to sleep before I took three steps."

"Maybe not."

She took him inside to bathe and patch him, and she took him to her bed to love him gently.

They wakened in the last of the night's darkness to find each other close. They kissed sweetly and stretched in the silence with only the lapping water in the basin reminding them of all that had happened. She laid her hand on his chest. "Any fire demons haunt your sleep?"

"None."

"I love you, Decker."

"Because I won?"

"Because you're a good man and you came to help a dying town."

"Not because I'm good in bed?"

She smiled. "That, too."

"And you'll marry me and live happily ever after."

"Yes."

After a comfortable silence of mutual pleasure in just being together, he asked in a cranky voice, "Are we going to go around being do-gooders all our lives?"

"Probably."

"Well, I *suppose* I can. But it sure takes a lot out of a man."

"Always."

"If you're there," he promised, "I can do anything."

She sat up, stretching, to look past him out of the window at the new lake. The beginnings of dawn reflected onto the new surface and into the room, casting Naomi's shadow onto the far wall and ceiling. The subtle lights and shadows of the restless water played lovingly over her nude body, making it mysteriously otherworldly. "Just look at that lake."

"It's yours." His voice was husky as he watched his magic woman. "I would never have helped with it, if I hadn't wanted to please you."

"That's a lover talking. You cleaned up this town, cowboy, because you can't stand to be idle. You are a marvelous man."

"I need to mention that I don't deserve you. You are perfect."

She agreed. "Yes."

"And you're mine."

"Yes."

"Dance for me." He only mentioned it. Why would she get out of their sleepy bed, put on a barbaric necklace, and dance at that time? A time not of night but not yet day?

She smiled down at him, taking much pleasure in seeing him in her bed. This man. He was so different from Brad but equally precious. How could she have come to know, to love two such remarkable men?

Naomi leaned to kiss his mouth, stretching over him but allowing only their lips to touch. She kissed him sweetly. And he lay deliberately lax, accepting her tempting salute.

His body tingled with the knowledge that she was going to seduce him. He disciplined himself to allow her to do so at her own pace. He'd never given her free rein of him, and the thought of her seduction made him steel himself to give her the freedom of him now.

She straightened away to smile at him, then she turned and slid off the bed. Decker frowned. He'd allowed her to escape. She left the room, he heard the squeaky stair boards and half rose to listen intently. What was she doing down there? Then he heard her coming back up and watched as she returned to him. She'd brought the cougar skin.

He almost lost his tight control and reached for her. But discipline did hold and he lay tensely anticipating her next move.

She came to their bed and spread the fur next to him, leaning over, her breasts moving in their independent sway. He was riveted, his breath picked up. He watched as she stood straight, both hands moving to lift her hair back from her neck as she invited his regard. Then she put on the tooth and claw necklace. She stood to display herself to him, and in that predawn water light, she was a magical woman of dreams.

His body gave him an urgent argument for action, and he did manage to curb himself but his muscles bulged and his sinews strained with the effort. His breathing sounded like an out-of-control bull pawing the ground, but Decker's stare never left Naomi.

The necklace was an alien thing on her slight and rounded civilized body. Her thick dark hair was down around her shoulders, and she smiled for him. She lifted her hands and instructed, "Clap, like this." And she set the rhythm.

He shifted restlessly on the bed, but managed to make the change in position appear as though he'd meant only to lean against the headboard. He clapped, his heated stare on her.

Slowly she danced, her movements like poetry, but gradually the dance changed and she became seductive. In the wavery water light, she turned, her movements designed to tempt him. She was breathtaking as the lights and shadows flickered over her shimmering body, highlighting only to obscure the lovely female snares and lures.

His breathing was shallow and rapid. He rose from the bed, still clapping the measure she'd set. His steps took him around her in his itinerant-cowboy stomp. His naked body, too, was caressed by the water's lights and shadows, which seemed to draw the two together in their mating dance.

Her steps kept her near him, and she had him riveted. She smiled, her eyelids heavy as she gave him steaming glances. Deliberately taunting, she did not quite touch his body with her own, but she was so close that she could feel the heat of him.

He was an innovative man. He then allowed his feet to stomp her commanded rhythm. That left his hands free. As she moved and turned, one hand of his or the other cupped and trailed along the silken turning of her body.

His head was bent forward; his stare never leaving her. His body was curled, his arms out and bent limiting her freedom without touching her. His hands were ready.

When he could survive no longer, he took her hand. His hand led her around him, in a finale of the dance, and his body waited until she again came to the front of him. His arms enclosed her, bending her back, and he kissed her the double-whammy killer kiss, the one that spun her senses entirely.

He lifted her into his arms, then he kissed her again.

He almost drew the essence from her, but he gave her of himself in return. And she was filled with love.

He laid her on the cougar pelt. The feel of it against her back, with the feel of his hard, haired flesh on her front, was excessively sensual. She moved and murmured with the sensations, her hands in his hair and down his tense shoulders and around to his face.

Their kisses were deep and hungry, and their seeking hands were bold and enflaming, building their desire to impossible tension. They seemed to feed on each other as their mouths sought to taste, as they explored their love.

Her surface was so sensitized that just the touch of his tongue was exquisitely felt. And he watched her avidly as he trailed his rough fingers up her stomach, to the bottom of her breast, and made her wait for its capture. She sighed and gasped and moaned, and he trembled with his need of her.

Their lovemaking touched another echelon of pleasure, and they were allowed to experience their delay. They could then experiment with kisses and touches and smoothing hands, hovering just at the brink of ecstasy. They could sigh and breathe as they postponed that final surge of love. And they learned the full measure of the mating sensation as she allowed him his every wish.

At last, they separated, lying apart, holding hands, their ardent gazes locked. They smiled. Then they kissed, gently, and they held each other. Their kisses slowly changed, and finally they made love, building their desire, allowing it free rein, rising to the emotional climax to cling, shuddering exquisitely at the scope of the experience and falling back to the thrilling lessening aftershocks of their passionate rapture. It was incredible.

Their mating had really been the cosmic clash he'd dreamed so scoffingly as he'd waited to meet with the squint-eyed, hard-nosed woman's libber.·

The two slept again and wakened in the early afternoon. They bathed sleepily and ate a breakfast meal out of sync, as they smiled at each other.

That day was Mrs. Billmont's funeral, and the sun shone as if it had never stormed so furiously. Trisha's birthing on the shed roof had been televised through the downpour from across the roaring stream. That, along with the search for the lady who was killed by the storm, and the Herculean effort to create the new lake, brought the area to the attention of the news media. The press recalled the gaudily painted Sawbuck, now half burned down. The town's struggle was given renewed publicity and, by coincidence, so was the town's water problem.

People are basically curious, Decker knew that. It's curiosity that makes the world go around, not love. Love is only the spice of life.

Much had happened in Sawbuck, and people came to look at the half-burned town, at the new lake, and since she was listed as having no kin, they came to Mrs. Billmont's funeral. Among those present were ... Frank and Elise Jones.

That caused a murmur among the actual but crowd-scattered townspeople. Meeting in the crunch, Buzz asked Decker, "Do you know that man from across the fence looks like you?"

"The devil disguised him. He wasn't supposed to be in our family."

In another shift of people, John told Decker, "He looks like any bastard. They have a special imprint, if you look at their eyes."

"My daddy loves him."

"No." John squinted at old Gimme. "I shall have to observe the man. Your father would not be foolish."

Decker's nod acknowledged the vote of confidence.

Joe said, "Him and the wife were nice about our doughnuts. They acted just like neighbors."

But it was Magdalena who said, "He will be a good man. It took some of your family courage for him to come here."

Decker tilted his head and looked across the crowd at his kinsman. Old Gimme had never been a stranger, anywhere, in all of his life. He never had to use courage for he'd never believed he wasn't welcome wherever he wanted to be. Courage? Frank hadn't ever known the need of it.

The circuit minister came, and the ceremony had to be outside because not even both of the surviving empty stores would hold the mob of people. Mostly strangers, they came to bid farewell to a lady they'd never known. In such a crowd, the commuters felt like home folks. When had they not felt that way?

Before her casket had been closed, Joe and Ann had sentimentally placed a raspberry tart in Mrs. Billmont's folded hands. And the children carried balloons as they all followed the casket to the little Sawbuck graveyard.

The preacher was another who'd never met Mrs. Billmont, but he proclaimed that she'd been a good woman. The day was lovely. The trees were washed as clean as the sky, and the air was pure. The people were quiet and respectful, and the setting was serene.

The children's balloons were then released as a symbol of the spirit going to heaven. All eyes turned skyward and the flight of balloons was colorful and charming.

The gathered mourners walked back into town, where the food left from the closed restaurant was served as the "family" dinner. The same door-tables had been set up along the wash by Naomi's house. Joe and Ann had loaned their restaurant crockery for the occasion, and all the townspeople helped with the chore of feeding all those people.

Dick mentioned leaving a monetary gift for the town. The strangers looked at that pitiful burned-out portion of Sawbuck, and their contributions were extremely generous. John asked Decker, "Did you hear what the man from over the fence did?"

But the crowd shifted, and Decker didn't hear. He only knew that whatever it was had been shocking. Decker frowned and looked around.

Buzz smiled across heads and shook his own, his eyes dancing.

Decker scowled and jerked his head in a what's-going-on? demand.

But Buzz only laughed and lifted a helpless hand as if incredulous.

Decker found Naomi and asked, "What's going on?"

Harried, she replied, "We're about out of bread."

Decker only then realized that Magdalena was the news center in Sawbuck. No one wanted her to feel left out, so everyone told her everything. He found her in a fan-backed cane chair and asked in her language, "Magdalena, what is occurring?"

"Frank Jones paralleled the money given by the strangers for the town."

"You mean he matched it? It is doubled?"

The old lady nodded.

Decker frowned at his kinsman, over yonder smoking a Cuban cigar, talking to a gathering of strangers to Sawbuck. Gimme's manner was expansive, and the strangers could easily think it was his town. That idea irritated hell out of Decker.

What was Gimme doing there in the first place? He was the one who'd sent Decker to clear out Sawbuck. It just didn't add up. Decker felt suspicious and sulky.

Naomi said, "Carry these over to the store."

Decker stomped off with the load of dirty dishes.

As he walked through people who had never before been to Sawbuck, who stood around visiting with each other, commenting, criticizing, and giving opinions, Decker remembered his warning to Naomi. He'd told her that the town would change. That things would happen that she might not agree about, and the people would make their own decisions which might not be her choices.

But he'd never thought that one of the decision makers, worming his way into *Sawbuck*, would be his uncle Gimme Jones, for crying out loud.

But wait, even after his warnings to Naomi, was it *he* who wanted to keep control of Sawbuck? Who was he to decide the future of that little nothing town?

Musingly he thought: Wouldn't it be interesting to watch Gimme Jones get involved with that town and end up fighting to get water for ... Sawbuck? What an irony. But it would give Frank something to sink his teeth into and keep him busy.

Decker decided he might just stick around, and if old Gimme was thinking to take over the town, he'd have his nephew Decker to watch him. Decker saw how easily that old wheeler-dealer charmed the people around him. He was home folks and ordinary to them, when actually he was an actor, a charlatan, a chameleon. Well, he'd have Decker as a counterpoint to his plots.

Then Decker saw that no one spoke to Elise. Everyone was sneaking looks at her, but the women wouldn't acknowledge her and the men were afraid to do that. Elise was a fine woman. She needed help if she was going to stay there. Not only Decker would monitor old Gimme, Elise would.

Decker took Naomi over to meet his kin. He introduced the two women and was surprised to see that Naomi was perfectly comfortable with that stunning woman. He looked at his love in some surprise. She could handle Elise. His "mouse" was no mouse.

And Decker understood that he really didn't know Naomi yet. However, he knew that not only he and Elise would watch out that Frank Jones didn't pull any fast ones on Sawbuck, but Naomi would share in that with them.

As Naomi helped Elise to feel comfortable in that bizarre situation, Decker went to his uncle Frank. "Want your truck back?"

"No, nephew. I have no use for it." Without even a flicker of memory of their last meeting, Gimme said that quite comfortably. "Keep it as a memento of an interesting time. It'll last for a couple of decades. Your first born will probably learn to drive with it. Although you might want to replace the rusted-out body parts."

Still a little hostile, Decker told old Gimme, "You're changing your ways. What's going on?"

"We're going to have a baby. We just found out

yesterday. Elise is hardly pregnant at all, but the tests say she is."

Decker understood they hadn't needed him. And he was glad for them.

His uncle was still talking. "I've got to get along with my neighbors," he confided in a manner that denied there would be any problem. "The kid will want to come with me to the new drugstore and buy wax juice babies, just like you did."

Old Gimme made his own histories. Decker looked at his uncle and said, "Gimme, you're an original." He held out his hand. "Congratulations."

Gimme shook Decker's hand with a routine acceptance of his nephew's regard. "Thank you, nephew. Have a cigar."

Decker took the Cuban cigar and put it in his mouth to chew on it. He looked across the way to Naomi. His love. He would never have met her if it hadn't been for his uncle Frank. So Frank was really responsible for that and, inadvertently, even for the town's rebirth in a strange domino effect of events.

Decker slowly shook his head at a droll feeling of gratitude to his uncle. But then he looked around and thought how good life was to him there in that nothing town. A town named for a crummy ten-dollar bill. He smiled at happenstance. Then Decker took a deep, contented breath. He was home.

Lass Small was born and raised in San Antonio, Texas. She went to the School of Fine Arts in Indiana and enjoys writing and traveling. She is the author of twenty-nine published books to date and currently lives with her husband in Fort Wayne, Indiana.

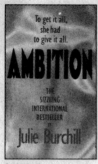